"Kiss it and make it better"

Jesse shoved up the sleeve of his sweater and revealed the tan Ace bandage around his sprained wrist.

"I think that only works when you're related by blood," Robin said, fighting the waver in her voice.

"Let's try it and find out."

"If I do try it, it'll be a miracle cure. You've got to admit you believe in miracles, Jesse, or it won't work."

His eyes met hers and his smile vanished. "I believe people make their own miracles." He raised his wrist in front of her, daring her.

She shyly touched her lips to his exposed thumb. "There. All better?"

"Miraculously." He ran his thumb gently over her lower lip, tracing the full curve of it. "Should I say hallelujah now? Sing your praises before heaven and earth?"

"No," Robin answered on a sigh, her body attuned to his, welcoming the kiss she knew was coming. "You only have to believe."

ABOUT THE AUTHOR

Judith Arnold can't remember ever not being a writer. She wrote her first story at age six and pursued a successful career as a playwright after getting her master's degree from Brown University. Judith, who now devotes herself to writing full-time, also pens novels under the pseudonym Ariel Berk. She and her husband and two sons live in Connecticut.

Books by Judith Arnold

HARLEQUIN AMERICAN ROMANCE
104–COME HOME TO LOVE
120–A MODERN MAN
130–FLOWING TO THE SKY
139–JACKPOT
149–SPECIAL DELIVERY
163–MAN AND WIFE
189–BEST FRIENDS
201–PROMISES*
205–COMMITMENTS*
209–DREAMS*

*KEEPING THE FAITH SUBSERIES

HARLEQUIN TEMPTATION
122–ON LOVE'S TRAIL

Don't miss any of our special offers. Write to us at the following address for information on our newest releases.

Harlequin Reader Service
901 Fuhrmann Blvd., P.O. Box 1397, Buffalo, NY 14240
Canadian address: P.O. Box 603,
Fort Erie, Ont. L2A 5X3

Comfort and Joy
Judith Arnold

Harlequin Books

TORONTO • NEW YORK • LONDON
AMSTERDAM • PARIS • SYDNEY • HAMBURG
STOCKHOLM • ATHENS • TOKYO • MILAN

Published December 1987

First printing October 1987

ISBN 0-373-16225-1

Chapter One

Robin tore her eyes from the paper turkeys tacked to the
bulletin board along the side wall and faced the front of
the room again. She felt like a restless schoolchild—
which wasn't surprising, given that she had spent nearly
half an hour squeezed into an undersized chair attached
to an undersized desk in Room 128 of the Brushy Plain
Elementary School, listening to Ms. Becker describe, in
an offensively chipper voice, what she had been doing
with her seven- and eight-year-old charges for the past
three months, and what she was planning to do with them
for the rest of the term. The classroom's overhead flu-
orescent lights buzzed, the bright yellow walls cloyed and
the green chalkboards gave off an aroma of dust. Every
time Robin tried to squirm into a more comfortable position at the tiny desk, the soft soles of her loafers
squeaked against the drab gray and beige linoleum floor
tiles.

She forced herself to pay attention to what Ms. Becker was saying. "So, as you can see," the young woman
at the front of the room chattered, "we did a great deal
to commemorate Thanksgiving." Robin found the
teacher's sunshiny smile and her singsong vocal quality
oddly irritating. "But kids will be kids," Ms. Becker

continued. "They're already badgering me about Christmas. So I've begun making plans for our class to celebrate that holiday, too. The turkeys were such a hit, I've prepared some lovely dittos of Christmas trees for the children to color in." She lifted from her desk a ditto stencil featuring an outline of a pine tree and displayed it for the parents.

Robin turned back to the side wall to study the turkeys. Twenty-four of them, each a blue ditto-ink outline decorated with individual touches by the children, each labeled with a student's name in the upper left-hand corner. Searching the row of drawings, Robin located the one with Philip's name printed on it. Bless him, she mused with a private smile. Not only had he crayoned most of his bird a garish orange, but in place of wings, he had drawn big purple hands.

Ms. Becker was less than inspiring. Robin should have given more weight to Philip's constant griping about his teacher. "She's *boring*," he frequently carped in his distinctive seven-year-old whine. "You know me, Mom, I can put up with a lot, but she's *boring*."

Robin had to agree. Her heart brimmed with sympathy for her son. The Branford, Connecticut school system wasn't the best in the world, but even here, teachers ought to know better than to stifle the creativity of their students by making them color already outlined pictures.

"In addition to decorating the trees, we'll be performing a classroom skit," Ms. Becker went on. "I've found a marvelous dramatization of Dickens's *A Christmas Carol* for the children to perform. I haven't cast any of the parts yet, but the children adore dramatic play. And, of course, it's a good learning experience for them. Dramatic play teaches co-operation . . ."

And it teaches how to take orders from a director, Robin added silently. She tried to catch Joanna's eye, but Joanna was sitting sideways in the neighboring desk, her legs extended to her left and her back to Robin, her head angled over her right shoulder in order to see the teacher. Joanna was a good three inches taller than Robin; she was wise not to have bothered trying to fold her lanky limbs beneath the minuscule desk. Even so, Robin preferred banging her knees on the underside of the built-in book tray to courting a stiff neck. She was sure that Joanna would be in dire need of a chiropractor by the time they got home.

Robin reproached herself for dreaming about returning home. Open School Night was too important; she owed it to Philip to learn everything she could about what was going on in his class.

"We're also going to have a grab-bag gift party," Ms. Becker announced. The perfect circles of her auburn curls bounced around her face as she spoke. Robin stared at the teacher's hair, attempting to guess whether it had been artificially permed. "If any of your children want to exchange presents on their own, I'd recommend that you make arrangements for that outside of class, so other children won't feel left out. But the grab-bag idea—about which you'll be receiving more details in a handout I'll be sending home with the kids—seems to me to epitomize the concept of Christmas as a time of giving. That's why I think it's so important that we celebrate these traditional rituals in class."

"Excuse me, Ms. Becker, but don't you think that celebrating Christmas in a public school might be riding roughshod over the Constitution?"

The voice came from the doorway, and, slamming her knees on the polished wood of the desk, Robin shifted in

her chair to locate its source. A man was lounging against
the doorjamb, clad in blue jeans and a suede bomber-
style jacket unzipped to reveal a ribbed white turtleneck
sweater that hugged his chest in a supremely attractive
way. His body appeared hard and lean and magnificently proportioned. Robin twisted deeper in her seat to
catch a glimpse of the face that accompanied such a terrific male body.

She wasn't disappointed. The man was gorgeous.

"Whose daddy is that?" Joanna whispered.

The same thought crossed Robin's mind, but she
brushed it off with the irrational notion that anyone who
was so utterly good-looking couldn't possibly be a daddy.
The man had a thick mane of coal-black hair that fell
about his face in long windswept waves. His eyes were
nearly as dark as his hair, and they were set deep beneath a high, fierce brow. He had a hawklike nose, thin
lips and a square jaw. Robin didn't know that men so
strikingly handsome actually lived in a town as sleepy and
predictable as Branford.

If they did, she surmised, they were already married,
the doting.fathers of second-graders. Only a handful of
fathers had chosen to come to this Open School Night,
and even if the man in the doorway hadn't bothered to
take a seat inside the room, the fact that he was present
informed Robin that he cared more about his child than
most fathers did.

Robin didn't condemn the other fathers for their absence. Some, like Joanna's husband Glenn, were undoubtedly at home baby-sitting for their children so their
wives could attend Open School Night. Others, like
Robin's ex-husband, were no longer in Branford, and
therefore were unable to fulfill their parental obligations. Robin had parked Philip at Joanna's and Glenn's

house for the evening. Their son Jeff was Philip's best friend, and Robin was grateful to Glenn for forgoing the Open School Night so Joanna and Robin could be there.

Although she would rather have continued her admiring inspection of the stranger in the doorway, Robin directed her gaze back to Ms. Becker, who seemed rather flustered by the man's question. "Hello, Jesse," she said, managing a smile. Robin was surprised by the informality of Ms. Becker's greeting; the teacher always referred to parents by their last names.

He must be a friend of Ms. Becker's, Robin concluded. If not a student's daddy, he must be the teacher's boyfriend. Any man that handsome had to be already taken. Robin couldn't smother a spiteful twinge of envy that a teacher as mediocre as Ms. Becker could have snagged a hunk like the fellow standing at the classroom door.

If they were friends, though, or lovers, why was Ms. Becker looking so defensive? "I don't think there's any need to worry about the Constitution," she rationalized, partly to the man she'd called Jesse and partly to the assembled parents contorted in their tiny desk chairs. "We discuss Chanukah in class, too, of course. We discuss the history of this special Jewish holiday. It isn't as if we deal with Christmas to the exclusion of all other religious holidays."

"You discuss Chanukah," echoed the man. His voice was low and smooth, a rich, lustrous baritone that might belong to a disc jockey. He quirked one black eyebrow skeptically as he regarded the curly-haired teacher at the front of the room. "Do you also discuss the Eastern Orthodox Christmas? Tet? Native American seasonal rites? And let's not forget the winter solstice. Perhaps there are one or two druids in your class."

"Well..." Ms. Becker moistened her lips anxiously and grinned. "The fact is, the children are the ones who want to discuss Christmas. I mean, it's all around them. Even before Thanksgiving, the stores were already starting to put up their Christmas decorations. And, let's face it, Christmas is a school vacation. I'm sure that makes it even more significant to them."

The man shrugged. Observing the graceful motion of his broad shoulders as they shifted inside his jacket, Robin sighed. She really ought to do something about socializing more, she chided herself. For all she knew, Branford was filled with plenty of equally stunning specimens of masculinity who weren't dating boring elementary school teachers. Being a divorced mother with a demanding job didn't leave Robin much time for meeting men, but . . . she ought to do something about reviving her social life. Maybe if she did, the man in the doorway wouldn't look quite so enchanting to her.

He made no move to enter the room, even though he had willfully intruded on the teacher's presentation. Robin wondered whether it was easier to attack Ms. Becker's methods when one wasn't doubled up on oneself inside a student-size desk and chair. She herself had a few critical remarks for Ms. Becker, but she preferred to wait until they could confer privately. Unlike the man in the doorway, Robin didn't want to embarrass her son's teacher in front of an attentive audience.

"Well," Ms. Becker said, tossing the man an edgy smile and then beaming at the roomful of parents. "I'd like the opportunity to meet each of you individually. So why don't you stand and stretch your legs and have a look at our displays, and I'll circulate among you."

Joanna immediately pried herself out of her seat and made a great show of unkinking her joints. Robin took longer to climb out of her chair, probably because she had been more deeply imbedded in it, and Joanna helpfully gripped Robin's arm to prevent her from falling while she wriggled her right leg out from under the book tray. "One more minute in that chair and I'd be crippled for life," Robin moaned.

Joanna laughed and tossed back the overgrown bangs of her shaggy brown hair with a flick of her head. "What do you think of Ms. Becker?" she asked Robin.

Robin rolled her eyes, then lifted her wool blazer from the back of her chair. "Not much, if you want to know the truth," she admitted quietly. "I'd like to think she's competent, but she certainly lacks pizzazz."

Joanna concurred with a nod. "Last August, when Dot Hasselhopf found out Joey was assigned to Becker's class, she made such a fuss that they reassigned Joey to Mrs. Greenblatt's class. Greenblatt's supposed to be the best of the second-grade teachers at Brushy Plain. Now I feel guilty that I didn't throw a tantrum, too."

"Don't feel guilty," Robin consoled her. Mothers had more than enough to feel guilty about these days without shouldering the blame for their children's fate in teacher assignments. "As soon as I get Becker alone for a minute," she warned Joanna, "I'm going to throw a very discreet tantrum. She probably isn't such a bad teacher—she's just young and relatively inexperienced. You and I know more about seven-year-olds than she could ever learn in her education courses."

"I'd like to join you in that tantrum," Joanna said wistfully. "But I've got to save my strength to face off with the snake. Jeff told me that if I didn't acquaint myself with the class's pet reptile, he'd never speak to me again." Shoring up her courage, Joanna stalked to the windowsill, which held a variety of science projects: incubating eggs, grapes drying into raisins, slices of Wonder Bread sprouting turquoise mold, and, inside a large glass tank, a corn snake that, according to Philip, was named Cookie Monster because the children liked to feed him cookies from their lunch boxes. Fortunately, Philip hadn't issued any ultimatums about Robin's developing a personal relationship with Cookie Monster, and she kept her distance from the tank.

Scanning the room, she noticed Ms. Becker standing to one side of her desk, surrounded by a throng of jabbering parents. Robin slipped her blazer on, smoothed her hair back and refastened the barrette holding it in a limp ponytail. Her hair was as fine and blond as it had been when she was a toddler, but she no longer had the time to set it and condition it. It was so much easier just to pin it at the back of her head and be done with it.

On the other hand, she ruminated, thrusting her hands into the pockets of her blazer and ambling to the periphery of the mob surrounding Ms. Becker, maybe a permanent wouldn't take much effort to maintain. A few springy curls—nothing as tight and foamy as Ms. Becker's, but maybe a body wave...

"You're Philip Greer's mother, aren't you?" Ms. Becker picked Robin out of the crowd and extended her hand. "I'm so glad you came tonight. There's something I wish to discuss with you. Excuse me," she said to the other parents, gripping Robin's elbow and steering her toward the bulletin board.

A subtle but sickening sense of dread curled through Robin's gut. Was Philip in trouble at school? Was he failing his lessons or acting incorrigible? Why else would the teacher haul Robin off, sidestepping all the other parents, for a one-to-one chat?

Inhaling to steady her nerves, she asked, "Is there a problem with Philip?"

"I'm not exactly sure, Ms. Greer," Ms. Becker confided. "He's such a bright boy, his reading and arithmetic skills are way above grade level and he seems popular with his classmates. But...well, look at this." She pointed at the bright orange turkey with the purple hands. "He drew this," Ms. Becker declared.

Robin gave the drawing a closer perusal. All right, so his orange scribbles had strayed across the dittoed outline in a few places. So he'd added nearly invisible blue antennae to the turkey's head. So what?

She turned to the teacher and awaited an explanation. *"Hands,"* Ms. Becker murmured ominously. "He drew *hands* on his turkey. Doesn't that strike you as...as somehow perverse?"

Robin suppressed a grin. If Ms. Becker hadn't already figured out that ninety-nine percent of all seven-year-olds were perverse, she ought to tear up her teaching certificate and try another line of work. "Did you question him about it?" Robin asked. "I'm sure he had a perfectly sound reason for giving his turkey hands instead of wings."

"Well, yes, I did question him," Ms. Becker conceded. "He told me that his turkey came from another planet— Geek or Bleep or something—"

"Gleek," Robin supplied. Gleek was a make-believe universe Philip had invented a few months ago. Whenever Robin ordered him to do something he didn't want to do, he would argue that on Gleek, the kids never had to make their beds or pick up their dirty clothes or do their homework when "Masters of the Universe" was on TV.

"That's right. Gleek," said Ms. Becker with a vigorous nod. "He told me that on Gleek the turkeys always have hands because turkeys can't fly anyway, so their wings don't serve any purpose, and because nobody likes to eat the wings at Thanksgiving. He told me that Gleekians—or whatever he called them—decided to breed their turkeys to have something useful, like hands, instead of wings."

The explanation struck Robin as brilliant; she had yet to meet anyone who liked to eat turkey wings. But she didn't want to come across as a gushing mama, so she only smiled. "Philip has an active imagination," she granted, "and I like to encourage him. Ms. Becker—it's only a suggestion, but instead of making the children color in your pictures, why don't you let them draw their own? Why not have them cut trees out of construction paper, any shape they want—and any color, for that matter—and then they can cut out decorations and glue them on. I know it's not my business to tell you how to run your class, but I think the children would enjoy the project a whole lot more if they got to design their own trees."

"Construction paper..." Ms. Becker gave the idea solemn consideration. "I'm afraid that's the art teacher's domain."

"Then let them make their trees during the art period," Robin advised, hoping she didn't sound too presumptuous. "I think it would be more challenging for them to make their own trees. And instead of having them enact *A Christmas Carol*, why not let them write their own skit? They might come up with a story closer to home, something they can identify with. Dickens is wonderful, but if you really want the kids to enjoy dramatic play, why not let them write their own dramas?"

Apparently she *was* coming across as presumptuous. Ms. Becker pursed her glossy pink lips and her eyes narrowed on Robin. "Ms. Greer, these are second-graders. If there's a budding Shakespeare among them, that's just fine. But really, they need direction, they need guidance—"

"And they need a little freedom to use their imaginations," Robin asserted. It was too late to back off; her only concern was that Ms. Becker shouldn't take out on Philip her resentment of Robin's attack. "They don't have to be Shakespeare. They just have to have the opportunity to invent their own worlds every now and then. Like Gleek. I'd be willing to bet at least half the kids in the class escape to an imaginary place like Gleek every now and then."

"Well," Ms. Becker said with a dubious huff. "I'll...I'll think about it."

"Good." Realizing the need to appease the teacher, Robin added, "I think you're doing a terrific job, and Philip's learning a great deal." The part about the terrific job Ms. Becker was doing was an overstatement, but Philip *had* learned a great deal in the class so far, and Robin felt that a compliment was in order. Thirty-three years of living had taught her the benefits of diplomacy.

Ms. Becker's face brightened. "Thank you, Ms. Greer. I confess, this has been an extremely rough autumn for me, but I'm glad to know I'm reaching the children."

Robin nodded and bade the teacher a polite farewell. *An extremely rough autumn,* she pondered, watching as Ms. Becker was engulfed by another swarm of avid parents. Although Robin's primary concern was for her son, she felt a pang of sympathy for the young woman. Obviously she was coping with problems that had nothing to do with her pupils. She was only human, a fact that

seven-year-old boys generally didn't take into account
when crabbing about their teachers.

"You told her off, didn't you."

The voice floated over Robin's shoulders from behind, deep and mellifluous. It seemed to enter her mind
not through her ears but through some other, secret
route. It was low, seductive, insinuating, and it made her
scalp tingle. She spun around and found herself staring
into the dark, luminous eyes of the man Ms. Becker had
called Jesse.

Close up, he was even better looking than he'd been
from afar—as if that were possible. He towered six or
seven inches over Robin, his eyes were adorned with the
thickest lashes she had ever seen on a man, he smelled of
leather and spice, his denim-clad hips appeared slim and
firm... She felt inundated by a disorderly barrage of
perceptions of the man. His smooth, bronze-tinged
cheeks. His laugh lines. His Adam's apple. His long legs.

And that honey-sweet voice. "Jesse Lawson," he introduced himself, reaching out to shake her hand. Jolting herself from her daze, Robin pulled her hand from
her pocket to accept his. "And you're...?"

"Philip Greer's mother," she said automatically, then
bit her tongue. With so many people—particularly in the
context of school—she identified herself not as an individual but as a parent. It had been that way ever since
Philip was born; she had gotten to know other parents in
terms of their children. "Hi, you're Becky's mom, aren't
you?" she'd greet a familiar woman at the supermarket.
Or, "I remember you—Eddie Romano's folks," when a
couple wandered into Woodleigh's and accosted Robin
at work.

Introducing herself as Philip's mother seemed natural
to Robin not only because it was Open School Night but

because she was busy racking her brain to recall if Philip had ever mentioned a classmate named Lawson. Maybe Jesse was someone's stepfather, and the child had a different surname. Like Philip, many children came from broken families, and some of those families entailed remarriages or mothers keeping their maiden names or whatever. It was hard to keep track.

The sound of Jesse's sonorous laughter brought her attention back to him. "Philip Greer's mother," he repeated. "That's an awfully long name. What do people call you when they're in a hurry?"

She laughed as well. "Robin. Robin Greer." Jesse's smile was cool but pleasant in an undefinable way, and she felt herself relaxing. "Which kid is yours?"

His smile remained. "I haven't got a kid. I'm here as a favor to Eileen. She asked me to drop off some documents she's been waiting for."

It didn't take Robin much effort to remember that Ms. Becker's first name was Eileen. Little more effort was required to conclude that Jesse Lawson's relationship with Eileen Becker was of a personal nature. Oh, well, she consoled herself. If a man with Jesse Lawson's physical attributes could exist, there must be others similarly endowed, somewhere. Three years of celibacy was enough. It was definitely time for Robin to start exerting herself to meet men.

Even knowing that Jesse was unavailable, she couldn't smother a vague insecurity about her appearance. At one time she had been totally confident about her beauty. Back then, however, during her teens and twenties, she had taken pains to make sure she always looked her best. Besides curling and fussing with her hair, she had lavished hours on her face, learning how to use the most stylish cosmetics in the most effective manner. She had dressed in chic apparel, and although there was nothing inherently wrong about the bulky crew-neck sweater and corduroy slacks she had put on before leaving the house that evening, there was nothing inherently right about them, either. The clothes just hung there, serving a function, concealing a body that might weigh one or two pounds less than it had during Robin's adolescence but lacked the nubile lusciousness of youth. Robin's breasts were flaccid, her skin was beginning to crinkle at the corners of her hazel eyes, her hands were perennially chapped and manicures were a distant memory. Divorced working mothers simply didn't have the time to pamper themselves.

Ordinarily, Robin didn't waste her energy worrying about the toll the years had taken on her. She was doing splendidly, considering. The divorce had been amicable, and Ray was as much a part of Philip's life as he could be, given his constant traveling. Robin's career was flourishing; a year and a half ago, she had been named manager of the Branford outlet of Woodleigh's. She had even had the good fortune to secure the services of Kate O'Leary, a widow who lived down the street from Robin and who welcomed the income Robin paid her to watch Philip every weekday from three o'clock until closing time at Woodleigh's. Robin couldn't complain.

Except that, standing barely three inches from Jesse Lawson, she felt peculiarly inadequate. Not that Eileen Becker was fashion-model pretty, not that the woman had revealed outstanding intellect or dazzling talent, but Robin suddenly found herself wishing that she wasn't just another suburban single mother trying to keep the scad of balls she was juggling from tumbling down around her head.

"I only caught part of her speech," he was saying, "but it sounded dull to me."

"Ms. Becker's speech?" Robin eyed the teacher, who was prattling to a rapt couple about their daughter's academic progress. "She's...a decent teacher," Robin allowed, figuring that it would be in poor taste to belittle the man's girlfriend to his face, even if he himself had just referred to her as dull. "I only wish that she spent a little more time encouraging the kids to be independent, instead of turning them into conformists. They're going to be regimented enough in the upper grades. But when they're this young..." Realizing that she was rambling, she cut herself off and smiled sheepishly.

"I agree," said Jesse. "Not that I'm an expert when it comes to children, but, sure, they ought to be independent. Independence is too important to squelch, no matter what the age."

Robin assessed his statement. Despite his charming smile, he sounded awfully solemn. Then she remembered his interruption during Ms. Becker's presentation, when he had alluded to the constitutional separation of church and state. He must be a fanatical patriot, she deduced, enamored of independence as an American birthright. "Did you really mean that, about how celebrating Christmas in class is riding roughshod over the Constitution?"

His eyes darkened briefly, and then he shrugged again, moving his shoulders in that delightfully languorous fashion of his. "I think there's too much emphasis on Christmas."

"Too much? How can there be too much emphasis on something so wonderful?" As far as Robin was concerned, there could never be too much Christmas. Woodleigh's was one of those stores that had put up

Christmas decorations before Thanksgiving, and Robin was all in favor of that. She loved the baubles and evergreen sprigs, the crystal snowflakes she and her staff had hung from the ceiling. She had already arranged for a delivery of a half cord of split logs to her house; she had considered and discarded at least three menus for Christmas dinner, and she was praying for snow. The holiday couldn't come soon enough—and it would be gone much too soon, she knew.

Jesse's attention had turned to the bulletin board. "Philip," he reflected, locating the bizarre orange-and-purple turkey. "Your son drew this?"

"Yes."

Studying the picture, Jesse frowned slightly. "Are the hands supposed to signify something?"

Robin laughed. "I guess they're supposed to signify that Philip has a mother who encourages independence rather than conformity."

Jesse's smile returned as he rotated back to her. "And what does Philip's father say about that?"

"Not much," Robin answered. "Philip's father and I are divorced."

"Ah." Something sparked in Jesse's eyes as they roamed across her small, hollow-cheeked face, and one corner of his mouth skewed upward in a lopsided smile. Then his gaze drifted past Robin and snagged on Ms. Becker. "If you'll excuse me for a minute, I think Eileen is temporarily free."

Robin watched him stride down the side of the room to the teacher, who had extricated herself from yet another cluster of parents. The babble of voices in the room remained at a steady, raucous pitch, and Robin sidled along the rows of desks to get closer to Jesse. Eavesdropping wasn't the most polite thing to do, but she was curious to know why her mention of her divorce had caused Jesse to abandon her. Besides, he had eavesdropped on her conversation with Ms. Becker. Fair was fair.

He reached into his hip pocket and pulled out a legal-size envelope. "Here you go," he said, handing it to Ms. Becker. "Signed, sealed, delivered. I imagine congratulations are in order."

Ms. Becker appeared flustered again, and then suddenly grateful. Her eyes glistened slightly as she accepted the envelope from Jesse. "I really appreciate your coming down to the school just to bring this to me, but since I'm going out with some of the other teachers afterward, and I probably won't be getting home till late—"

"I saw your note, Eileen. And I assure you, it was no problem."

"It's just—I wanted it in my hands, tonight. Just to get it over with, to have it with me—"

"I understand."

Ms. Becker's teary eyes met Jesse's for a moment. "Are you sure I can't pay you for this?"

"Positive," he said gently. "All it entailed was a couple of telephone calls."

"Perhaps you'd let me treat you to dinner or something?"

He shook his head. "No thanks, Eileen. Really. It wasn't any trouble. I'm glad I could help."

If he refused an invitation for dinner with Ms. Becker, Robin analyzed, then they couldn't be lovers. That understanding shouldn't have made any difference to her, but an unjustifiable sense of elation filled her. Not that a rusty, dowdy, out-of-practice divorced mother like her could ever instill more than a passing interest in a man like Jesse Lawson. But if he wasn't taken, then there must be others who weren't, either. Robin instantly began her mental list of New Year's resolutions with a promise to start putting forth an earnest effort to meet men.

She hadn't expected Jesse to turn around so suddenly. He found her standing indefensibly close to him, and her abashed expression informed him that she had overheard his conversation with Ms. Becker. Yet instead of appearing angry, he smiled. "That's my good deed for the day," he said. "I think I deserve extra credit for doing it in front of a witness."

"Your good deed?" she mumbled, trying unsuccessfully to hide her chagrin.

"Eileen's a neighbor of mine." He didn't owe Robin an explanation, and she considered pointing that out to him, but he didn't give her a chance. "She needed some minor legal assistance, and I was able to help her out with it."

Legal assistance. The man was a lawyer. That would explain the luxurious suede jacket.

That Jesse Lawson was rich as well as handsome struck Robin as almost unreasonable. No man deserved to have that much going for him. "Your assistance couldn't have been all that minor if you raced all the way here on Open School Night just to make a delivery."

Jesse shrugged. "I was going to drop the papers off at her house this evening, but by the time I got home she had already left for school. She had taped a note to her front door, asking if I wouldn't mind bringing the papers here. She didn't want to have to wait until tomorrow."

The only legal paper Robin had ever been that anxious to have in her possession was her divorce decree. The divorce had been so long in coming, and the negotiations, although devoid of bitterness, had seemed to take forever. Robin's attorney had offered to mail her the decree, but she had insisted on driving over to his office on her lunch hour the day it was ready, just to have it in her possession.

An extremely rough autumn. Ms. Becker's words resounded inside Robin. "You handled her divorce," she blurted out, her exasperation with the teacher abruptly replaced by a tide of sisterly compassion. No wonder Robin's mention of her own divorce had spurred Jesse to perform his good deed.

He appeared surprised by the accuracy of Robin's guess. He glimpsed the teacher, whose smile as she conferred with another student's mother seemed more genuine than it had appeared when she'd been lecturing the parents en masse. Then his gaze returned to Robin. "I don't think she wants the news broadcast in a big way," he said.

"I won't breathe a hint of it," Robin promised, herself surprised that she'd guessed right. Then another surprise jolted her—Ms. Becker had offered him payment, and he'd refused. What sort of lawyer didn't take money for his services? Although Robin's and Ray's divorce had been completely free of acrimony, although they had worked out all the details without a quibble, although Ray had willingly left her the house, given her custody of Philip, and volunteered both generous child support and a small monthly stipend until she had been promoted at work and insisted that the alimony was no longer needed—in spite of all that, their lawyers had pocketed hefty retainers for doing little more than filling out the proper forms.

"Why won't you let her pay you?" she asked Jesse, assuming that if he minded her probing he would have walked away from her by now.

He shrugged. "I didn't do much. She had her own lawyer negotiate the settlement, but he's away on vacation now, and the other side was sitting on the papers too long. I just called them for her and gave them a nudge."

Despite his modest claim, Robin was impressed by his refusal to accept money from Ms. Becker. Most lawyers would charge hundreds of dollars for making a single telephone call. Inspecting the fine suede of his jacket, she realized that Jesse must be so wealthy that a few hundred dollars more or less didn't matter to him. Even so, his gesture in helping out his neighbor was generous.

She turned away, following Ms. Becker with her eyes for a moment. Then she shook her head. "I'm sorry for her," she commiserated.

"Are you? You don't seem sorry for yourself."

Her head snapped back to Jesse. His face was impassive, and she recognized that he had simply stated the truth. "I'm not. It's hard at the beginning, but after a while, you become so involved in other things that it doesn't hurt anymore."

"If you're lucky," Jesse noted. "What other things are you involved in?"

"Philip," she said, then grinned. "Of course, Philip. And I've got the house, my job—"

"Where do you work?"

"Woodleigh's," she told him. "On the Post Road."

"Woodleigh's," he repeated uncertainly. "Is that a store of some sort?"

His ignorance startled her. Woodleigh's served an affluent clientele. Her store specialized in hand-blown crystal and hand-painted Ironstone, fine linens, Danish modern flatware, butcher-block computer desks, ceramic napkin rings, and all sorts of elegant knickknacks. There were currently four Woodleigh's outlets, all located in shoreline Connecticut towns, all catering to the upwardly mobile, the yuppies, lawyers who were likely to wear expensive leather jackets.

"Yes," she remembered to answer him. "It's a store. I'm the manager. And—especially at this time of year—I'm much too busy to sit around moping—"

"Green!" a familiar voice squawked shrilly into her ear. "Oh my God, it's green!"

Spinning around, Robin found Joanna glaring at one of the crayoned turkeys on the bulletin board, her hands on her hips and her face contorted in a grimace. "Hi, Joanna," Robin hailed her. "How was the snake?"

"Either he was sleeping or he was dead. I didn't bother to ask. But look at this, Robin! Jeff colored his turkey green!"

"What's wrong with green?" Robin asked, laughing. "At least his turkey has wings."

"Robin," Joanna said sternly. "I happen to make the best roast turkey this side of Chicago. You know that—you've had Thanksgiving dinner at our house two years running. Now, what do you think Jeff is trying to tell me when he colors his turkey green?"

"I think he's trying to tell you that green was the first crayon he pulled out of the box. Don't take it so personally," Robin comforted her.

Joanna started to laugh, too. Then her eyes wandered past Robin and she fell momentarily silent. "Oh," she said contritely. "I'm sorry, I didn't mean to interrupt."

Robin bailed her out with a smile and a courteous introduction. "Joanna, this is Jesse Lawson. Jesse, Joanna Calloway."

Joanna shook Jesse's hand, then shot Robin a quizzical glance. "Lawson? I didn't know there was someone named Lawson in the class."

"There isn't," Jesse smoothly corrected her. His gaze shuttled between Robin and her friend, and he nodded. "It was a pleasure meeting you both," he said by way of parting. "Green is great, but—" his eyes lingered on Robin for a split-second longer "—purple hands are exceptional. You must be quite a mother, Robin Greer."

With an economy of motion Robin found strangely hypnotic, he pivoted on his heel and strolled out the door.

Robin and Joanna stared for a wordless minute at the empty doorway through which he'd vanished. Then they simultaneously turned to each other. "So?" Joanna prodded Robin, obviously brimming with curiosity. "I'm all ears."

"There's nothing to tell," Robin declared truthfully. "We talked for a few minutes, that's all."

"If he isn't someone's daddy, what was he doing here?"

"He's a neighbor of Ms. Becker's," Robin informed her. "He had to bring her some . . . some documents she wanted." Sworn to secrecy about the teacher's divorce, she wasn't about to say anything more, not even to her close friend.

"Is he single?" Joanna asked.

"How should I know?" The question irked Robin, mostly because she had failed to find out that vital piece of information. "All we did was talk about the hands on Philip's turkey."

Joanna assessed Robin dubiously. "He approached you," she pointed out. "I was watching."

"You were supposed to be looking at the snake," Robin scolded.

"Which would you rather look at, a comatose snake or that spectacular man? I hope for your sake he *is* single," Joanna said, zipping her jacket. "I'm all done here if you are. Let's go home and rescue Glenn."

Rummaging in her purse for her car keys, Robin followed Joanna from the classroom. As they walked through the building to the parking lot out front, she listened with half her brain to Joanna's report on what Matthew Florio's mother had said about the gym teacher and on the gossip about Emily Gelb's father's transfer to Dallas. With the other half of her brain, Robin mulled over Joanna's remark about how she hoped Jesse Lawson was single.

Why should Robin care whether he was? They'd passed the time for a few minutes, that was all. She wasn't apt to see him again. If she ever started dating— *when* she started dating, she silently amended—she would be smart to stick with safe men for her first few outings. Her definition of "safe" was not too affluent, not too good-looking, not too suave. Not possessed of a voice that could tame wild lions and croon colicky babies to sleep, that could cause a woman to suffer heart palpitations merely by saying, "You must be quite a mother, Robin Greer."

His voice had sounded so sweet when he'd uttered her name. Sweet, velvety, seductive, as if those two bland words contained intimate secrets. Robin fleetingly wondered what Jesse Lawson would sound like murmuring *real* intimacies, whispering erotic incantations, caressing Robin's soul with flattery, with vows . . .

Starting the station wagon's engine, she clicked on the radio. The car filled with a buoyant rendition of "Deck the Halls,'' its rousing melody effectively erasing the memory of the man's mesmerizing voice. Indeed, Robin concluded with a wry smile, someone like Jesse would sound absolutely foolish singing "Fa-la-la-la-la."

Chapter Two

Loosening the knot of the navy-blue scarf at his throat, Jesse climbed the stairs to Mrs. Selby's third-floor apartment. The elevator still hadn't been fixed, which was both good and bad. Good, because the broken elevator was a major item on the list of grievances that Jesse had filed with the court on the tenants' behalf. Bad, because women like Mrs. Selby shouldn't have to trudge up and down several flights of stairs every time they wanted to run an errand or visit a friend.

The elevator was broken, and bags of garbage were heaped along the curb outside. The corridors were strewn with more garbage, and the front door lock had been broken for nearly a year. A couple of the windows were laced with cracks. Most of the tenants had already moved away, but Mrs. Selby and a few others were staying on because they had no place else to go.

The exposed lightbulb on the ceiling of the third floor hallway had burned out, Jesse observed. He pulled a pad and pen from an inner pocket of his tweed blazer and made a note of it. One more grievance. He hoped that there wouldn't be too many more before the landlord felt compelled to rehabilitate the building. It was too close to being condemned—and if it was, Mrs. Selby and the others would have no choice but to move. Mr. Cabot was probably hoping for condemnation. He had made little secret of his desire to remove the rest of the tenants, raze the building, and sell the land. Even in the rundown New Haven neighborhood of Newhallville, a person could turn a tidy profit on the sale of a double-size lot like the one on which the tenement sat.

Jesse knocked on Mrs. Selby's door—the doorbell had stopped functioning ages ago—and listened to her plodding footsteps approaching the door from the other side. He heard the click of the peephole lid opening, and then the slip of the bolt being released. "Mr. Lawson," she greeted him, smiling and stepping aside so he could enter the apartment. "You're early. I was just making some lunch. You hungry?"

"No, thank you," he declined, closing the door behind him. His polite smile faded as soon as he heard the orchestrated melody emerging from the television set in the living room. *Blessings at Noon,* he identified the show from its familiar theme music. He walked briskly into the living room, where he found Mrs. Selby's one-year-old grandson asleep on the floor in front of the television set, a blanket covering him and a pacifier protruding from his mouth. *I don't blame you for wanting to sleep through this,* Jesse muttered silently, stepping over the baby to shut off the television.

"I was just watching that," said Mrs. Selby, squatting down to tuck the blanket more snugly around the baby. "I just love *Blessings at Noon.*"

"It's a stupid show," Jesse snapped, then berated himself for responding so sharply. Lots of people loved *Blessings at Noon.* According to last year's Neilsen ratings—

"Well, the choir, they sing so nice," Mrs. Selby explained. "And today, well, the Reverend Robert Shepherd had on this amazing girl. You wouldn't believe it, Mr. Lawson. Paralyzed from the neck down in a ski accident, and then she prayed and prayed and the Lord saw fit to let her regain the use of her hands. It was a miracle, Mr. Lawson, and I saw it with my own eyes, right there on the show. I saw that girl write her name and throw a baseball from her wheelchair."

"It wasn't a miracle," Jesse argued, unable to modulate his scathing tone. "Chances are, the girl's spinal damage wasn't as severe as originally thought. When people recover like that, it isn't because of divine intervention. It's because of excellent medical care and physical therapy. And hard work."

"I don't know," Mrs. Selby debated him. "She and the Reverend said, right there on the show, they said they prayed together and the Lord saw fit to make this girl's hands work again. And right now I'm just praying and praying that the Lord see fit to fix up this apartment before it falls down on our heads."

Jesse permitted himself a dry laugh. Prayer wasn't going to fix the apartment building. Even if the Reverend Robert Shepherd, his enormous staff and the entire Grace Cathedral Choir prayed for the tenement's redemption, it wouldn't do any good. The only way to save Mrs. Selby's home was through legal maneuvers, the class-action civil suit Jesse had just initiated, and a lot of pressure on the recalcitrant landlord. In other words, hard work.

"Come on," Mrs. Selby said, urging him into the tiny kitchen where a couple of frankfurters were boiling in a pot on the dilapidated gas stove. She waved Jesse to one of the vinyl chairs by the table, then busied herself pulling two hot dog buns from a plastic bag. "You sure I can't feed you one of these?" she asked as he took a seat.

"I'm sure," he insisted.

"Some coffee, then," she decided, filling a kettle with water and setting it on another burner. "You must be hungry, a big man like you. I know my boy Gerald, when he's home on leave, he'd as soon clean out the refrigerator with his bare hands."

Gerald was Mrs. Selby's oldest child, and he was in the Navy. Lucky for him, Jesse thought, surveying the cramped kitchen. As it was, Mrs. Selby lived in the three-bedroom apartment with her four other children and the baby one of her daughters had given birth to, out of wedlock, at the age of fifteen. At least that daughter had returned to high school.

The weight of Mrs. Selby's life seemed to rest heavily on her shoulders. In her mid-forties, she looked at least ten years older. Her hair was more gray than black, and her posture was hunched, as if she were too fatigued to stand up straight. Not that Jesse could blame her. Her husband had died eight years ago, leaving her a minute widow's pension on which she was trying to raise her huge family. And she was desperately close to joining the ranks of the homeless, thanks to the mendacity of Mr. Cabot. It was no wonder she watched trash like *Blessings at Noon* and looked to the Lord for help. Until Jesse and the staff of New Haven Legal Assistance had entered her life two months ago, nobody else had bothered to lend a hand to Mrs. Selby and the other few stubborn tenants.

She handed him a cup of instant coffee and sat facing him at the table, her frankfurters rolling about on a chipped plate. Jesse took a dutiful sip of the coffee. It was weak but hot, and it thawed his chilled bones. His shirt, V-neck sweater, tweed blazer and scarf hadn't succeeded in keeping out the midday chill. Jesse never wore a suit and tie when he visited his clients. If he did, they wouldn't trust him. They'd think he was "The Man."

"Still having problems with the heat?" he asked Mrs. Selby.

She chewed, then swallowed and shrugged. "It comes and goes," she said. "Mostly comes, these days."

"That's good." He set his cup on the table and wrapped his hands around it to warm them. "I spent an hour this morning at the building inspector's office, and so far I've managed to persuade them not to condemn the building."

"Praise God," Mrs. Selby said with a sigh, and Jesse pressed his lips together to prevent himself from rebuking her about her useless faith. "They condemn this place, and we'll be on the streets. Or they'll put us in one of them hotels. You know as well as I do, there's no room in any of the projects."

"I've put you and the other tenants on the waiting list for public housing," Jesse informed her. "Just in case. But you're right—the list is long. We can't have this building condemned. Most of the building code infractions here are inconveniences, but they don't really constitute a risk to life or health. The light is out in the hall, by the way."

"Been out for four days," Mrs. Selby lamented. "I figure, Gerald's got leave for Christmas, I can get him to fix it."

"Don't," Jesse instructed her. "By the time he gets home, maybe we'll have prodded Mr. Cabot into action. I've begun formal proceedings against him. I filed the civil suit this morning."

"You did?" Her round brown eyes met Jesse's, glimmering expectantly. "How much you asking for?"

"A hundred and fifty thousand dollars per tenant," Jesse told her.

Mrs. Selby dropped her hot dog. "A hundred fifty thousand? Are you kidding?"

"No, but—"

"A hundred and fifty thousand dollars!" She clasped her hands to her breast, evidently transported. "I can't hardly think that big! What we could do with money like that—"

"Mrs. Selby, you're not going to wind up with that much money," he cautioned her.

"Well, I know, you take your cut, Mr. Lawson, but—"

"I don't take a cut," he explained patiently. "I'm on a salary from Legal Assistance. However, you should understand that the amount we're asking for is only a starting point. We want to shock the landlord into action. By asking for a large amount, we hope we can drag him to the negotiating table. We'd be willing to settle for much less."

"How much less?" Mrs. Selby asked suspiciously.

"If we can arrange to have all the infractions taken care of—plus a settlement of, say, two years' back rent plus interest . . ."

"Two years back rent." Mrs. Selby closed her eyes and calculated the amount. Her face fell. "That's less than five thousand dollars."

"Plus interest," Jesse reminded her. "Maybe more, maybe ten thousand per unit. And the repairs. It's better than living in a hotel, Mrs. Selby."

"I suppose it is," she allowed, nibbling on her frank-furter. "Better than we got now, too. 'Tween you and me, Mr. Lawson, I'd settle for a working elevator."

"You'll get that and more," he said. "At least, I hope you will. Now, as far as December's rent, did you write it out to the escrow account, like I told you?"

She scowled. "I don't see why I got to pay it at all, the way this place is falling to pieces."

"I understand your feelings. But you've got to keep paying the rent until this matter is resolved."

"I know you'll resolve it," Mrs. Selby said confidently. "I got faith in you, Mr. Lawson."

That's better than having faith in God and the Reverend Robert Shepherd, he grunted to himself as, a few minutes later, he took his leave of Mrs. Selby. She was typical of the sort who wasted their time with junk like *Blessings at Noon* and Shepherd's Sunday morning show, *Holy Hour.* His audience comprised the poor, the benighted, people struggling under a burden they were unable to comprehend. How much easier it was to send a check to the Reverend Shepherd's Grace Cathedral and send their prayers skyward than to raise arms against their self-serving landlords, to roll up their sleeves and exert themselves to improve their lot.

It had taken Jesse a long time to reach this level of cynicism, to break away from the powers that had once dominated his world. He, too, had believed, at first. Like the child he had been, he hadn't known any better, and so he'd tried his hardest to believe. Then he'd grown up and discovered the truth about outfits like the Grace Cathedral and its television empire. The money that flowed in was obscene in its quantity, and where did it go? Into the coffers of Shepherd and his henchmen, into the grotesque enormity of the cathedral, into the TV studio.

"The more people we reach," Shepherd liked to preach, "the better we can do the Lord's work. So dig deep, brothers and sisters, and send us whatever you can. Let us extend our network into every home, into every heart, so we can bring our good work to all people."

"Hah," Jesse snorted out loud at his memory of Shepherd's sermons.

He had already visited the other tenants to update them on his legal action at the court and his success in stalling a condemnation of the building. Settling himself inside the Volkswagen Rabbit he'd bought second-hand when he moved to Branford last June, he remembered the Mercedes he'd left behind in Los Angeles. It didn't take a fleet of extravagant automobiles to do good work, any more than it took a religious broadcasting network or a flashy cathedral. It didn't take millions upon millions of dollars subtracted from the skimpy savings of impoverished believers. All it took to do good work was a humane attitude and a willingness to skip lunch every now and then.

Newhallville was dressed for Christmas, Jesse noted with another surge of cynicism. Some of the tenements were adorned with strings of colorful lights, and a number of windows had electric candles or silver stars displayed in them. The people who lived in those tenements could barely afford to live from one paycheck—or welfare check—to the next, yet they wasted money on inane decorations instead of buying themselves food, clothing, things that would truly make their lives better.

Jesse didn't consider himself a Scrooge—Scrooge was a miser, after all, and Jesse believed in giving. On the other hand, the hoopla attached to Christmas, the gaudiness and commercialism, set his teeth on edge. People called themselves Christians, yet they gave of themselves only one day a year. The whole thing was hypocritical, overdone, superficial. Doing good that one day freed people to be selfish and thoughtless the other three hundred and sixty-four days. The emphasis was wrong.

Something so wonderful... For not the first time that day, Jesse heard a soft, gentle voice echoing inside his skull, counteracting his irritation about the holiday. *How can there be too much emphasis on something so wonderful?*

Robin Greer. More than her voice had haunted him after he had departed from the elementary school the previous evening. At least a dozen times—hell, at least a hundred times—since he'd walked out of Eileen Becker's classroom, an image of the petite blond woman with the bright hazel eyes and even brighter smile had floated across his mind. Something in the intensity of her defense of Christmas struck Jesse as almost childlike in its exuberance, childlike and innocent and immensely appealing.

Not that Robin Greer was an innocent child. The woman managed a store, she raised a son, she was divorced...

That was part of it, too, he acknowledged as he started up the engine and waited for it to warm up so he could turn on the heat. Most of the divorced women Jesse knew were like his neighbor Eileen, infused with bitterness or brittle with rancor. Women like Eileen, or like that hardbitten lady to whom Bill and Sally Hammond had introduced Jesse at their Thanksgiving party last week. Still something of a newcomer to the New Haven area, with absolutely no desire to fly back to Los Angeles to spend the holiday with his parents, Jesse had been delighted by the Hammonds' invitation. He hadn't known that within minutes of entering their house, he would be dragged across the living room to meet Tracy LaPorte. "She's a knockout, eh?" Bill had whispered to Jesse some time later, when Jesse had escaped from the woman's clutches long enough to flee to the kitchen for a drink of water.

Tracy LaPorte was a knockout—except for the rage seething just below her pretty surface, the resentment emanating from her. Less than ten minutes after they were introduced, Tracy had been enumerating for Jesse all the sins of her ex-husband. Her gripes differed from Eileen Becker's in the particulars, but in tone they were no less petulant than those of Eileen, or of any other divorcée's.

But Robin Greer—if she hadn't told him, he never would have guessed that she was divorced. She seemed so happy, so lively, so much at peace with herself.

He admired her feistiness in criticizing Eileen's teaching methods. He admired the fact that she had produced a son who drew hands on a turkey. When Jesse was seven, he would never have dared to commit such a bizarre act. He might have considered it, but he would have lacked the gumption to go through with it. Years of training, discipline and force-fed piety had driven his independence out of him. No wonder it had taken him this long to find the courage to leave that whole scene and forge a new life, faithful to his own ideals and nothing else.

He was still thinking about Robin Greer a few hours later when he'd finished up at his office and begun the short commute from New Haven to Branford, eight miles east of the city. He was still thinking of Robin's silky yellow hair and her delicate cheeks, her stunningly bright eyes. What he wasn't thinking about was the route he was taking until he found himself coasting off the turnpike several exits before the one he usually took. He would be able to get home from this exit; the Post Road paralleled the turnpike throughout most of southern Connecticut.

With an amazed smile, he understood why he'd taken the wrong exit onto the Post Road. If he traveled home this way, he'd pass Robin's store. Woodson's, he thought it was called. Woodson's, or Woodmont's, or Wood-something. Crossing the town line into Branford, he slowed enough to read the signs marking the numerous stores that bordered the road. Woodson's could be anywhere along the route; it could be any one of those countless stores trimmed with blinking lights and electrified Santa Clauses, plastic wreaths and tinsel garlands.

Woodleigh's. That was it, Woodleigh's. Applying the brakes, Jesse navigated into the parking lot and coasted to the first parking space he found. Then he locked the car, strode to the building and shaded his eyes as he peered through the broad panes of the glass front wall. The displays lining the windows featured attractive modern stained-wood tables festooned with holly and poinsettias, red and green tapers protruding from silver candlesticks, decanters wrapped in red ribbons and delicate, hand-crafted Christmas tree ornaments. Beyond the window display, he saw more of the same—elegant housewares, table settings and carved wooden train sets, all sprayed with tiny flecks of rainbow created by the light from the overhead fixtures passing through the crystal stars dangling from the ceiling. A dwarf Christmas tree stood on one end of the polished wood sales counter at the center of the store.

The sight of so much seasonal detritus almost caused Jesse to leave the shop without entering. Stores like Woodleigh's lived for Christmas—he assumed that they raked in unconscionable profits at this time of year.

And yet... and yet he couldn't shake the image of a lovely blond woman somewhere within that room full of holiday merchandise, a cheerful woman with penetrating eyes and a son who gave his turkey hands. Jesse drew in a deep breath and entered.

GLANCING UP from the cash register, Robin saw him standing beneath the mistletoe.

The mistletoe had been hung above the front door by the salesclerks as a gag. It was hardly noticeable to unwary customers, and the clerks had strung it up with the notion that if a foxy-looking man happened to venture into the store, they'd have a perfect excuse to fling themselves upon him and bury him in kisses. Not that they would actually do anything that forward—they'd have to answer to Jack Woodleigh himself if they did. But since they were supposed to approach any customer who remained loitering too long near the front door, the mistletoe gave them an added incentive to do their jobs.

The man unknowingly standing beneath the mistletoe right now went beyond foxy, however. In his well-tailored blazer, pale gray sweater and open-collared oxford shirt, his scarf draped untied around his neck, his long legs flattered by his slate-gray corduroy slacks and his hair, adorably unruly and so black it put Robin in mind of such concepts as midnight and infinity... Jesse Lawson was easily the best-looking man ever to plant himself under that wicked sprig of green leaves and white berries.

Not surprisingly, Kirsten was the first of the clerks to spot him. A tall, well-groomed woman with ash-blond hair and discerning eyes, Kirsten was easily the prettiest member of Robin's sales force, and the most overtly man-hungry. Robin spied on her employee, who managed to look seductive even when she was wearing a plain white sweater and tan flannel slacks beneath her starchy brown Woodleigh's pinafore, as she wandered over to Jesse and offered him her most winning smile. *If she kisses him, Jack Woodleigh's going to have a connip-tion,* Robin mused, watching and wondering just how brazenly Kirsten would behave.

A customer jarred Robin by plunking seventy dollars' worth of Christmas linens—napkins, place mats, and hand towels—onto the counter and demanding gift boxes. Robin reluctantly turned her back on the door and began to punch numbers into the computerized register. "Lisa, could you put these things in boxes?" she called to her assistant, who had just finished bagging another order.

"Do you think she's going to kiss him?" Lisa murmured, her eyes glued to the doorway as she reached for the stack of unfolded white boxes on the shelf below the counter.

"If there's anything Kirsten likes more than men, it's money," Robin answered with a chuckle, accepting the customer's credit card and fitting it into the charge machine. "I doubt she'd risk her job, even for him."

"I'd risk mine," Lisa said with an exaggerated sigh. She joined Robin's laughter for a moment, then caught herself. "He's coming over here," she whispered, dropping the box she had been assembling in order to preen and fuss with her hair.

If Robin had wanted to run her hands through her own hair, she wouldn't have been able to. As usual, it was pinned back into a ponytail. Even so, as Kirsten led Jesse among the display tables to the counter, Robin dropped her gaze to her pinafore, hoping her skirt and blouse hung straight beneath it. She knew she looked better now than she had last night at the Brushy Plain School, but better didn't seem good enough.

"Hello, Robin," Jesse said in that delicious voice of his.

She raised her eyes and presented him with a surprisingly relaxed smile. "Hello, Jesse. I see you've finally decided to find out what Woodleigh's is."

Lisa and Kirsten exchanged a glance at this proof that their boss, good old Robin, for whom no man had ever come to call at the store, was actually on a first-name basis with such a fantastic-looking gentleman. Robin's smile widened at the comprehension that her acquaintanceship with Jesse might win her a bit more respect from her underlings.

"I've got to finish this order," she said, excusing herself to fill out the charge slip.

"Take your time," said Jesse.

Needless to say, she completed the charge slip in record time. As soon as the customer signed it, Robin abandoned her to Lisa, who had resumed assembling boxes for the linens, and glided around the counter to Jesse. "Are you looking for something special?" she asked.

He opened his mouth, then shut it and gazed around the shop. "Just curious," he said. "What is all this stuff?"

Robin laughed. "All what stuff?" She surveyed the bustling store. "It's what we sell here. Housewares, decorator items—"

"Stationery," he mumbled, lifting a box of note cards featuring a silkscreened winter scene on the front. He turned the box over, saw the price tag and winced. "Expensive stationery."

"High-priced, but worth it," she justified. "These note cards feature one-of-a-kind designs on recycled paper, and..." She trailed off. Somehow she knew that Jesse hadn't come into the store to listen to a sales pitch.

His gaze circled the room again, pausing at one of the butcher-block tables with its matching cane-and-Haitian-cotton chairs, pausing again at the colorful array of place mats and tablecloths exhibited against one birch-paneled wall, and again at the hand-painted toy-soldier nutcrackers lined up in formation on a shelf covered with green felt and bedecked with holly. When he turned back to Robin, his eyes seemed darker, shadowed by an undefinable sadness. "What's wrong?" she asked instinctively.

He shook his head and grinned. "I was just thinking about some people I visited today, through work. I was thinking about their apartments, and how out of place these things would be inside them."

Visiting some people through work? "I thought you were a lawyer," she said.

"I am."

"Do lawyers make house calls?"

"Legal aid lawyers do, sometimes."

A legal aid lawyer? Since when could legal aid lawyers afford extravagant suede jackets? Or, for that matter, Harris Tweed blazers? Jesse's clothing fit him too well to have been purchased off the rack at Sears. That sweater had to be angora, and his loafers appeared hand-stitched. The scarf looked like cashmere.

"Would this stuff be out of place in your home?" she asked. It was admittedly a nosy question, but she couldn't imagine a man like Jesse Lawson living in the sort of house a legal aid lawyer might be able to afford.

He shrugged. "At the moment, anything would look out of place in it," he confessed. "I moved here from Los Angeles six months ago, and except for a few pieces of necessary furniture, I haven't done much with my place."

"Do you live in Branford?"

"In one of the condominiums off Brush Plain Road," he replied with a nod.

"Mondo Condo," Robin let slip. That was the derogatory name she and Joanna had given to the sprawl of condominium developments north of the elementary school. The developments had proliferated in the last few years like toadstools after a downpour. When Robin and Ray had first bought their modest Cape Cod house in Branford, the town had been little more than a quiet, underdeveloped bedroom community for people who worked in New Haven. In the nine years since then, however, the town had been built up beyond recognition. Robin had signed petitions and attended town meetings calling for a halt to the development, but the condos kept sprouting.

Jesse apparently wasn't offended by the epithet. "Mondo Condo," he repeated. "That about sums it up."

She didn't really have to make amends for having slighted his residence, but she felt she ought to, anyway. "Some of those condominiums are pretty classy. Your home would probably look nice with a few fancy items in it. A wine rack, maybe, or some of these crystal tree ornaments from Denmark—"

"I don't plan to have a tree," he said curtly. "What would I want with ornaments?" Then he relented, his smile returning. "But I do drink wine on occasion."

No tree? The notion seemed incomprehensible to Robin, but she refrained from blurting out any more impolitic remarks. She was lucky that he hadn't been insulted by her comment about his condominium-infested neighborhood. Even if not having a Christmas tree was, to her mind, a lapse bordering on inexcusable, she didn't dare to question him about it.

Instead she ushered him through the store to a display of wine racks. Some were constructed of varnished wood, others of brass. He appraised their price tags first, then their designs. "I'd probably do better at K-Mart," he muttered.

"In terms of price, maybe," she said loftily. "Not in terms of quality."

Abruptly he turned to her. He dug his hands into the pockets of his trousers and gazed down at her, his eyes unnerving in their resonant force, in their vividness. "I didn't come here to shop," he admitted quietly. "I came here to see you."

Robin laughed. She often laughed when she was shocked, and Jesse's announcement shocked her. A series of emotions clamored through her—that she was immeasurably flattered, that she wished she were as beautiful as Kirsten, that she didn't have to be as beautiful as Kirsten because Jesse was here to see her and not the statuesque salesclerk. That she truly wanted to start dating again, and that Jesse seemed much too attractive, much too perilously intriguing, to become her first boyfriend in thirteen years.

"What did you want to see me about?" she asked guilelessly.

A tender smile danced across Jesse's thin, strong lips. "About your son, I think."

"Philip?" Had Eileen Becker confided in Jesse about her concerns regarding Philip? Had the teacher told her neighbor she thought Philip Greer was perverse? And why had Jesse added, "I think"? Wasn't he sure why he had come to see Robin?

"I'd—I'd like to meet him," Jesse said.

"Why?"

"Because..." He hesitated, taking time to sort his thoughts. "Because any boy who's got the guts to draw hands on a turkey must be pretty special."

A wave of maternal pride flooded through Robin. Philip was special—he was the most special, darling, brilliant, magnificent little boy in the world. "He also drew antennae on his turkey," she reminded Jesse.

"More power to him." He reflected for a minute, shoving his hands deeper into his pockets and striking an almost diffident pose. As diffident as it was, however, the motion of his arms pulled back the flaps of his blazer, revealing the fine, soft wool of his sweater and, beneath it, the fine, hard shape of his torso. "Am I out of line?" he asked. "Asking to meet your son, I mean."

"No, of course not," Robin said quickly. She wondered what Philip would say if she brought Jesse home— she wondered what he would say if she brought *any* man home. That particular situation had never occurred before, although Robin assumed that if she started dating, it was bound to crop up sooner or later.

Not that she was dating Jesse. It was Philip he was interested in, not Robin.

And yet the idea of bringing Jesse home had an undeniable appeal to it. "We close up in half an hour," she told him. "If you want to stick around until then, sure, you can meet my gutsy son."

"I'll stick around," Jesse promised.

Her gaze locked with his for an instant. Despite his affable smile, there was something somber in his dark, piercing eyes, something earnest and oddly wistful. Before Robin had a chance to interpret it, Lisa raced over to her and jabbed her arm. "Robin? Are we out of the Swedish votive candles?" she asked. "Ginny went downstairs to the stock room, but she couldn't find any there."

"We just got a delivery of them yesterday," Robin said, snapping into her professional mind-set. "If I know Kevin, he misplaced them." She grinned apologetically at Jesse. "Crisis time," she explained. "Heavy is the head that wears the crown, or however the saying goes."

"Don't let me interrupt your work," Jesse said swiftly, taking a step backward and then bending down to examine one of the wine racks more closely. "I'm not going anywhere."

Chapter Three

Forty-five minutes later, he *was* going somewhere. He was following the red taillights of Robin's compact station wagon off the Post Road and onto a winding back lane that lacked adequate lighting. He hadn't bothered to purchase a wine rack—for a thirty-four-year-old man, he knew pitifully little about wines, and he tended to buy bottles singly, on impulse. He had browsed through Woodleigh's, engaged in silent debate about whether the toy-soldier nutcrackers were cute or tacky, whether food tasted better when eaten off expensive dishes than when eaten off cheap ones, whether someone like Mrs. Selby, unexpectedly bestowed with a hundred fifty thousand dollars in an out-of-court settlement with her landlord, would choose to spend any of it in a place like Woodleigh's.

At six o'clock, he had stood by while Robin locked the shop's front door, reminded her salesclerks to double-check the pre-Christmas schedule of store hours, which had been extended to accommodate the holiday shoppers, removed her brown apron and shut off the lights. Her car was parked in back, and he had waited until she'd driven around to the front parking lot and flashed her station wagon's lights at him before he started his engine.

Now he was going to meet Philip.

He wanted to meet the boy. He wanted to see for himself this child who had been raised to give his imagination free rein, to invent a make-believe universe—Jesse had overheard Robin and Eileen discussing the alien planet from which Philip's turkey had allegedly descended. He wanted to befriend a child who was allowed to believe whatever he wanted and to create whatever he wanted. Although Jesse didn't know much about children, he wanted to meet the son Robin Greer had produced.

That was the other reason he was trailing those beacon-like red taillights through the darkness: Robin herself. There was something so alive about her, something so vibrant, so warm. From a distance, he had observed her banter with her clerks at the store, her competence in solving the mystery of the temporarily missing votive candles, her sedate control over her domain. Jesse didn't particularly care for the items Woodleigh's sold, but he liked the way Robin ran the store. She seemed capable and strong and...at peace. Again it occurred to him—she was at peace with herself.

They entered a quiet area of modest but lovingly tended Cape Cod houses that backed on a dense forest. Their front lawns were neatly mowed and their walks lit. Many of them were trimmed with Christmas lights. The driveway up which Robin turned led to a blue house with a woven willow wreath hanging on the front door.

Jesse's car trailed hers onto the long driveway, and he killed the engine and climbed out. Robin had parked inside the garage and was pulling down the garage door when Jesse reached her. "Let me give you a hand," he said. She seemed much too delicate to be able to yank the massive door into place.

She waved off his assistance with a simple "I've got it," and sure enough, the door slid into position. Then she accompanied Jesse up the walk. "You're welcome to stay for dinner if you'd like," she invited him matter-of-factly. "Philip is always starving by the time I get home, and the roast is probably ready. It's too big for two people, anyway."

"Roast? Your son cooked a roast?"

She laughed and jiggled her key ring to select the right key for the front door. "No. Kate O'Leary put it in the oven. She's Philip's baby-sitter." The door swung open, and Robin hollered, "Phil? I'm home!"

A wiry tow-haired youngster bounded into the living room from a hallway behind the staircase. "Hey, Mommy!" he shouted, springing into her arms and giving her an exuberant hug. "I did all my homework and I watched *Masters of the Universe* and I fed all my cookies to Cookie Monster at school so that means I can have more cookies for dessert tonight, okay? Hey, who's this?" he asked, releasing his mother and fixing his gaze on Jesse.

Jesse was only subliminally aware of the redolence of cooking meat that filled the air, the homey furnishings in the living room, the broad brick fireplace on the far wall and the sturdy maple occasional tables scattered about the room. The bulk of his attention was focused on the boy.

Philip looked exactly like Robin—or at least, exactly like a seven-year-old male version of Robin. His hair was the same flaxen shade, the same flyaway texture. His eyes were as bright and multicolored as hers, his cheeks as cleanly defined, his jaw as pointy. His build, like hers, was slim yet strong, exuding energy. And his greeting was just as down-to-earth and accepting as Robin's "Hello, Jesse" had been when he'd entered her store.

"This is Jesse Lawson," Robin said. Jesse had wondered how she would explain his presence to her son, whether she would introduce him as a friend or an acquaintance, or, perhaps, as a cheapskate who didn't give a hoot for one-of-a-kind silkscreened notecards. But she avoided labels and simply provided his name. Jesse liked that. "Jesse, my son Philip, on leave from the planet Gleek. Hi, Kate," she greeted the plump silver-haired woman who had entered the room behind Philip. "How did it go today?"

"No problems," Kate O'Leary reported, eyeing Jesse curiously as she moved past Robin to the entry closet for her coat. "Philip just gave you the whole story—except he pestered me for cookies. I thought it best to leave that up to you."

"Thanks," Robin said with a laugh. "Phil knows I'm more of a pushover than you are when it comes to sweets. By the way, Kate, I'm going to have to work late a couple of nights this week—"

"No problem," Kate assured her, slinging on her coat and reaching for the front doorknob. "Just let me know your schedule when you've got it."

"'Tis the season," Robin reminded her with a contrite smile. "Our hours are going to be crazy for the next few weeks."

"I don't mind, I really don't," Kate insisted. "I could use the extra money—lots of presents to buy."

"You gonna buy me a present?" Philip asked, climbing up to the second step of the staircase and then jumping down dramatically. "I ask only on account of I'm gonna buy you one."

"You are?" Kate feigned utter astonishment. "In that case, I'd better revise my shopping list. I'd be mortified if you gave me a present and I didn't have one to give you!" She winked at Robin, gave Jesse another interested glance, and said, "So long, everybody. See you tomorrow."

"Thanks, Kate." Robin left the porch light on for Kate, then locked the door and removed her jacket. "Give me five minutes to change my clothes," she requested, "and then we'll have some dinner."

"You staying for dinner, Jesse?" Philip asked, climbing up the stairs again and leaping down with death-defying courage. "I think maybe we'll have cookies for dessert. What's your favorite kind of cookie?"

"Chocolate chip," Jesse answered the child, though his gaze remained on Robin, watching the playful bounce of her shiny blond hair, the graceful motion of her hips, the slender curves of her calves and her small, dainty feet carrying her up the stairs and out of sight.

BY THE TIME Robin returned to the living room, Jesse and Philip were gone.

She had taken longer than the promised five minutes to change her clothes. Ordinarily when she got home from work, she threw on her old jeans and a sweat shirt, washed off what little makeup she was wearing, and bounded down the stairs to spend the evening with her son. But tonight she had taken an unreasonable amount of time combing through the double closet in her bedroom, searching for an outfit that would look both casual and flattering. The jeans and sweat shirt met the first of those conditions, but definitely not the second.

After donning a pair of wool slacks and a patterned blouse, Robin headed for the bathroom, not to scrub off her makeup but to freshen it. She pulled the barrette from her hair, brushed it out, and then decided to leave it loose. Hurrying down to the living room, she hoped that Philip wouldn't be a big-mouth and question her about her uncharacteristic dinnertime appearance.

She gazed about the empty living room for a moment, spotting Jesse's blazer draped over the back of a chair, and wondered where Philip had dragged him off to. Then she heard her son's piping voice floating out of the den.

She strode to the doorway and found Jesse seated on the sofa and Philip kneeling on the coffee table facing him, holding the poor man captive as he displayed for him various stamps, papers and envelopes, which he pulled from an old shoe box. "This one, it's from Mexico," Philip announced. "See? It's got Spanish words on it. That's what they speak in Mexico," he explained with great self-assurance. "This one's from Brazil. And you know what, Jesse? It looks like Spanish, but it's not. Guess what it is."

Jesse labored to appear ignorant. "I don't know, Philip. What is it?"

"Portuguese!" Philip crowed, obviously thrilled to have shown up an adult with his superior knowledge. "They speak Portuguese there. Did you know that? My dad doesn't really understand Portuguese, but he speaks Spanish real good. I'll show you—he wrote me this message in Spanish . . ." Philip rummaged through the shoe box and withdrew a sheet of white note paper. "Here, he wrote, *'Hasta la vista, Filipo.'* Do you know what that means?"

"What does it mean?" Jesse asked politely.

"It means, Goodbye, Philip. Mostly my dad goes to Spanish places, like in South America and the West Indies and stuff, so he can talk to the people. Sometimes he gets stuck going to Brazil or something, though. Then he needs a translator."

Clearly, Philip and Robin were novices at this business of entertaining a strange man in their home. If she had been more savvy about such situations, she would have trained her son not to besiege a male guest—a potential boyfriend, at that—with the collection of letters and exotic postage stamps Philip had received from his father. Robin was glad that Ray corresponded regularly with Philip, but she didn't think that having the boy chatter nonstop about his father was exactly the proper way to make Jesse feel welcome.

"Philip?" she said, trying not to sound disapproving as she entered the den. Not only had Philip been sharing his father's letters with Jesse, but he'd brought Jesse into the messiest room in the house—not counting Philip's bedroom, of course. With Kate O'Leary's help, Robin managed to keep the living room and kitchen relatively tidy, and the dining room was practically immaculate since it was used so rarely. The den, however, was a place for unwinding, kicking back, overlooking the rubble of scattered toys and games, half-read books and magazines, two-month-old issues of *TV Guide*s and piles of sewing projects yet to be completed.

At the moment the den seemed even more cluttered than usual because Robin and Philip had recently lugged the cartons of Christmas decorations down from the attic storage area. Robin had insisted that it was too early to start decking the house with holiday adornments, but Philip was so eager for Christmas to arrive that he'd cajoled his mother into bringing the cartons downstairs. He had also begun badgering her about buying a tree, but she had maintained that if they bought one too early in December, it would be all dried out by Christmas Day.

"Please put the letters away," she firmly ordered her son. "And what's the rule about climbing on the tables?"

At the sound of her voice Philip jumped off the table and spun around. Collecting a few scattered postage stamps into his box, he grinned. "Did you know that on Gleek, kids are allowed to climb on tables all the time?"

"Then I'm glad I don't live there," she said succinctly. "Speaking of tables, Philip, perhaps you could give me a hand setting the one in the dining room. We're going to eat there tonight."

"Yeah? How come?"

"Because Jesse is here, and we use the dining room when we've got company."

"We don't use it when Mrs. O'Leary stays for supper," Philip reminded Robin as he set the lid on the box and returned it to a shelf.

Were all children of divorced mothers this difficult the first time a new man entered their home? "Mrs. O'Leary," Robin said as evenly as she could, "spends more time in this house than I do. She's practically one of the family."

Philip shrugged. "Okay. The dining room, huh. I guess I gotta wash my hands, then." He pranced out of the den and vanished into the downstairs bathroom.

Robin risked a glance at Jesse, who was rising from the sofa. If Philip had made him uncomfortable by discussing Ray, Jesse didn't show it. He had shoved up the sleeves of his sweater and rolled up his shirt sleeves beneath it, exposing his slender, sinewy forearms. He had bony wrists and long, tapered fingers, and his skin was a gold-tinged color just a shade lighter than the skin of his face. Robin wondered what he would look like in the summer, his entire body shimmering with a rich, toasty tan, and then she swallowed a shocked laugh. That she should be thinking of viewing Jesse's unclothed body startled her, and she swiftly chased away the image by concentrating on the subject he and Philip had just been discussing—her ex-husband. Surely fifteen minutes listening to Philip sing the praises of his peripatetic father was enough to smother any romantic inclinations on Jesse's part.

He offered her an amiable smile and crossed the room to join her at the doorway. "Gleek—that's Philip's make-believe planet, right?"

She nodded. "Among other things, Gleek is a place where seven-year-old boys do everything they aren't supposed to do on earth, and don't do anything they are supposed to do on earth. Ten'll get you twenty that during dinner Philip's going to announce that on Gleek kids don't have to eat their vegetables." With that, she marched down the hall to the kitchen, removed the bag of already washed green beans from the refrigerator, and dumped them into the steamer to cook.

In spite of the fact that they ate in the dining room instead of the kitchen, Philip was as rambunctious as usual. He monopolized the mealtime conversation with a long-winded description of his day in school. "Cookie Monster is such a pig," he informed Jesse. "He eats grapes, lettuce leaves, bugs and cookies. He gobbled up all my cookies and all of Adam Worblin's. Did you know that Adam Worblin is the worst speller in class? We're having a spelling test on Friday. Spelling is dumb, don't you think, Jesse? When I grow up, I'm gonna have a secretary and she'll check my spelling for me."

"When you grow up," Robin asserted, "maybe you'll be a secretary."

"Uh-uh." Philip soberly shook his head. "I wanna be a scientist. I wanna have lots and lots of snakes."

Robin didn't bother to hide her grimace. Jesse chuckled. "What you want to be is a herpetologist," he told Philip. "That's the name for a scientist who specializes in snakes."

"Yeah?" Philip's eyes grew round. Clearly he considered Jesse a genius for knowing such an arcane fact, even if the man had to be instructed by a mere second-grader that people in Brazil spoke Portuguese. "That's what I want to be, then. What's the word again?"

"Herpetologist."

"Herpetologist," Philip murmured, cementing the term in his memory. "I think Jeff Calloway wants to be one, too. We could have a snake farm together, and then we could spend all day catching bugs to feed our snakes. And buying cookies for them, too. Can I have some cookies now, Mom?"

Robin eyed her son's plate. He had distributed his uneaten green beans around the dish, as if by dispersing them he would give the impression of having consumed most of them. She considered nagging him to finish his vegetables before he requested dessert, then decided not to. It was a special night; Jesse was present. She didn't want to have a face-off with her son about something as trivial as beans.

"I tell you what," she negotiated. "Why don't you help me clear the table, and then you can have some cookies and milk in the den."

Philip let out a hoot. This was a double treat—Robin rarely permitted him to bring food into the den. He bolted from the table, gathering his plate and silverware, and charged into the kitchen.

Robin smiled at Jesse. "We can have some coffee in the living room, if you'd like," she offered. Then she remembered that he had asked to come to her house specifically to meet her son, and she added, "Or you can have cookies and milk with Philip."

"Coffee sounds great," he said, standing and lifting a few more dishes.

It didn't take long to clean up the dishes and cram the leftovers into the refrigerator. After preparing a pot of coffee to brew, Robin arranged a few cookies on a plate, filled a tumbler with milk, and carried the snack into the den. "Can I watch TV, too?" Philip asked hopefully.

"All right," she said. "You can watch reruns of *WKRP*. No news, though." Turning to Jesse, she explained, "Whenever he watches the news, he wants to ask me a thousand questions about each story. Not that I mind—I'm glad he has an interest in the world—but it would be nice to have our coffee without interruptions."

Philip switched on the television, then flopped onto the couch and balanced the plate of cookies on his knees. Pivoting to leave the room, Robin noticed that Jesse was gazing at the shoe box in which Philip stored his mail from his father. She cringed, then forced a faint smile and left the room. Jesse followed.

A vision of his intense stare fastened to the shoe box remained with her while she filled two cups with coffee, asked him whether he took cream or sugar, and carried the cups to the living room. Although Jesse didn't mention the letters Philip had shown him, Robin couldn't keep herself from contemplating his reaction to them. Had he felt uncomfortable listening to Philip go on and on about his father? In Jesse's place, she would have felt uncomfortable.

Her smile still felt forced as she sat on the chintz-covered sofa and gestured for Jesse to take a seat beside her. She watched him as he lifted his cup, sipped, and lowered it. "I'm sorry about that stuff with my ex-husband's letters," she said finally, to alleviate her own awkwardness if not Jesse's.

Jesse eyed her steadily. His lips shaped a hesitant smile. "Don't be." He took another sip of coffee, then leaned back against the cushions, stretching his long legs out under the table. "I take it your son and your ex-husband are close."

"As close as they can be, given that Ray travels so much."

"I think that's terrific," he said. He sounded as if he meant it, and Robin felt her tension abate. "It's probably one reason Philip is such a well-adjusted child. So many kids of divorce aren't."

Robin nodded.

"Does he get to see much of his father?"

"They get together about twice a year," she answered. "Whenever Ray is stateside, he spends as much of the furlough as possible with Philip."

"Furlough?" Jesse questioned her. "Is he in the armed forces?"

Robin laughed and shook her head. "Just a habit of speech," she explained. "I spent my youth as an army brat. I've gotten most of the military jargon out of my system, but every now and then a word slips in."

Jesse mused for a moment. "Can I get personal, Robin?"

A frisson of anxiety rippled through her. Was he going to kiss her? Proposition her? With her child in the next room? As Jesse's dark, piercing eyes met hers and his sensual lips curved in an enigmatic smile, she found herself almost wishing that he would make a pass at her. She would have to reject him if he did, but still... How heavenly it would be to have a man like him getting personal with her.

Mustering her courage, she said, "Go right ahead."

Jesse continued to study her, mulling over his thoughts before he verbalized them. "Why did you get a divorce?" he asked.

Personal, granted—but hardly what Robin had been bracing herself for. She felt the muscles along her spine go slack and her heartbeat slow. She wasn't really ready for him to make a pass at her anyway, she consoled herself. "What do you mean, why?" she countered.

His smile widened, growing warmer. "It's more than just that Philip seems well-adjusted. You seem well-adjusted, too. Most divorced women I know are so bitter and vindictive about it."

"Do you know many divorced women?" she asked.

He chuckled. "Enough to make totally unsupportable generalizations," he conceded. "Seriously, Robin. You seem so sweet and open. You invited me to dinner on the spur of the moment, without making a big deal about it—"

"Around here, eating in the dining room *is* a big deal," she joked. Then she accepted his question in the spirit in which it had been posed. "When I was growing up, we moved around a lot. Every two or three years, my father would be reposted, and we'd ship off to a new base. We never had roots, we never had a real home. And I was always being thrust into a new community where I didn't know anybody, where I had to start all over again making friends. To make it easier for me, my mother had what she called her 'Open Door Policy.' Whenever I met anyone I thought might become a friend, I could bring her home with me for dinner, without advance notice. My mother often dragged acquaintances home, too—army wives and their kids. You had to work fast making friends in that kind of environment." She shrugged. "It amazes me that Philip and Jeffrey—you met his mother, Joanna, at the Open School Night—it amazes me that the boys have known each other practically since their conception. Until I moved to Branford, I had never lived in any one place for so long."

"And now your ex-husband travels all over the world," Jesse noted.

Robin grinned. "Bingo. You figured it out."

"I did?" He appeared perplexed.

"You asked me why I was divorced." She drank some coffee, then nestled deeper into the couch's plush upholstery and folded her legs underneath her. "Ray had traveled a lot as a child, too. He wasn't an army brat, but his father was an executive with one of the airlines, and they were always moving. When we met, I told Ray that my dream in life was to have a real home, to settle down someplace and know that this was *my* house, *my* place, my little corner of the world. He understood and he agreed with me, at first. He took a job teaching economics at Yale, and we bought this house, and I dug in my roots. And then..." She sighed wistfully. "He began to get restless. Neither of us was used to living in one place for so long, but I loved it. He never got used to it. So he took a job with the Agency for International Development. The next thing I knew, he was being shipped off to Honduras for on-site observation. And..." She sighed again. "I stayed here."

"Your choice?" Jesse half asked.

"My choice. Ray knew how I felt about moving. A good wife would have gritted her teeth and packed up and followed her husband wherever he went, but . . ."

The tiny lines framing Jesse's eyes deepened as he laughed. "Is that what good wives do?"

Robin smiled reluctantly. "It's what my mother did. I always assumed that she loved the transfers and the life of an army wife. But then Ray and I were facing this crisis, and I called my mother for advice, and she admitted that she had despised the constant moving, that she had always resented my father for denying her a home, and that if I refused myself what meant the most to me, I'd wind up resenting Ray, too. I didn't want that to happen. So, yes, I made my choice."

Jesse took a minute to digest what she'd told him. "Your ex-husband's the bitter one, then?"

"No, he's not bitter, either. He knew that gallivanting about Central and South America wouldn't necessarily be the healthiest thing for Philip, and that I had a right to live the kind of life I wanted to live. We just grew apart—literally, I guess. His career meant more to him than I did. And my desire to have a home meant more to me than he did."

"And now you have your home," Jesse concluded.

"A home, a job, a son . . . a place where I can plant perennials and get to watch them bloom, year in and year out. And Philip can grow up secure, belonging to a neighborhood and knowing that his friends are here where he is. He isn't going to have to spend his childhood memorizing dozens of different addresses and guessing which drawer the silverware is in, and being a chameleon at school, trying to fit in with a new crowd of kids every couple of years."

Her gaze journeyed around the cozy living room, which was furnished with pieces she'd selected specifically for this room. Growing up, she had lived in so many strange houses where the furniture that had been bought three houses earlier never quite fit and the wall colors and carpet never quite suited her family. Those temporary residences had never represented home to Robin. This unassuming Cape Cod house did.

"The tree is going to go in that corner," she murmured, pointing to a nook beside the fireplace. "It always goes there. And we'll wrap holly and red ribbons around the balustrade, and put red candles in the windows. That's why having a tree is so important to me," she said, justifying her affection for Christmas. "It's a part of home. Christmas means being with Philip and having our tree in that corner."

Robin hadn't consciously intended to introduce the subject of Christmas trees. Yet it was all part of a whole to her. The house, the tree, her son and the spirit of the season. Christmas equaled home in Robin's mind.

Jesse's expression changed as soon as she mentioned the holiday, however. A shadow flickered within his eyes, and he shifted slightly on the couch. Then he smiled crookedly. "I don't condemn other people for having trees," he remarked, apparently sensing the need to reassure Robin.

She had already told Jesse a great deal about herself, and she found talking to him surprisingly easy. Hoping that he would find it as easy to talk to her, she twisted on the cushions to face him fully and inquired, "Why don't you want to have one?"

He glanced at his coffee cup, which was empty. Robin was about to ask him if he wanted a refill, thoughtfully giving him a chance to avoid responding to her blunt question. But before she could speak, he answered, "I don't believe in it."

"In what? In Christmas trees?"

"In Christmas."

She gaped at him. There was nothing defensive in his claim; he'd stated it as bluntly as she'd stated her question. And since Jesse was already to blame for having directed their conversation into the personal, she felt free to grill him as he'd grilled her. "Are you Jewish?" she asked.

"No."

"Druid?" She recalled his having commented in Ms. Becker's classroom that some of the students might be druids. Robin had little understanding of what druids were all about, other than what Jesse had said at Open School Night about the winter solstice.

He chuckled, apparently amused that she remembered his remark. "No," he said. "I'm an atheist."

"An agnostic, you mean?" She'd met a few people who admitted to having their doubts, which made them agnostics. But she'd never met anyone who declared himself an actual atheist, refusing to hedge his bets on the possibility of God's existence.

"I mean I'm an atheist," Jesse insisted.

"Just like that?" she pressed him, fascinated. "You don't believe in anything?"

"Oh, I believe in some things, Robin," he claimed. "I believe that every person has the inherent ability to do good in this world, and that it's his or her choice whether or not to do good. I believe that strength comes from knowledge, not faith, and that it comes from within, not without. What I don't believe is that there's some old geezer in a white beard who lives in the clouds and pulls the strings."

Surely that was as absurd a definition of God as any Robin had ever heard. "Then you don't believe in Santa Claus, either, do you?" she said, unable to stifle a laugh.

"Other than the guys who stand on corners in funny costumes and ask for handouts, no, I don't."

"Please don't tell Philip," she whispered conspiratorily.

Jesse nodded in understanding. "It'll be our secret."

She settled against the throw pillows, pondering what Jesse had revealed. Because of her childhood on army bases, Robin hadn't had much formalized religious instruction. The chapels on most army bases offered nondenominational Christian services—when they weren't being used for Jewish services. She couldn't quite say that she was a Methodist, as her father had been, or a Lutheran like her mother. But she did believe in God. It seemed much too depressing *not* to believe.

She peered curiously at the man beside her: an atheist, without any sense of a guiding power larger than himself, without any faith, without any belief in a greater being to whom he could turn in times of stress or despair. Jesse appeared unconcerned about what he'd just confessed to, although he looked as if he was willing to answer more questions from Robin. "Don't you believe in heaven?" she asked.

"As a place where people go after they've died? No."

"Then what do you think happens when they die?"

She noticed another shadow hovering over his sharply chiseled features, a pensiveness tugging at the corners of his mouth. Then he shrugged resolutely. "I think that when people die, they get buried—or cremated—and their remains are absorbed by the earth."

"What about their souls?"

That shadow again, that brooding sadness darkening his eyes. He turned to gaze out the window, staring into the darkness beyond the glass. "I don't think of the soul as something separate from the body," he explained haltingly, addressing the cold night outdoors. "I think of it as a person's mind, his personality, the capacity for goodness inside him. When he dies, it's gone."

"Jesse." It was such a bleak thought, Robin felt compelled to refute it. "If there's nothing beyond that, then why do people bother to be good at all?"

He turned back to her and snorted. "Most people bother because they *do* believe in heaven. It's a bargain they're cutting: 'I'll be a decent human being now, and I'll get my payback later.' I do my best to be decent, too, Robin, but I'm not expecting a payback. I just do it because it's nicer and fairer to live my life that way." He stood and ambled to the window, gazing past the swagged curtains into the moonlit front yard. Rotating, he leaned against the windowsill and shoved his hands into his pockets. "When I was thirteen years old, my sister died of leukemia."

"Oh, God," Robin groaned, not even thinking that, in the context of atheism, such a statement was meaningless. "That's terrible, Jesse. I'm sorry."

"It was terrible," he confirmed. "But . . . you see . . ." He grappled with his thoughts. "When I tried to comprehend Marybeth's death, everybody said, 'God loved Marybeth so much, He wanted her in heaven with Him.' That was the answer religion provided. And all I could think was, if there *was* a God, how could He be so selfish? If He really loved Marybeth, He would have let her live a full, happy life. He could have waited fifty or sixty years before snatching her away and flying her up to heaven. What's fifty years to God, right? But no, He was selfish. He must have hated the rest of us to have taken her away from us. And He must have hated her, too, to make her suffer so much before she died. If God did exist, He seemed far too capricious and self-centered and thoughtless to believe in.''

''But that was one thing, Jesse, one incident. I could see where it might shake your faith. If anything ever happened to Philip—'' Robin cut herself off, unwilling to imagine such a horrible possibility. ''Yes, it might shake my faith, too. But—''

''And take war,'' Jesse posited. ''Or famine, or earthquakes. Would a loving God let such things occur? If He's truly in control of the world, why has He fouled it up so much?''

''But then other things happen,'' Robin argued. ''Wonderful things. Miracles. And when the bad things occur, many people turn to God to help them through.''

''Sure. Religion offers easy answers. It's a lot easier to say 'God works in mysterious ways' than to say Marybeth got unlucky, her blood cells got screwed up and she died.''

''Did losing your sister turn your parents away from God, too?'' Robin asked.

He issued a short, dry laugh. ''Hardly. They're superreligious. They've made a full-fledged career of their devoutness. I tried it their way, Robin. I honestly tried. But it never really made sense to me.''

''And *not* believing does make sense to you?''

''It allows me to be who I am and to do what I want,'' he explained cryptically. ''It enables me to help someone simply because I want to see them smile, without worrying about whether I'm scoring points for the hereafter.''

Robin lapsed into a bewildered silence. She hadn't expected that she would wind up describing the circumstances of her divorce to Jesse this evening—she discussed them only with people she had known close to forever. She suspected that Jesse didn't explain his atheism to near strangers, either.

Yet she hadn't expected that he would enter her store several hours ago and ask to meet her son, and she hadn't expected that she would impetuously invite him to join them for dinner. Nothing that had happened since she'd noticed Jesse standing beneath the mistletoe at Woodleigh's could have been predicted.

Even so, it seemed natural that she should be having this conversation with him. Debating the existence of God with Jesse seemed as reasonable as talking about her childhood as the daughter of an army colonel, and her decision to remain true to her ideal of home rather than trying futilely to salvage a shaky marriage. Jesse Lawson might indeed be a near stranger, but she felt close to him.

She wasn't going to persuade him to rethink his view of religion. She saw no need to. He was entitled to his beliefs—or his non-beliefs—and he was a decent human being. In his profession, he could be raking in hundreds of thousands of dollars in fees, but instead he made house calls to his indigent clients as a legal aid lawyer. Whether the goodness came from within or without didn't matter. Jesse was a good man.

"Maybe," she said, grinning whimsically, "the reason you don't like Christmas is because you haven't experienced one of Philip's and mine. Some pine wreaths, a bit of tinsel, the smell of evergreens and wood smoke and baking cookies, and you'd be a believer, too."

"Or maybe I'd turn into a snake," he quipped. "Depending on what kind of cookies they were, of course."

His allusion to Philip's dinnertime discourse on Cookie Monster prompted Robin to check her wristwatch. A quarter to nine. "Yikes," she groaned. "It's past Philip's bedtime. God knows what he's been watching on TV all this time."

"No," Jesse said with a laugh. "God doesn't know. Only Philip knows."

Robin chuckled, too. "Well, his mother is about to find out." She sauntered into the den and found Philip seated on the floor, barely ten inches from the television, watching a shoot-em-up scene of mayhem on the screen. "Bedtime, pal," Robin announced, lifting the empty cookie plate and milk glass from the coffee table.

"Awww!" Philip automatically whined, although he obediently stood and turned off the set. "Is Jesse still here?"

"Yes. Now how about some pj's, pronto?"

"Can I say good-night to him first?"

"As long as you don't make a two-hour production out of it," Robin warned, carrying the dishes to the kitchen sink. Reentering the living room, she found Philip swinging on the newel post at the bottom of the staircase and squawking to Jesse about how he wanted to buy a remote-control Jeep for Mrs. O'Leary for Christmas. "They're really neat, Jesse," he went on. "They just showed an advertisement for them on television. They're four-wheel-drive, with big fat tires, so you can drive them on gravel and everything."

"I'm sure that's exactly what your baby-sitter's been dreaming of owning," Jesse muttered wryly, though his eyes sparkled with humor. "Are you sure that's not what you want for yourself?"

"Uh-uh," Philip swore. "I want some new Masters of the Universe stuff, and another Transformer, and maybe a rocket ship. And I don't want anything with Smurfs on it. I'm too big for that," he added pointedly, glowering at Robin. He still hadn't forgiven her for her assertion that the Smurfs lunchbox he had pleaded for when he started first grade was in excellent shape and she wasn't about to buy a replacement. According to Philip, he was the only boy in the entire second grade who had to use a Smurfs lunchbox. Smurfs were strictly for girls and wimps.

"You know what I want for Christmas?" Robin declared sternly. "I want a certain seven-year-old boy to be in pj's and brushing his teeth by the time I count to twenty."

Philip pretended to be annoyed, but when he swung back to Jesse he was smiling. "Was your mother this mean, Jesse?"

"She was much, much meaner," Jesse said soberly. "If I were you, I'd count my blessings and put on my pajamas."

"Oh, all right," Philip relented, issuing an exaggerated sigh. "'Bye, Jesse."

"Goodnight, Philip."

Philip plodded up a few steps, then leaned over the railing and, in a stage whisper that was undoubtedly audible three houses away, commented, "Jesse's pretty nice for a grown-up, Mom."

Robin laughed. "We grown-ups do the best we can. Now git!" Philip scampered up the stairs.

"I guess I should be leaving," Jesse said, lifting his blazer from the chair where he'd left it. "I didn't mean to impose myself on you for half the evening—"

"Don't be ridiculous," she interrupted, silencing him. "It was my pleasure. Philip's pleasure, too. Anybody who can distract his mother for a few hours so he can watch blood and gore on television is tops in his scheme of things."

Jesse turned to the front door, then hesitated and spun back to Robin. "I'd like to see you again," he said.

She remembered the way he'd looked a few hours ago at the store when he'd asked if he could meet Philip—diffident, earnest, vaguely unsure of himself. He didn't seem at all unsure of himself now. His eyes pored over her face, and the hand that had reached for the door-knob instead alighted on her shoulder. "You're always welcome for dinner, Jesse," she assured him.

"That wasn't what I had in mind."

A date. He was asking her for a date. Her first date in over a decade, the first time in thirteen years that she was faced with the possibility of a date with a man other than Ray. She tried to recollect the apprehension she'd felt when she had first seen Jesse at the school—that he was too handsome, too debonair, too much for her to handle on her first social outing in eons. But that was before she'd gotten to know him, before he'd exposed his soul to her—if atheists were allowed to have souls.

Whether or not they were allowed, she knew that Jesse had one. And her reply came easily. "I'd like to see you again, too."

"What night's good for you?"

"Friday?" she suggested. "The store's open late, but I won't have to be there past six."

"Friday," Jesse confirmed. "I'll be here at seven. Get a baby-sitter." Then, so swiftly Robin couldn't prepare herself for it, he bowed and kissed her. It was a light, friendly kiss, landing half on her lips and half on her cheek, but it was tantalizing in its promise.

Too handsome, perhaps. Too risky. But as she watched Jesse open the door and stride down the front walk to his car, she knew intuitively that she was right to trust him.

SHE DID HER BEST to conceal her nervousness at work on Friday. The only three people, other than Jesse and herself, who knew about the date were Mrs. O'Leary, who agreed to baby-sit for Philip, Philip himself, and Joanna. Joanna was beside herself with delight. "That gorgeous guy from Open School Night? I knew it, Robin, I told you I saw him approach you. I could tell he was interested!"

Joanna's excitement about Robin's date only fed her own anxiety. She could trust Jesse, but could she trust herself? Not that she was worried about losing control around him, hurling herself at him and engaging in irresponsible orgiastic pleasures, but rather, could she trust herself not to botch things up? What if she dressed wrong? What if she spilled her soup? What if she accidentally smudged her mascara, or tripped on a step and wound up sprawled across a parking lot with her skirt around her waist? What if, when she got home from work today, she discovered a pimple on the tip of her nose?

Had dating been this frought with tension when she'd been a teenager? She supposed that it had been, but she'd been younger and more resillient in her youth. Everybody had pimples back then.

"Relax," Mrs. O'Leary ordered her when she finally arrived home, ten minutes later than she'd hoped because one of the salesclerks had returned late from her supper break and because a sleety rain was falling, slow-ing the rush-hour traffic to a crawl. "Everything's going to go fine. He's a good-looking fellow. If he were thirty years older, I'd ask him out myself. Now go upstairs and get dressed. Philip and I will go ahead and have dinner."

Robin raced upstairs, took the quickest shower since indoor plumbing was invented, and then pawed through her closet in search of a suitable outfit. She put on her gray wool dress, decided that it made her look pale and flat-chested, and traded it for a bright red sweater and skirt ensemble. That looked too Christmasy, and she pulled it off and put on the gray dress again. Then she darted into the bathroom, fixed her makeup, brushed her hair back, brushed it up, brushed it down, and exhumed her curling iron from the back of the linen closet. She curled the droopy ends of her hair, jogged back to her bedroom to slip on her shoes and grab her purse, and discovered in the mirror above her dresser that the curling iron hadn't done its job. Her hair appeared just as limp and lackluster as usual.

Relax. Kate O'Leary's command echoed inside Robin's skull. This wasn't the high school prom, and if Jesse didn't already like her, he wouldn't have asked her out. If he didn't like her, he wouldn't have kissed her. Closing her eyes, she relived in her mind that brief, glancing kiss. She recalled the whisper-soft pressure of his lips on hers, the subtle flavor of him, his musky scent. Of course he liked her, and everything was going to go perfectly. Confidence washed through her, and she was smiling when she went downstairs to keep Kate and Philip company while they devoured the chicken Kate had broiled for their supper.

By a quarter after seven, they were done eating and the kitchen was clean. That Jesse was fifteen minutes late wasn't unforgivable, Robin tried to convince herself. She joined Kate and Philip in the den, where Philip wolfed down an apple and three cookies and grilled Robin interminably about the stories presented on the network newscast. Where exactly was Nicaragua? he wanted to know. Had Daddy ever worked there? Which of the candidates did Robin support in the upcoming presidential primary?

Robin answered all of Philip's questions as calmly as she could. She didn't want him to know how overly conscious she was of the ticking of the clock, of the passing of the minutes. But soon it was seven-thirty, and then it was a quarter to eight, and Jesse didn't come.

Her first date, and she had been stood up. So this was the way atheists viewed their obligations, she fumed. Oh, Jesse might be noble when it came to his poor clients, but when it came to Robin, a woman he'd invited out for dinner, a divorcée who believed, just a little bit, in Santa Claus...

At nine o'clock she tucked Philip into bed. Then she changed out of her dress and into her sweat shirt and jeans. She told Kate she could go home, but Kate insisted on staying a little longer. Obviously she felt that Robin shouldn't be left alone when she was in such a foul mood.

After washing off her makeup, Robin stormed to the kitchen and helped herself to a leftover drumstick. Once she had nibbled it to the bone, she again requested that Kate go home. Sighing, shaking her head and mumbling about the disproportionate number of men who were cads, lice, and assorted other vermin, Kate pulled her coat from the closet and slipped it on.

And then the phone rang.

Chapter Four

"I'm sorry," said Jesse.

Just those two words, delivered in a tired monotone, as if they'd dropped off his lips rather than risen from his heart. He had ruined Robin's evening, skewered her ego, and all he could say was "I'm sorry."

An inane memory visited her, of Philip when he was about three years old. Whenever he did something naughty back then, she used to remand him to the corner, where he had to stand until he said he was sorry. It didn't take him long to conclude that the sooner he said he was sorry, the sooner he'd be released from his sentence. So when she'd confine him to the corner, he would jam his little nose against the wall and, within a second, holler "I'm sorry!" and then romp out of the corner to resume playing. As if all he had to do was verbalize those two words and his transgression, no matter how severe, would be overlooked.

Did Jesse actually believe that uttering "I'm sorry" was enough to win him Robin's instant forgiveness? The way she was feeling, she'd like to send Jesse to the corner for a few years.

"Robin? Are you there?" he asked as her silence extended beyond a minute.

"Yes." She stared at the yellow kitchen wall to which the phone was attached, hoping that the daffodil color would soothe her bruised, bristling nerves and keep her from letting Jesse know how hurt and angry she was.

"I'm sorry about our date," he said. "I'm calling from Yale-New Haven Hospital. I was in an auto accident on my way home from work this evening."

Robin felt deluged with remorse. An accident! If ever a man had a valid excuse to break a date... "Are you all right?" she asked, frantic.

"I'm fine."

"Then why are you in the hospital?"

He emitted a short, humorless laugh. "I'm a lawyer, Robin. I know enough to plan ahead, in case there's a lawsuit. I feel all right now, but if I wake up six months from now and find myself paralyzed, I want it on record that I sought immediate medical attention."

"Jesse—"

"I'm fine, Robin," he insisted. "Really. I only wish I could say the same for my car." When she didn't speak, he added, "The doctors looked me over and released me. I'm free to leave."

"Maybe you should be spending the night there," she suggested, dubious. "For observation or something."

"There's nothing to observe. They've told me to go home."

"Then let me come and get you," she offered.

"No, that's all right. I think the policeman who brought me here can take me home. I don't want you driving when the roads are so bad."

"Don't be ridiculous," Robin argued. A little sleet was no big deal to someone who'd viewed nine New England winters through her windshield.

On the other hand, someone who hailed from Los Angeles, as Jesse had, probably thought that ice was something that came out of the freezer compartments of refrigerators, never out of the sky. Immigrants like him ought to be forced to take special driving courses the minute they arrived in the northeast. "I'll be at the hospital as soon as I can," she told him, resolved. "Where are you, in the emergency room?"

"That's right—but really, Robin, you don't have to—"

"Stay put," she ordered him. "I'll be right there." Before he could dispute her, she hung up.

Turning, she found Kate O'Leary unbuttoning her coat in the doorway. "No problem," Kate assured her, evidently having heard enough of the conversation to recognize that Robin needed her baby-sitting services for a while longer. Her round, generous face registered dismay. "Is he hurt?"

Robin shook her head. "According to him, not as badly as his car. I don't know how long I'll be, Kate, but—"

Kate shooed her out of the kitchen with an impatient wave of her hands. "Go and take care of him. And don't you ever let him know I referred to him as vermin."

Robin donned her parka, grabbed her purse and keys, and hurried through the front door. In the hours since she'd left Woodleigh's, the temperature had risen a few degrees, converting the sleet into fat drops of rain, which quickly drenched her hair and face. Robin opened the garage, climbed into her car, flicked on her lights and windshield wipers and backed down the driveway.

She was no longer anxious. Jesse had insisted that he was all right, and she believed him. Certainly no physician facing the current malpractice crunch would release

a patient if there were the slimmest chance that he might
not be in perfect health.

It took her twenty minutes to reach the hospital. She
found a parking space not far from the emergency entrance, locked the car and went inside. The waiting area
was well lit and crowded, an assortment of people occu-
pying the vinyl chairs and hovering around the nurses'
station. One dingy-looking elderly man appeared to be
drunk; he swayed and mumbled to himself. A few family groups huddled here and there, some with sick-looking
children. A uniformed police officer was conferring with
one of the nurses at a desk.

Jesse sat alone near an end table covered with outdated magazines, a trench coat and a leather attaché case
lying on the chair next to his. He had on a dark blue
business suit, his tie gone and the collar button of his
white shirt unfastened. His hair was rumpled, his jacket
creased. Robin was unable to see his face because he was
hunched over, perusing an official-looking form.
"Jesse," she said, approaching him.

He peered up and smiled hesitantly at her. A large
bluish welt marked his cheekbone below his left eye, and
his lower lip looked puffy. The front of his shirt bore a
splotch of dried blood.

"What's that from?" she asked, pointing at the small
stain.

He glanced down, then lifted his face to hers again.
"My lip," he said quietly. "I bit it."

She sighed, feeling the last of her tension ebb away. As
composed as she'd felt during the drive to the hospital,
she'd had to see him with her own eyes to make certain
that he was truly safe and sound. One bruised cheek, one
bitten lip. He hadn't lied; he was all right.

"I'm so sorry," she murmured, closing the distance between them.

He shrugged and reached for his attaché case. His actions were slow and deliberate, Robin noticed, and his left wrist was taped.

"Your arm?" she asked, requiring a full inventory of his injuries, no matter how minor they were.

"A slight sprain," he told her as he slid the papers into the briefcase and snapped it shut. Then he stood and slipped on his coat, moving woodenly. "From fighting the steering wheel. They x-rayed it, Robin. Nothing was broken. Seriously."

Her gaze roamed down his body, searching for further hints of physical damage. If he was bloodied or bandaged anywhere else, she found no evidence of it. Still, his stride lacked its usual grace. His limber legs carried him cautiously to her side, reminding her of the stiff way her mother sometimes moved when her arthritis acted up. "Are you sure you're free to leave?" Robin asked.

"Yes. And I'd love to. This place is beginning to get to me."

Nodding, Robin accompanied him outdoors. The pounding rain pasted her hair to her cheeks, and she thought wryly of her wasted effort with the curling iron earlier that evening. She also thought of her concern about her outfit, her exertion with her seldom used makeup applicators, her attempt to appear ravishingly beautiful for Jesse. Instead, here she was in her faded jeans, her University of Wisconsin sweat shirt, her loafers and parka, saturated and bedraggled.

Yet the way that Jesse gazed at her, the way his eyes glowed with gratitude and relief, made her feel as if she did look ravishingly beautiful.

She unlocked the passenger door of her station wagon, and Jesse gingerly lowered himself onto the seat, balancing the attaché case on the floor between his knees. She dashed around the car to the driver's side and climbed in, shaking the excess rainwater out of her hair and off her hands.

Jesse watched her for a moment as she started the engine and steered out of the parking lot. Then he turned to stare out the window. Robin respected his silence until they merged with the traffic on the turnpike. "Where did it happen?" she asked.

"On Brushy Plain Road," he answered, still facing forward. He sounded incredibly weary. "The vast majority of automobile accidents occur within ten minutes of home, isn't that right?"

She wasn't about to discuss statistical probabilities with him. "What happened? Did you forget to put snow tires on your car?"

"It wasn't my fault," he grunted.

She smiled gently. "I'm not blaming you, Jesse. This is your first winter in Connecticut, isn't it?"

"Just because I'm from Los Angeles doesn't mean I've never driven in bad weather before," he asserted. He sank into the seat, rolling his head back to the headrest and closing his eyes. "Some clown was tailgating me," he told her. "When I slowed down at a curve, he rear-ended me, and that put me into a spin. If it weren't for a strategically placed electrical pole, I'd probably still be spinning. The road was awfully slick."

A rear-end collision, a spin, a crash into an electrical pole. Robin shuddered. "It's a miracle you weren't hurt worse."

His eyes still closed, he issued a dry laugh. "I wasn't saved by a miracle," he disputed her. "I was saved by my seat belt."

Of course. Atheists didn't believe in miracles. "How's the other driver?" she asked.

Another bitter laugh escaped him. "The poor guy—his bumper was dented."

She accepted his sarcasm without question. Wasn't that always the way it went—the person responsible was the person to suffer the least. "It must have been very frightening," she commiserated. She'd never been in an accident herself; she could only imagine how dreadful the experience must have been.

"It was," Jesse confirmed.

"I'm so sorry," she repeated, reaching across the seat to squeeze his hand.

Still leaning against the headrest, he turned to her and opened his eyes. Her attention was glued to the road ahead, but she could feel the intensity of his gaze as it coursed over her. "So am I," he admitted. "This wasn't the night I had planned for us."

"What I mean is—" She surrendered to a strong compulsion to confess. "I'm sorry that I was mad at you for standing me up. There you were, going through this terrible thing, and—"

"You were entitled to be angry. You didn't know."

"Where's your car now?" she asked, coasting onto the exit ramp in Branford.

"It was towed to that Mobil station on the corner," he said, gesturing with his arm. "They said I could leave it there overnight. The insurance adjuster has to have a look at it before it's salvaged for scrap metal."

Succumbing to curiosity, Robin turned right instead of left, heading for the Mobil station. "Can I see it?"

"Be my guest."

She turned into the dimly lit lot and cruised around the building to the back. Her headlights cut through the slanting rain to illuminate the mangled wreckage of Jesse's Volkswagen, which had been left at the edge of the asphalt lot. The rear end of the car was smashed in on one side, with the bumper and taillight missing. The entire front end of the car had accordioned inward from the impact of its skid into the electrical pole, and the windshield was a spiderweb of cracks.

Robin let out a cry at the gruesome sight. The image of Jesse's body trapped inside that heap of twisted metal and broken glass, the comprehension of what the car had undergone to have wound up so demolished... "I don't care what you say," she declared. "It *was* a miracle. Simply surviving would have been a miracle. But to have been able to walk away from a mess like that—"

"It was a seat belt," Jesse tersely refuted her.

Tension emanated from him as he stared through the downpour at the wreck. Robin suspected that looking at it was forcing him to relive the accident in his mind. She hastily shifted into gear and sped around the building, fleeing from the ghastly sight.

Neither of them spoke for a few minutes. Robin drove north toward her house, wondering exactly where on the road the accident had occurred. Would there be skid marks etched into the pavement? Shards of glass lying around? The missing Vokswagen bumper? She hoped that the scene had been cleaned up; she didn't want Jesse to have to view it. For that matter, she didn't want to view it herself.

Near the turnoff leading to her house, she slowed. "Come home with me," she suggested. "I'll fix you a drink—some brandy, soup, whatever—and you can unwind."

"No." His resolute gaze seemed to penetrate her, seeping beneath her skin as he studied her from across the front seat. "I appreciate the invitation, Robin, but... I think I need some time alone."

"I understand," she said. She wasn't sure how wise it was to leave him all by himself after what he'd just been through, but he must know his own needs. She had no right to question his decision.

Bypassing her turnoff, she continued up the road to the neighborhood she and Joanna had dubbed Mondo Condo. Eventually, Jesse directed her to turn left, and at the bottom of a hill they entered his condominium complex. "That's my house," he said, pointing to a spacious-looking town house at the bottom of a rolling hill of grass, and then to a staircase leading down the hill from the road. "Park anywhere near the stairs."

Robin shut off the engine and scrutinized the stairs. They appeared slippery with rainwater. Recalling how stiffly Jesse had moved in the emergency room, she climbed out of the car and around to his side. "I'm walking you to the door," she announced before he could ask what she was doing. "You're creaky and sore; I don't want you taking a spill on those steps."

"Yes, ma'am," he complied, grinning reluctantly. He refused to let her carry his attaché case, however. As creaky and sore as he was, he clearly wasn't going to let Robin treat him like an invalid.

The steps were as slippery as they looked, and Robin gripped Jesse's elbow to steady herself as much as him. When they reached the bottom, he led her along a winding walk to his front porch, which was protected from the rain by an overhang. He set down his briefcase, dug into

his pocket for his keys, then paused and turned to Robin.
"Thank you for bringing me home," he said.

"It was the least I could do."

"Sure. After I stood you up." He offered a lopsided
smile, then cupped his hands over her shoulders. "I . . ."
He seemed momentarily at a loss, and then his eyes came
into focus on her upturned face, on the raindrops trapped
in her eyelashes and skittering down her cheeks. "Thank
you," he whispered, his tone freighted with a meaning
Robin was unable to interpret.

She checked herself before protesting once more that
she hadn't done anything particularly wonderful, that
picking him up at the hospital hadn't been such an oner-
ous task, that she cared about him and acted accord-
ingly. Jesse's gaze seemed to impale her, numbing her
ability to think, let alone speak.

His mouth descended to hers, and their lips met cautiously, tenderly. Remembering that he'd bitten his lip
deeply enough to bleed from it, Robin didn't dare to lean
toward him or press her mouth too eagerly to his. She
didn't want to hurt him.

The pressure came from him. He seemed oblivious of
his wound, his mouth moving with surprising force
against hers, his arms winding tightly around her and his
fingers digging possessively into her wet hair. His tongue
thrust past her teeth and deep into her mouth, filling it,
consuming, shocking her with the sudden throbbing desire it aroused within her.

It wasn't just that she hadn't been kissed like this since
her divorce—since long before her divorce, if she wanted
to be honest about it. Her response to Jesse's kiss defied
logic, just as his kiss itself did. Reeling with sensations
that had lain dormant inside her for so long she had all
but forgotten about them, she slid her hands beneath the

flaps of his trench coat, circling his waist and holding him close, absorbing the warmth and hardness of his body, feeling the shift of his muscles, his hips, the tension in his thighs as they met hers.

When he finally drew back, he was gasping for breath. "Oh, Robin...Robin." He cradled her head against him, combing his trembling fingers through her hair. "I don't know what I'm doing."

"You're kissing me," she breathed.

"Yes." His lips brushed over her forehead. "I'm kissing you." His arms pinned her to him for a moment longer, then relented. He drew his hands forward to frame her face, tilting it up so their eyes met. "I want to ask you in," he whispered. "But I can't."

"I know," she murmured. She knew that he wanted to ask her in, and that he couldn't, but she didn't know why. Nor did she know whether, if he had asked her in, she would have said yes or no. In fact, she wasn't sure what she knew, beyond the fact that Jesse was about to go inside by himself and she was about to get back into her car and drive home. His kiss had left her with the disturbing notion that she didn't know anything at all.

"Can I see you tomorrow?"

"Tomorrow," she echoed, scrambling to resurrect her sanity. "I've got to be at Woodleigh's till three, and I promised Phil I'd take him to the Milford Mall afterward to do some Christmas shopping."

"I could come with you."

"Christmas shopping?" She laughed. It was a delayed laugh; his kiss had shocked her, but she couldn't have laughed then. The possibility that Jesse would want to go Christmas shopping was nearly as shocking, however, and the familiar sound of her own laughter relaxed her.

"I've got to meet with the insurance adjuster tomorrow morning, and make arrangements for a rental car until I can buy a replacement," he explained. "But I should be done by three o'clock."

"Do you really want to go to a holiday-infested mall?" she questioned him. "With Philip?"

"I want…" He sighed, his fingers raveling through her hair again. "I want to be with you. It doesn't matter where."

The extravagance of his claim disconcerted her. She understood that he hadn't said it simply to compliment her. It had been an expression of need, and she wouldn't deny him what he needed. She didn't want to. "Come by around three-thirty," she said. "We'll be ready to storm the mall by then."

He nodded slightly, then bowed and touched his lips to hers one last time. Then he released her, unlocked the front door and stepped inside. "Tomorrow," he murmured. He remained in the open doorway, watching until she returned to her car, backed out of the parking space, drove down the road and away.

PEOPLE OFTEN SAID that, at such times, your life passed before your eyes. Jesse had never before had the opportunity to test that hypothesis, but he now knew that it was true.

It hadn't been what he might have expected, though. He would have guessed that a person viewed his life as if it were a chronological film, from birth to the present, running in fast-forward. In his case it had been quite different: a series of strobelike images, out of sequence, defying order or rationality. In those few agonizing seconds, from the first sickening thud and lurch of the car, through the nauseating spin and into the final, horrifying crunch of metal against solid wood, he'd seen instants, tasted memories, experienced split-second slices of personal history.

Mrs. Selby's face, that was the first. Her worn, demoralized expression as she'd sat across his desk that very afternoon, moaning, "You got to help me, Mr. Lawson! I want my boy home for Christmas!" Then his mother's face, her distant half smile as she benignly announced, "Marybeth's gone." His father's voice, floating to Jesse from another room, crowing, "It's mine, they've chosen me, but they want me to change my name." Anne, her lush auburn waves tumbling about her lovely face, muttering, "If you won't stay in line, then you don't belong here." A crystal star shooting rainbow lights into his eyes, temporarily blinding him. A towering palm tree casting a shadow across the swimming pool behind his parents' house. And then another swimming pool, a huge public one, seemingly miles below an eight-year-old Jesse as he stood on the high diving board. Mickey Santangelo had dared Jesse to jump off, and he'd been petrified. But he'd filled his lungs with air, bounced on the spring end of the board, and heard Mickey behind him, shouting, "Cross yourself, Jesse, cross yourself!"

And then the jump, the breathless, endless, shapeless fall, the deafening roar of water in his ears, water below him, above him, around him, the disorientation, the certainty that he was sinking, that he would never see the sky again ... and then the triumphant burst to the surface, to light, to life.

To the sight of his car's front end molded around an electrical pole, to the sound of sleet drilling against the roof of the car, to the throbbing of his pulse in his temples, the fierce ache in his wrist and on his cheek.

To the melodic whisper of a woman's voice. *Something so wonderful. A home, a job, a son...* That sweet, mantric whisper, a vision of truth, stability, morality. A glorious woman with blond hair and steadfast eyes and the most genuine smile Jesse had ever viewed, whispering; *Other things happen, wonderful things. Miracles.*

Gradually he came to grips with what had occurred. He returned to full consciousness, to the fact that his car was demolished and he himself wasn't, that he was really alive, essentially unscathed. As his mind clarified itself, he realized that that whisper, that chant had been with him throughout, a counterpoint to all the other images, an affirming continuum, a guide to lead him out of the nightmare.

The time he had plunged off the high board at Mickey Santangelo's goading, Jesse had been certain he was going to die until the moment he opened his eyes and saw the rippling surface of the water just inches above him and, beyond the surface, the sun. This time, as he'd fought his way to that glittering surface separating death from life, it hadn't been the sun directing him upward to life. It had been Robin, her face, her voice, her strength, her golden hair and her smile.

"Guardian angel," he mumbled, trudging up the stairs to his bedroom. He dropped onto the bed and stared at the ceiling, utterly drained. He ought to remove his clothing, take a hot shower—or maybe a bath. He ought to soak his traumatized body until it felt whole again. Then he ought to fix himself a drink. He didn't have anything as strong as brandy in the house, but he supposed a glass of wine would do. Or a bowl of soup, wasn't that what Robin had offered him? A bowl of hot soup, a couple of aspirin, a night of uninterrupted sleep.

But he couldn't do that as long as the concept of a guardian angel was lodged inside his skull. Jesse didn't believe in angels, guardian or otherwise. He didn't believe in miracles. He believed in seat belts.

Then why was it that, when he reviewed the accident in his mind, he kept coming to the conclusion that what had saved him wasn't his seat belt but rather a small, beautiful woman with a halo of yellow hair, murmuring, *Something so wonderful . . .*

When he finally heaved himself up to sit, he discovered that he'd been lying on the bed for over an hour. He was exhausted. He barely had the energy to peel off his clothes. The suit could be dry-cleaned, and the shirt— maybe bloodstains were removable, but he wasn't going to bother. He tossed the shirt into the garbage pail and stepped into the bathroom to take a shower.

The hot water pounding down on his aching body felt excruciating at first, but eventually it began to affect his knotted muscles and joints, loosening them, restoring them to their former elasticity. He remained beneath the spray until the water began to cool off, then wrapped himself in his terry-cloth robe and went downstairs for a drink. He didn't have a bottle of wine open, and he opted for hot chocolate instead.

He carried his mug into the living room and sank onto the leather sofa, which was positioned across the room from a bentwood rocker, a pedestal table, a lamp and a blank wall. The room looked stark, lacking any of the intimate touches that would make it a real home. Jesse wasn't good at decorating. It hadn't mattered out in Los Angeles; once he and Anne had gotten together, he'd wound up spending more time at her place than at his. She knew how to fix a place up, how to select pictures for hanging, how to arrange objets d'art. Her apartment hadn't been nearly as warm and lived-in as Robin's house, but it had been nicer than Jesse's sterotypically characterless bachelor pad.

They both had been earning huge incomes, but one of the differences between Anne and Jesse was that she knew how to spend money on herself and Jesse didn't. Anne had helped him to pick out his leather sofa and his leather jacket. "Being rich and living well isn't a sin," she used to say.

To that, Jesse would silently reply, "Then why are we living in sin?"

Not that Anne wanted him to marry her. "It doesn't matter, as long as we're discreet," she would insist. "Let's face it, Jesse, you and your father have different last names. Nobody has to put two and two together. You aren't going to embarrass him. I like things the way they are now. If we decide to get married down the road, then we have that option."

What she hadn't predicted was that Jesse had another option: leaving. Turning his back on the hypocrisy of it all.

The cocoa felt good going down. Jesse wondered whether Robin ever made cocoa for Philip. Of course she did, he recognized. If Philip had a rough day, Jesse imagined that Robin would give him cocoa, cuddle him to her, sing him lullabies. Even if the kid protested that only girls and wimps enjoyed lullabies, Robin would continue to croon to him—and Philip would secretly love being crooned to.

Jesse hadn't meant to kiss her.

He hadn't even expected to see her that night—the policeman had been hanging around the emergency room for hours, taking Jesse's statement between sessions with an X-ray technician and then taking more statements

from the doctors. Jesse was sure the officer would give
him a lift back to Branford.

But even if Jesse had expected to see Robin, he hadn't
meant to kiss her. Not like that.

Yet he hadn't been able to help himself. It had started
as a kiss of thanks and then escalated, until he was
drinking her in like a drug, savoring her sweetness, her
womanly warmth and power. Until he'd felt all over
again as if she were beckoning him back to life, to
triumph, to the miracle of his own survival.

"It *wasn't* a miracle," he grumbled, setting down his
empty mug. A physicist, a highway safety expert, anyone with a bit of knowledge about momentum and resis-
tance, centrifugal force or whatever it was that had
buffeted Jesse could provide a perfectly reasonable, un-
miraculous explanation for his having been able to walk
away from such an accident. If it had been a miracle, that
would imply divine intervention. And God didn't exist.

After all, if God did exist, why would He be putting a
religious woman like Mrs. Selby through the wringer?
Why, on top of the threat of losing her home, had God
decided to foul up her son Gerald's Christmas leave so
the poor woman had to drag herself all the way to Jesse's office that afternoon, sobbing about how if Gerald
couldn't be home for Christmas she might as well just
die, and please, *please*, couldn't Jesse do anything to get
the Navy to see its way clear to send Gerald home for
Christmas, because he had nothing to do with the outbreak of violence on board his ship and he shouldn't have
to be sequestered along with the rest of the crew for the
term of the investigation.

Jesse had explained to Mrs. Selby that taking on the
United States Navy was a tall order, and he doubted that
much would come of any effort he made on her behalf to

get her son released in time for the holiday. But she'd been so plaintive, so desperate, that he'd yielded and promised to make some inquiries. And she, in turn, had promised that she'd go home and pray to God to bring Gerald home for Christmas.

If God existed, Jesse mused, He shouldn't have arranged to have Gerald and his shipmates sequestered in Newport for Christmas. And if God existed, He shouldn't have given drivers the ability to tailgate other drivers on sleety, dusklit evenings. For that matter, God should never have invented sleet.

But then...then there were other things. Wonderful things. Miracles. Sunshine, and air, and life.

And women like Robin Greer.

Chapter Five

Robin lay awake for hours, writhing beneath the comforter, punching her pillows, tangling her feet in the hem of her nightgown and listening to the rain hammering against the roof that sloped above her head. She lay awake, picturing Jesse as he'd hovered in his open doorway watching her departure. Then she pictured him before her departure, when they'd stood together on his porch. She could still feel his arms around her, his hands coursing through her hair, his body, despite its injuries, strong and firm against hers. She could still taste his lips on hers, his tongue, his breath filling her. Hours after she'd bade him good-night, his presence was still with her.

His kiss hadn't been romantic, she realized in retrospect. It had been passionate—no question about that—and her passionate reaction to it had been understandable. She could accept the possibility that Jesse desired her, but desire hadn't been his motivation when he'd kissed her so powerfully outside his door. What she'd sensed in Jesse's kiss was raw, desperate need.

He'd been straightforward about not wanting her to enter his house. Surely, after a nearly devastating automobile accident, only a sex-crazed animal would want to race home and bed down a woman he hardly knew. Admittedly, Robin was flattered that Jesse had bothered to mention the idea, that he'd confessed that he did want her—but she wasn't surprised that he'd chosen not to follow through.

Yet he'd needed her. For that one devastating moment when his mouth had taken hers, and his arms had clung to her, he'd needed her. Not the way he'd needed her to pick him up at the hospital and ferry him home, but some other way, some mysterious way.

And now he wanted to go Christmas shopping with her and Philip. She wondered whether he was still intrigued by her son, or whether he would have agreed to anything just for the opportunity to spend the following day with her. Oddly enough, she found herself hoping that the former, and not the latter, was the truth. She wanted Jesse to like Philip. As Philip's mother, she wanted the entire world to like him—but especially Jesse. And as moved as she was by his kiss, as fascinated as she was by him, she wasn't at all certain she was ready for an attachment to develop between them.

Even though she slept poorly that night, she didn't require her alarm clock to awaken her in the morning. Philip took care of that, rising at seven and engaging in a strident game of fire chief—complete with vocalized sirens—right outside her closed bedroom door. "It's about time you got up," he chastised her once she stumbled groggily from her room. "We're going to the mall today, remember?"

"After I get home from Woodleigh's," she reminded him. "I'm sending you to Jeff's house till I get home."

"Okay," Philip said agreeably. "Santa Claus is going to be at the mall, right?"

"I'm pretty sure he is," Robin answered. "Jesse's going to be coming with us, too," she added, praying that Jesse wouldn't balk or make snide remarks when Philip demanded to sit on Santa's knee. He had promised that he wouldn't disillusion Philip about Santa Claus, but—

"Jesse?" Philip squawked, trailing Robin to the bathroom and gaping at her as she brushed her teeth. "Did he ever come last night?"

"No," she replied after spitting out the toothpaste. "He was in a car accident. A very minor one," she fibbed, hoping not to frighten Philip. "But he's all right, and he's going to come to the mall with us this afternoon."

"I guess he's got to do his Christmas shopping, too," Philip commented.

Did he? Robin wondered as she returned to her bedroom to dress. Would a confirmed Christmas-tree-hater like Jesse bother to do Christmas shopping at all? Or was he so negative about the holiday that he didn't even exchange gifts with his family and friends? Did atheists refuse to believe in green-and-red foil wrapping paper, ribbons and bows, stockings stuffed with goodies? Did they refuse to believe in fruitcake and eggnog and rolled sugar cookies shaped like bells and stars? There was a whole lot more to Christmas than simply the religious aspects—they were important, of course, but the holiday entailed so much else. How could anyone, no matter what his faith, thumb his nose at such delights?

She probably should have refused Jesse's offer to join her and her son this afternoon. He might turn out be a grouch, bah-humbugging throughout the mall and transforming Philip's favorite annual outing into a miserable episode. But it was too late to disinvite Jesse. All she could do was hope that he behaved himself around the child.

Despite the hectic activity at the store, Robin was able to escape a few minutes before three. She drove directly to the Calloway house, around the corner from her own, to pick up Philip. Joanna answered her ring and hastened Robin inside. "Come on in," Joanna welcomed her. "I'm just fixing some coffee."

"I can't stay," Robin said, not bothering to open her jacket. "Philip and I are going to—"

"The Connecticut Post Mall," Joanna completed with a phony yawn. "He hasn't shut up about it all day. But you can spare a minute," she insisted, ushering Robin into the kitchen. "Glenn and the boys are downstairs, tearing up the rec room. I want to hear about what happened last night with Jesse."

"Nothing happened." As soon as the words were out, Robin acknowledged their falseness. Too much had happened last night—the accident, the drive to the emergency room, the pilgrimmage to view Jesse's crushed car. The kiss.

Joanna filled two cups with coffee and presented one to Robin. "What do you mean, nothing happened?"

"He had to cancel," Robin told her. "He was in a fender-bender on the way home from work."

"A fender-bender?" Joanna appeared indignant. "He canceled for that?"

"It was a little worse than a fender-bender," Robin conceded. "He sprained his wrist and got a black eye."

"Oh, no," Joanna moaned, now persuaded that he'd been justified in breaking his date with Robin. "That poor man. Did he make another date with you, at least?"

Robin took an obligatory sip of coffee, then set the cup down on a counter and sighed. Joanna was her closest friend, yet she didn't feel up to divulging what had happened when she'd taken Jesse home. She could scarcely make sense of it herself; she wasn't about to describe the moment to Joanna. "He's coming with us to the mall today," she answered carefully. "That's why I can't stay."

Joanna's face brightened. "He's going shopping with you? How romantic!"

"Shopping is hardly romantic," Robin argued.

Joanna shrugged. "Humor me," she said. "I'm an old married lady. I've got to get my thrills vicariously."

"Shopping isn't thrilling, either. The mall is going to be overcrowded and noisy. We're going to spend more time standing in lines than getting things accomplished. You know what a zoo that place is at this time of year." Robin knew she sounded surly, but she refused to allow herself too much optimism about how the remainder of the day would proceed. Jesse was definitely not the sort of man who would consider Christmas shopping either thrilling or romantic. "I'd better get Phil and go home," she resolved, jingling her key ring. "I've got to change my clothes before Jesse comes."

Descending to the finished basement, Robin found Philip, Jeff, and Jeff's younger brother Brian dueling with the bolster cushions from the couch while, oblivious of the circus around him, Glenn watched a college basketball game. As soon as he saw his mother, Philip threw down his cushion. "We're going to see Santa!" he shouted, practically knocking Robin over as he raced across the room. "Maybe we'll even get a tree tonight!"

"It's much too early for a tree," Robin objected, although Philip gave no indication of having heard her. In a trice, he was upstairs, buttoning his jacket and bounding out the front door to the station wagon. Robin quickly thanked Joanna for having watched Philip, then dashed down the walk to join him in the car.

As soon as she turned the corner, she spotted the small white automobile parked at the curb in front of her house. Her gaze shot to the door, where she saw Jesse seated on the porch step, clad in jeans, a crew-neck sweater and his suede jacket. "There's Jesse," Philip announced unnecessarily. "We can leave right away."

"No, we can't," Robin cautioned him, coasting to a halt in the driveway and turning off the engine. "I'm not going shopping in my work clothes."

Jesse stood as Philip sprang from the car and scampered up the walk. Robin moved at a more leisurely gait, appraising Jesse's face as she neared him. The bruise was still visible below his eyes, but it had faded from a vivid purple to a subdued grayish-blue. His wrist was still taped. "Are you sure you're feeling well enough to do this?" she asked as she climbed the step to the porch.

Jesse smiled and grabbed Philip by the arm, halting him before he'd executed a complete circuit around the adults. "Hello to you, too," he greeted Robin before admonishing Philip, "slow down, pal. You'd better save your energy for the mall."

Relief swept through Robin. Jesse's remark assured her that he had the correct attitude about Christmas shopping. At least in front of Philip, he was willing to display the proper enthusiasm. "I'll be five minutes, guys," she said, unlocking the front door and leading them inside. "I've got to get out of this skirt."

"Five minutes is all you're getting," Philip warned her as she headed up the stairs. "Any longer and I'm gonna make Jesse take me without you."

It would serve you both right, Robin countered silently, although she was laughing as she hurried into her bedroom to exchange her skirt for a pair of slacks. Clearly, Jesse was fond of Philip, and sensitive to the youngster's need to believe. He wasn't going to spoil the day.

True to her word, she was downstairs before five minutes had elapsed. The three of them trooped out to the station wagon, and Jesse didn't quibble when Robin volunteered to drive. "I'm not crazy about that rental car," he admitted, glaring at the white automobile as Robin backed past it. "It's an automatic, and I'm used to a standard transmission. And it doesn't have enough leg room."

"Why didn't you rent something bigger?" she asked.

"My insurance wouldn't cover it," he explained. "Anyway, I don't plan to have it long. The adjuster said he'd process my claim today, which means I should be receiving a check by the end of the week. I'll get a replacement as soon as I can."

"Is Santa bringing you a new car?" Philip called from the back seat.

Jesse twisted to look at the boy. Robin held her breath, awaiting his reply. "Actually, I'm buying myself a new car," he told Philip. "December twenty-fifth is a long way off. I don't think I want to wait till then."

There was definitely no cause for concern, Robin mused, relaxing in her seat and steering toward the turnpike. Jesse couldn't have provided a better answer to Philip's question.

"How are you feeling?" Robin asked Jesse once Philip had subsided in the back seat.

"Pretty good."

"You aren't moving as stiffly as you were yesterday," she observed.

Jesse gazed thoughtfully at her. Her mention of the previous night evidently stirred his memory of what, besides the accident, had occurred the last time they were together. "Look, Robin," he murmured softly. "About last night—"

She cut him off with a brisk shake of her head, then angled it toward her son in the back seat. "Some other time," she whispered. In a louder voice, she asked, "I take it you had no problems with the insurance adjuster?"

"None at all. The whole thing took less than two hours." He turned to face the windshield, studying the smoothly flowing traffic on the highway. "I wound up spending most of the morning working."

"Really? On a Saturday?"

Jesse chuckled. "Lawyers who make house calls also work on weekends," he rationalized.

"It must be an important case if you'd work half of Saturday on it, right after totaling your car."

He shrugged. "It's an impossible case, actually. One of my clients found out that her son, who's in the Navy, had his Christmas leave revoked. She's asked me to take on the Pentagon and get him home for the holiday."

Robin groaned. She was naturally interested in tales about the hassles the armed forces regularly visited upon its personnel. How many times had her father's transfers been subjected to last-minute alterations? How many times had a transfer date been changed, so that her father had to ship off weeks ahead of Robin and her mother, stranding them to pack everything and empty the house without him? How many times were their belongings rerouted by mistake, leaving them living in a strange new residence without any clothing or furniture for days on end? "Don't tell me the Navy's as bad as the Army about these things. How come they revoked the kid's leave?''

"There was a violent incident on his ship," Jesse related. "Some sort of gang rivalry. A small fire was set, and a few seamen were injured. Once they dock in Newport, the whole crew is being held for questioning."

"At Christmastime?" Robin exclaimed. "That's terrible! Why can't they do their investigation at sea?"

"I may be a lawyer, but I don't pretend to understand military logic," Jesse countered with a dry laugh. "Nor do I expect to be able to help my client. But she's so heartbroken about it, I promised her I'd make some inquiries."

"Of course she's heartbroken," Robin concurred. "If I couldn't have Philip with me for Christmas, I'd die."

Jesse shot her a skeptical glance. "You wouldn't die, Robin. Christmas isn't worth dying over."

Robin glimpsed Philip, who was staring out the window, apparently not listening to the adult conversation. She turned her attention back to the road. "All right, so maybe I've overstated the case," she allowed. "But not by much. Christmas is the most important time of the year when it comes to family. Philip's my family. If I couldn't have him with me . . . what point would there be in celebrating the holiday?"

"I don't know," Jesse answered slowly. "I'm not sure there is a point, even in the best of circumstances."

Robin grimaced. This was not the proper attitude. "I take it you aren't going to celebrate Christmas with your family," she presumed, not caring if she sounded judgmental.

"No." His tone was lighter when he asked, "How do you want to work this shopping expedition, Robin?

Would you like me to keep Philip occupied while you buy his presents?''

The gloom that had momentarily settled around Robin lifted at his generous offer. "Would you? That would be great, Jesse. I'd really appreciate it. If you wouldn't mind—"

"If I minded, I wouldn't have suggested it."

"He's going to run you ragged," she warned.

Jesse laughed. "I'm bigger than he is. I can handle him."

The parking lot outside the mall was crammed with cars, and residual puddles and patches of ice from the previous day's storm marred the paved surface. Robin had to park at the far end of a row of cars. As soon as Philip climbed out of the car, he stepped on an ice patch and took a spill. His anguished roar resounded throughout the parking lot.

"Where did you hurt yourself?" Robin asked swiftly, kneeling down beside him and arching her arm around his heaving shoulders. He didn't appear to be seriously injured, and she wondered whether his overreaction was a result of embarrassment or simply of being so keyed up. Or maybe it was a prophecy of what the rest of the day had in store for them, she thought grimly.

He held up his hand. The palm was scraped, and a few pebbles of gravel stuck to the skin. She dusted them off and kissed his hand several times. "There. All better?"

"All better," he said, bravely sniffling away his tears and heaving himself to his feet.

As she trekked to the nearest entrance with Jesse and Philip, passing countless cars and dozens of scowling people burdened with packages, she cringed at the comprehension of how crowded the mall would be. Her expectations bore out. Massive swarms of shoppers milled around the mall's interior, blocking the store entrances and promenades, jamming their rear ends onto benches, littering the floor with food wrappers and cigarette butts. The throngs wouldn't have bothered Robin, except for Jesse. He must hate this sort of thing, she realized—thousands of people spending hundreds of thousands of dollars in honor of a holiday he didn't consider worth celebrating. And, to top it off, the mall was decorated to the limit with evergreen bowers, artificial snowmen, glitter and tinsel and electric candles with flashing flame-shaped lights. Overhead speakers boomed sprightly renditions of Christmas carols down to the shoppers.

At the center of the mall, across the fountain from an enormous spruce tree dripping with electric lights and painted balls, a fenced-off area covered with fake snow housed a cute little red-and-green hut bearing a sign reading Santa's Workshop. Plastic reindeer—including one with a glowing red nose—and red-garbed elves were positioned inside the fence. In front of the hut, a huge man in an impressive Santa Claus costume sat on a throne. A snaking line of children waited their turn to sit on Santa's lap, and a photographer was on hand to preserve on film each child's encounter with Santa.

"Santa Claus!" Philip shrieked, racing to the fence and gawking at the bearded, pot-bellied character. "Can I talk to Santa Claus before we go shopping?"

"It's a very long line," Robin pointed out. "Maybe later, when everybody goes home for dinner—"

"I'll wait in line with him," Jesse declared. "Why don't you take care of your shopping?"

Robin hesitated. She couldn't imagine Philip having the forebearance to wait in the line for more than fifteen minutes, and her shopping would take much longer than that. Still, if Jesse was willing...

"Better yet," he recommended, "why don't we arrange to meet somewhere in, say, an hour and a half?" He surveyed his noisy, teeming surroundings in search of a good meeting place. "The entry to the steak house," he decided. "By five-thirty we'll be ready for dinner."

Robin wavered. "Are you sure you don't mind?"

He gazed down at her, his eyes dark and constant, glittering with good-natured tolerance. "I wouldn't mind sitting on Santa's lap myself. I want to ask him for a Porsche, preferably silver, with a sunroof, delivered two weeks ahead of schedule."

Robin laughed. "Well, if you insist. The steak house at five-thirty." Before Jesse could change his mind, she kissed Philip's cheek, ordered him not to give Jesse a hard time, and slipped away.

"I'VE ALREADY TOLD Mom what I want for Christmas," Philip solemnly informed Jesse as they inched along the line. "But just to be safe, I think I ought to tell Santa, too."

"That sounds like a wise strategy," Jesse confirmed.

At another time he might have found all the seasonal hoopla repulsive. But his current mood left no room for disgruntlement. Ever since he'd awakened that morning, feeling well rested and not at all achy, his spirits had been high. He was glad to be alive, glad and grateful. All of this holiday nonsense—the mannequins spruced up in silver furs and red stocking caps, the silver-foil snowflakes dangling from the vaulted ceilings, the screaming children competing with the choral performance of "Little Drummer Boy" oozing from the overhead speakers, the tight grip of Philip's small hand within his—it was all a part of being alive.

Christmas was just the outer trapping. The inner truth of this frenzied environment was that these people, these frazzled parents and demanding children, were alive, too. They were all survivors. That was what they were here to celebrate.

"Are you really gonna ask him for a Porsche?" Philip questioned Jesse. "I used to have a Matchbox Porsche, but I don't know where it is. I think Jeff's kid brother Brian lost it. He loses everything. He's four years old."

"That's a rough age," Jesse noted, nudging Philip forward in the line. "Does your mom want a picture of this?" he asked, scanning the placard posted by the fence listing the prices the photographer charged for his snapshots and enlargements.

"Nah. Too expensive," Philip said rationally. "I've got to get a present for her, too. And for Mrs. O'Leary. I've got almost fifteen dollars. You know what? Adam Worblin, he's the worst speller in our class, he said he's gonna give Ms. Becker a Christmas present. Ms. Becker's my teacher."

Jesse nodded. "She's my neighbor."

"She is?" Philip confronted him with a saucer-eyed stare. "She lives near you?"

"She lives next door to me."

"Wow." Philip took a minute to absorb Jesse's astounding revelation. "Is she as boring at home as she is in class?"

Jesse laughed. One of the best things about children was that they weren't hypocrites. They said exactly what was on their minds. "She isn't that boring at home," he told Philip. "Maybe what's boring about your class isn't the teacher but the schoolwork."

Philip considered that possibility, then discarded it. "Nah. It's her. She's really boring. My turn's next!" He strained at Jesse's hand, leaning toward the gate. "What a wienie," Philip whispered to Jesse after listening to the wish list of the child on Santa's lap. "He wants books."

"What's wrong with books?" Jesse asked.

"You can get them for free at the library. It's my turn!" After practically colliding with the young bookworm leaving the fenced enclosure, Philip hopped onto Santa's knee. Jesse stood to one side of Santa's throne, signaling to the photographer that he wasn't interested in a photograph. "My name's Phil Greer," Philip announced, "and here's what I want: another Transformer, some more Masters of the Universe things, and a rocket ship. Maybe a battery-operated one, with lights that go on and off. Okay?"

Grinning, Santa glanced at Jesse to make sure he'd heard Philip's requests. He winked, then bowed to address the boy on his lap. "That's a lot of stuff, Phil. Have you been a good boy this year?"

"I've been so good it's disgusting," Philip asserted.

"Well, I'll see what my elves can do for you."

"Okay, but no clothes," Philip implored him. "My grandma's going to send me clothes. She always does."

"That's what grandmas are for," Santa allowed. He reached into a sack at his feet and pulled out two candy canes. "Here you go, Phil, one for you and one for your dad. Merry Christmas! Ho-ho-ho!" With that, he lifted Philip off his lap, eyed the line, and sighed wearily.

"Hey, did you hear that?" Philip asked Jesse, handing him one of the candy canes and tearing the wrapper off the other. "He thought you were my dad. Pretty funny, huh?"

Jesse was too nonplussed to find Santa's error funny. He liked Philip a lot, and he liked Philip's mother at least as much. But to be mistaken for Philip's father was a bit unnerving.

"You got any kids, Jesse?" Philip inquired, taking Jesse's hand and leading him toward the department store at the center of the mall. He playfully hooked the rounded end of his candy cane over his lower lip, smirked, and bit off an inch of minty candy.

Jesse pocketed his candy cane and tightened his hold on Philip, afraid of losing him in the surging throngs of customers. "No, I don't," he answered as nonchalantly as he could.

"Maybe you ought to have some," Philip advised him.

Jesse closed his eyes and tried to sort his thoughts. First Santa had taken him as Philip's father, and now Philip was counseling him on paternity. Was this what the Christmas spirit did to people?

"My mom told me where kids come from," Philip claimed. "It sounds pretty gross to me."

"It isn't gross," Jesse calmly corrected him. "It's the most beautiful thing in the world." He was surprised to hear himself make such a statement. The subject of birth and babies had never been particularly relevant to his life. Anne hadn't wanted children—if she had, she might have been keener on the idea of marriage—and Jesse had assumed that if children were ever to enter his world, it would be sometime in the distant future.

Yet what he'd said to Philip was the truth, and as soon as he'd said it, he understood how right he was. "I bet your mother looked beautiful when she was pregnant with you," he mused aloud. "I bet those were some of the happiest days of her life, Philip."

"Call me Phil," he said, effecting a mature tone. "Wow. Look at that necklace. Maybe I'll get that for Mom."

Jesse followed Philip's outstretched finger to the diamond-and-gold pendant on display inside a locked glass showcase. Grinning, he shook his head. "I think that might be beyond your means," he commented gently.

"Yeah? How about those gloves, then?" Philip asked, pointing to a pair of fur-lined leather gloves inside another showcase.

Jesse chuckled. "Rule of thumb, Phil—if it's locked up and doesn't have a price tag showing, you can't afford it."

Philip considered Jesse's observation and accepted the sensibility of it. "What are you gonna get my mom?" he asked.

Jesse swallowed. He hadn't planned to buy any Christmas gifts this year. But then, he hadn't planned to meet someone like Robin. Or like Philip. "I haven't given it much thought," he admitted.

"Maybe I ought to get Mrs. O'Leary's present first," Philip resolved. "Where do you suppose they've got those remote-control trucks?"

"I don't know that she'd really want one of those," Jesse remarked. Not that he was on intimate terms with Philip's baby-sitter, but he felt it safe to assume that an elderly woman like Mrs. O'Leary wouldn't be enamored of such a toy. "How about a book?" He recalled the boy Philip had called a wienie at Santa's Workshop. "That might be within your budget."

"Hey, that's a good idea," Philip agreed, masterfully weaving among the crush of shoppers and dragging Jesse out of the store. "She likes crossword puzzles. Maybe I could get her one of those books of puzzles."

"She'd love that," Jesse heartily concurred. They made their way across the mall in the direction of a book emporium.

Philip paused near the workshop and studied Santa for a moment. "You know what?" he whispered. "That guy—he isn't really Santa Claus."

"Oh?" Jesse didn't bother to temper his smile. No wonder he'd liked Philip right from the start—he must have recognized the boy as a fellow cynic. "How do you know that?"

"Two things," Philip explained. "Number one, the real Santa doesn't have time to sit around shopping centers. He's too busy supervising the elves at the North Pole right now. And number two, the real Santa would've known that you weren't my dad. This guy's a fake. But that's okay," he concluded with a shrug. "Maybe he'll get my message to Santa, anyway."

"I'm sure he'll do his best," Jesse said solemnly as he led Philip into the bookstore.

ROBIN JOGGED PAST the lengthy rows of cars and back into the mall. It was five-thirty-five, and she'd just locked her packages inside the station wagon. The crowds had thinned slightly with the arrival of dinnertime, and she had little difficulty locating Jesse and Philip near the entrance to the steak house. Jesse was holding a large paper bag with a bookstore's logo printed across it.

"Didn't you buy me anything?" Philip asked, his face registering disappointment as he stared at her empty hands.

"It's in the car," she told him before lifting her face to Jesse. "You seem to have survived," she observed.

"By the skin of my teeth," he complained, though he was smiling. "Can I interest you in some food? We menfolk are starving."

They entered the steak house. The restaurant was doing a brisk business, but they didn't have to wait long for a table. Jesse and Robin ordered steaks, Philip a hamburger. He scrutinized his mother while they waited for their food. "Did you get lots of stuff?" he asked.

"I got what I came for," she answered cryptically. Part of the fun of Christmas was to keep Philip fretting and guessing, even though he had to know that she wouldn't let him down on the big day.

"You didn't get me clothes, did you?"

Robin laughed. "I'm leaving that for your grandmothers. And don't worry—I've already sent them both linens from Woodleigh's. With your name on the cards."

Philip's relief was palpable. He twisted to Jesse. "Mom takes care of everything," he boasted. Then he turned back to Robin. "Did you get something for Jesse?"

Her cheeks colored slightly as she glanced across the table. Jesse leaned back in his seat, obviously amused by Philip's lack of discretion. While she'd been running from store to store, purchasing toys for Philip, a sweater for Kate O'Leary, yo-yos for Jeff and Brian Calloway and a box of chocolates for Joanna—Joanna loved chocolates but Glenn refused to buy them for her because he didn't want her to get fat—Robin had searched for something that would be right for Jesse. But other than a new car, she didn't know what he could use, what he might want. She had decided to wait until she knew him better. Maybe she could find something for him at Woodleigh's. Given what he'd told her about his condominium, she felt safe in assuming that he could use a household item of some sort. Maybe one of the brass wine racks.

She hadn't yet made up her mind, but she knew she was going to give Jesse something.

"So, listen, Mom," Philip ventured. Their food had arrived, and he was drowning his hamburger in ketchup. "I think we ought to get our tree tomorrow."

"Philip, we've already discussed this. It's too soon to get a tree."

"They've got a tree here," Philip argued. "And it isn't an artificial one, like the one you've got at Woodleigh's. Jesse and I checked. It's a live one."

"This is a huge mall," Robin pointed out. "If their tree dries out, they can afford to get a replacement for it. If ours dries out, all we'll have by Christmas morning is a carpet full of brown needles."

"Not if we water it a lot," Philip maintained. Then he glanced at Jesse, seeking an ally. "Tell her, Jesse. Tell her we should get a tree tomorrow."

"You should get a tree tomorrow," Jesse obliged.

Robin's eyes widened. She had concluded from his happy, exhilarated mood that Jesse hadn't had too terrible a time with Philip. But to hear him state that Robin ought to buy a Christmas tree—let alone that she ought to buy one tomorrow—astonished her. "Get serious," she chided him.

"I am serious," he insisted, carving his steak. "It won't dry out if you keep it watered."

"Jesse. I thought you didn't . . . well . . ." She refused to finish the sentence; she didn't want to reveal to Philip that Jesse cared little for the holiday rituals.

"It's for Phil, not for me," Jesse reminded her.

Phil. Apparently things had gone quite amicably between her son and Jesse, if Philip had given him permission to call him by that name. Yet, as amicably as they'd gone, she couldn't imagine why Jesse was exhorting her to buy a tree. "Jesse—"

"What's the point of having a tree for only a few days?" he posed, his eyes meeting hers above the table and twinkling enigmatically. "If you're going to have one, you may as well enjoy it for as long as you can."

"I can't believe this," she muttered, unable to disguise her pleasure. "I can't believe that you, of all people—"

"Having trouble with your beliefs?" he teased. "Perhaps it's time you revised your philosophy."

"There's nothing wrong with my philosophy."

"Then get the kid a tree."

"Two against one, Mom," Philip chimed in. "You lose."

Robin laughed. There *was* nothing wrong with her philosophy. She believed in miracles, and Philip had obviously worked a miracle on Jesse to get him excited about a Christmas tree, of all things.

And the truth was, two against one notwithstanding, Robin didn't feel the least bit as if she'd lost.

Chapter Six

It was one thing for Jesse to argue that Robin ought to buy a Christmas tree. It was another for him to insist on accompanying Philip and her when they went to get it.

In saner moments, she told herself that her relationship with Jesse—if "relationship" was the proper term—was downright peculiar. Weren't men and women supposed to get acquainted, go out on a few dates, explore their sexual attraction gradually, and, much later, attempt to build a friendship with each other's offspring? Once she had decided, during Open School Night, that she was going to reactivate her social life, she had assumed that this was the route she would take.

She had also decided that night that Jesse Lawson wasn't the man with whom she was going to embark on her new life as an available single woman. Perhaps she had sensed intuitively that he wasn't the sort of man with whom one could follow a predictable pattern in developing a relationship.

Everything about the times she'd spent with him seemed fragmented, backward, bewildering. And yet in her less sane moments—and she seemed to be having more and more of them—she was too delighted by what-

ever it was she had with Jesse to care about the route she
was supposed to take.

Abandoning him to spend most of Saturday afternoon with Philip at the mall might have been incorrect,
but it had worked out wonderfully. Driving to his condominium late Sunday morning to pick him up for their
tree trip made just as much sense to her. The fact that
Philip was as excited about seeing Jesse as Robin herself
informed her that Jesse and her son had struck a fine
friendship.

Maybe Philip needed a man in his life—a mentor, a
role model, someone with whom he could act macho.
Unlike so many children of divorce, he didn't have a father who neglected him. But Ray simply wasn't around
most of the time. Twice a year might not be enough time
for Philip to spend in a man's company. Maybe he saw
Jesse as a substitute daddy.

Which was well and good, Robin supposed, except...except shouldn't she and Jesse be forging something, too? Or did Jesse merely view the Greers as a
family that conveniently afforded him an opportunity to
be a Big Brother without joining the national organiza-
tion?

He had to view them as more than that. If that was all
he wanted he wouldn't have kissed Robin the way he had
Friday night. But was he ever going to kiss her again?

She turned onto his street and braked. "Which house
is his?" Philip called from the back seat. He had cour-
teously left the front passenger seat empty for Jesse.

"That one," she said, pointing to one of the town
houses as she pulled into a parking space. The door to the
adjacent town house swung open and a curly-haired
woman in a stylish pink sweat suit emerged, lugging a
huge evergreen wreath.

"Yucch!" Philip moaned, slinking down in his seat. "It's Ms. Becker!"

"Don't you want to say hello to her?" Robin asked as she opened her car door.

"Uh-uh." Philip slouched lower, covering his face with his arms. "I don't want her to see me. It's Sunday."

Robin shrugged. "Suit yourself. I'll get Jesse." She shut the door, strolled around the car to the steps, and started down them.

As soon as Eileen Becker spotted her, Robin suffered a twinge of apprehension. How would Philip's teacher view the fact that the mother of one of her students was involved with her neighbor? Ms. Becker might be privy to information about Jesse, knowledge about his affairs with women. Maybe Ms. Becker had seen him escorting numerous young lovelies into his house at odd hours. Maybe Ms. Becker herself was one of those young love-lies.

"Ms. Greer?" Ms. Becker called out, obviously star-tled. Drawing closer, Robin noticed that Ms. Becker had a hammer and a nail in her hand.

"That's a beautiful wreath," said Robin, figuring that the only way to handle this potentially awkward encoun-ter was to behave as unruffled as possible.

"Isn't it? It used to be my husband's job to hang the wreath every year, but..." Ms. Becker bit her lip to cut herself off, and Robin felt a new swell of sympathy for the woman. Her own experiences the first few months after her divorce hadn't been too trying since Ray had been gone for long stretches of time during the preced-ing year, flying off to Bolivia and Honduras in his new job with the Agency for International Development. By the time they were legally divorced, Robin had grown accustomed to his absence. Yet certain jobs, chores that she'd always associated with Ray, had been difficult to tackle. It had taken her nearly a year to check the oil in her car, not because she didn't know how but because that had always been Ray's responsibility.

Evidently hanging the wreath had been Mr. Becker's responsibility. But since Robin wasn't supposed to know about Ms. Becker's divorce, she couldn't offer her condolences. "Do you need any help?" she said instead.

"No," the woman refused. "I've got to learn how to do these things for myself." She tapped the nail into her door, banged a couple of times on it, and then turned back to Robin. "Are you here to see me?"

"Actually, I'm, uh, I'm here to see Jesse Lawson."

Digesting this bit of news, Ms. Becker eyed her neighbor's front door with curiosity. "Legal business? I swear, he does more work at home than at his office."

"It's personal." Robin admitted, adding, "We're friends."

"You are?" Ms. Becker grinned broadly. "I didn't know that. I wonder why he didn't say anything that night he dropped by the school."

Because we weren't friends then, Robin answered silently.

"He's such a sweetie," Ms. Becker effused. "I have never in my life known anybody so eager to give of himself. The fact is, if I started to have trouble with this wreath, I would have asked him to help me. He's such a dear man, always lending a hand to everybody around here."

Robin wasn't sure whether she was surprised by Ms. Becker's remark. Jesse was helpful; his willingness to watch Philip yesterday while she shopped was probably something he would have done for anyone. On the other hand, his obstinacy about rejecting God didn't seem particularly sweet or dear to Robin.

She wondered whether Ms. Becker expected confirmation of her opinion of Jesse. But, without waiting for Robin to speak, the schoolteacher once again busied herself with her hammer, pounding the nail into the door and then hanging the wreath on it. "There," she announced, taking a step back and beaming at her achievement. "Looks good, doesn't it?"

"It looks terrific," Robin agreed.

Ms. Becker opened her door. "Say hi to Philip for me," she requested before vanishing into her house.

Robin analyzed their exchange and decided that it hadn't gone badly at all. As a divorced woman, Ms. Becker must assume that other divorced women had male friends. Indeed, if she wasn't already one of Jesse's ladies, the recently divorced teacher might herself have designs on her good-looking neighbor. But that was between them, none of Robin's business. She resolved not to succumb to jealousy.

She rang Jesse's bell, and when he answered, he already had on his jacket. "Good morning," he greeted her. Then his gaze circled the porch and the sidewalk beyond. "Where's Philip?"

"Hiding in the car," Robin said. "Ms. Becker was out here when we drove up, and he didn't want to talk to her."

"Ah." Jesse glanced at the vacant porch abutting his and then at the station wagon parked beside his rental car in the lot. Finally his eyes returned to Robin. He ran his index finger down her cheek to the underside of her chin, then tilted her face up and bent to kiss her.

His lips felt delicious on hers, so warm and tender and inviting that she had to muster all her willpower not to give herself over to his kiss as she had a few nights ago. She allowed her mouth to revel in the feel of his for only a moment, then pulled away.

"Okay," Jesse whispered, clearly requiring no explanation for her reticence. "Let's go."

Maybe he required no explanation, Robin pondered as they walked together along the walk to the stairs, but she required one. She needed to know what was going on between them, what he thought of her, what he expected of her. She needed to know whether Jesse considered them something more than friends—and, if so, exactly how much more. She needed to know why he was so interested in joining her and Philip when they went to pick out their tree.

But these were questions that would have to wait. She and Jesse arrived at the station wagon, and Philip pulled himself up to his usual posture. "Hey, Jesse, we're getting our tree!" he hooted as soon as Jesse opened the door.

"That's right."

"Did you get your tree yet?" Philip asked Jesse as Robin started the engine.

"I'm not going to have one," he replied.

Robin winced, afraid of how Jesse would react to the inquisition she knew Philip had in store for him. Jesse had been so good with Philip yesterday. Was he going to ruin everything now?

"How come you aren't going to have a tree?" Philip demanded to know.

Robin cast Jesse a quick glance, but he ignored her, twisting to look at Philip. "Not everybody gets trees, Phil."

"Why not?"

"Because it takes all kinds," Jesse answered. "Some people believe that having a Christmas tree is great, and some people don't."

"How come you don't?" Philip persisted.

"I think..." Jesse paused, shaping his words with care. "I think that the people who really want trees ought to have them. And that's why you're going to have one."

"Don't you like Christmas trees?"

"I'm going to like yours," Jesse promised. "I bet your tree is going to be the best one in the world."

That seemed to satisfy Philip, who smiled and settled contentedly in his seat. Robin cast Jesse another glance, this one filled with awe. She was impressed that he'd managed to parry all of Philip's questions without lying, and without burying the child in anti-Christmas claptrap. Yet Jesse didn't appear smug about his superlative performance under pressure. Nor did he seem uncomfortable. His smile reflected his pleasure at the bright sunshine, the crisp blue winter sky, and—she hoped—the company he was in. Nothing more.

She drove to the same tree vendor she patronized every year; buying a tree at the abandoned fruit stand on the Post Road was a tradition, and that particular vendor's trees were usually fresh, healthy and reasonably priced. Philip was the first out of the car. By the time Robin and Jesse climbed out, the boy had vanished between the tagged rows of cut pine trees. "Have you ever done this before?" Robin asked Jesse, her eyes sparkling with a mixture of humor and concern.

"Not in ages," he said. "When I was very young, we lived in northern California, in the foothills of the Sierras, and we used to cut our own trees there. But once we moved to Los Angeles, an evergreen would have been as out of place as a blizzard. Everyone had artificial trees down there. My parents had a white one.''

Robin wrinkled her nose. A fake white Christmas tree would probably sour the whole holiday for her, too.

Philip ran to them, breathless. ''Come on, Mom! I found the perfect one!'' He grabbed Robin's hand and yanked her between two rows of cut trees to the biggest, fullest tree on the lot. Robin didn't even bother to check the price. ''It's too tall,'' she said, rejecting it. ''We'd have to saw it in half to fit it into the living room.''

''We could cut a hole in the ceiling,'' Philip recommended.

''Forget it, Phil.'' She guided her son back to a stand of smaller trees. ''Pick out one from here,'' she advised him. ''These aren't too tall.''

''They're puny,'' Philip complained, even though they weren't.

''We go through this every year,'' Robin muttered to Jesse. ''He always swears that the one we picked is puny until we get it home and untie it.''

Jesse gallantly came to the rescue. ''Check this one out, Phil,'' he suggested. ''It's nice and full all around.''

''It's puny,'' Philip sulked, although he held Jesse in enough esteem to give the tree a reluctant perusal.

Robin lifted the tag. Forty dollars. ''We'll take it,'' she told the vendor.

Once the limbs were tied, Jesse insisted on helping the vendor carry it to the car. ''Don't!'' Robin tried to stop him. ''Your wrist—''

Shrugging off her solicitude with a good-natured grin, he hoisted up the trunk with his right hand, using his injured left one to balance it. Obviously he didn't want to be pampered. The bruise on his cheek was still visible, and his wrist was still taped, yet he stubbornly carried the heavier end of the tree and assisted the vendor in wedging it into the back of the station wagon.

He was just as stubborn about carrying the tree into the house, once they'd driven home with it. Robin had already spread an old waterproof tablecloth on the floor in the corner of the living room to protect the carpet, and she had dug the tree stand out of one of the Christmas boxes in the den. Philip eagerly played the boss man as the two adults set up the tree, commanding Robin to tilt the trunk slightly forward, slightly to the left, slightly back again, while Jesse tightened the screws around the base. Once they were all in agreement that the tree was perfectly straight, they untied the limbs.

"Wow!" Philip whooped, darting to the den. "Let's get the decorations."

"Not now, Phil." Robin attempted to halt him. "We've got to let the branches settle for a day before we start hanging things on them." In truth, her primary concern was not the branches but Jesse. After yesterday's trip to the mall and this morning's purchase of the tree, he might be dangerously close to overdosing on the holiday.

To her astonishment, he pulled off his jacket, tossed it onto a chair and gave the tree a comprehensive inspection. "I think you could decorate it now," he remarked. "The branches can settle with the decorations on them."

Robin eyed him speculatively. Did he intend to help hang the decorations? Was that why he had removed his jacket? And why was he trailing Philip into the den to fetch the boxes? "I'm going to like yours," he had said when Philip had grilled him about why he wasn't going to have his own tree. "I bet it's going to be the best tree in the whole world." Perhaps, she mused as she hung the strewn jackets in the coat closet, decorating a tree didn't necessarily offend an atheist's sensibilities, as long as it was someone else's tree.

Jesse emerged from the den with a carton cradled in his arms and Philip at his heels. Jesse set the carton down near the tree with a thud and straightened up. "You sure have enough stuff in those boxes," he muttered, his dark eyes twinkling with amusement. "You could open your own store."

"I've already got a store," she countered, crossing to the box and pulling back the flaps. "There's only one more box with tree ornaments besides this one. The other boxes are filled with things for the rest of the house. We won't be unpacking those today."

Philip knelt by the box and began lifting items from it. "Remember this little rocking horse, Mom?" he shouted, displaying the wooden ornament for her. "Remember this felt Santa?"

Ignoring him, Robin studied Jesse. She gazed into his eyes; their powerful radiance offered her no hint of his thoughts. "You don't have to do this if you don't want to," she reminded him quietly.

"I know that," he responded. Then he gave her a reassuring grin, squatted down next to Philip, and helped him to unload the decorations.

It took the three of them nearly two hours to adorn the tree. There were strings of lights, garlands of tinsel, reflecting balls, and all the individual ornaments, each with a story attached to it. Philip took it upon himself to fill Jesse in on their significance. "This star, it came from Woodleigh's," he announced. "Mom's boss gave it to her. This little stocking, my Grandma Greer sewed it. The snowman came from the Calloways. Jeff Calloway's my very best friend, Jesse. See this little teddy bear? I got this when I was a baby. I don't remember it, but Mommy does." He turned to his mother for the full account.

She smiled apologetically at Jesse. "One of Ray's colleagues at Yale gave it to Phil," she explained. "I'm sure this can't be as interesting to you as it is to Phil."

Jesse laughed. "I'm hanging on his every word. How about this silver bell, Phil?" he asked, dangling another ornament in front of the boy's eyes.

"That's the 'Jingle Bell'," Philip informed him. "Shake it, Jesse—it really rings. Mom found it in the street a few days after Christmas one year, and she polished it up. It fell off Santa's sleigh, right?"

"That was my guess," Robin said, offering Jesse another sheepish smile. She refused to feel guilty about using a fortuitously placed prop to buttress the Santa myth for her son. But if Jesse condemned her for feeding Philip malarkey about St. Nick, he didn't show it. He shook the bell, producing a gentle tinkling sound, and mirrored Robin's smile.

By one-thirty, the tree was embellished with every item from the cartons. Philip and Jesse stood back to assess the result of their labor while Robin plugged in the lights. This year's tree looked essentially the same as last year's, but the moment the chains of bulbs were illuminated, Robin viewed the tree as something unique, a symbol of both continuity and newness. Every year it was like this: the lighting of the tree instilled a feeling of rebirth deep within her, a blossoming in her soul, softly glowing and magical. If only Jesse could feel it, too, if only he could allow himself to know the wonder of it . . .

"I'm starving," Philip declared, shattering her brief reverie. "I want lunch, Mom."

"Lunch. Of course." Forcing herself back to reality, she marched into the kitchen, followed by Philip and

Jesse, who thoughtfully deposited the empty cartons in the den on his way.

"Peanut butter," Philip requested, flopping onto a chair. "Cut the sandwich in triangles, okay?"

"How about a 'please'?" Robin remonstrated as she pulled a jar of peanut butter and a loaf of bread from the refrigerator.

"Please," Philip obliged.

Spreading the peanut butter on the bread, Robin glanced at Jesse. "Would you like lunch, too?"

"I'd like dinner," he answered, leaning against the counter next to where she was working. "Just you and me. Tonight."

Jesse's decision to ask Robin for another date in front of Philip struck her as indiscreet, but it was too late for her to silence him. The boy at the table immediately piped up. "Yeah, Jesse—you owe her one, after standing her up Friday night. She was real sore about that."

"Philip!" Robin's cheeks burned with embarrassment.

Jesse indulged in a low, warm laugh. "She couldn't have been as sore as I was," he commented before turning to Robin. "How about it, Robin? Dinner tonight?"

Robin set down the knife and faced him. "You obviously don't know the first thing about baby-sitters," she lectured, her pleasure at his invitation tempering her discomfort about having this conversation in front of Philip. "They have to be booked days in advance. Weeks, sometimes. I'll never be able to find anybody on such short notice."

"It can't hurt to try," Jesse noted, lifting the receiver from the wall phone and handing it to her, then delivering Philip his sandwich.

"Go ahead, Mom," Philip urged her. "Try Mrs. O'Leary."

Two against one, her son's voice echoed inside her. *You lose.* Grinning at the irrepressible team Philip and Jesse made, she pushed the buttons for Kate O'Leary's number. "Well, Jesse," she said a few minutes later, after bidding Kate goodbye, "if you don't already believe in miracles, you'd better start."

"Mrs. O'Leary's available?" he asked.

"Not exactly. She was planning to have a friend over for an evening of canasta, but when I told her she could bring her friend along, she said she'd come. That means you've got to be twice as well behaved tonight, Phil," she concluded, shooting her son a warning look.

"Canasta," he groaned, curling his lip. "Mrs. O'Leary once tried to teach me that game. It's really boring."

"She'll be playing canasta in the kitchen with Mrs. Lindblad," Robin explained. "And you'll be watching television in the den. Until eight-thirty, and then straight to bed. Do we understand each other?"

"Yeah," Philip said before slugging down a drink of milk. "I'm not allowed to call it boring in front of Mrs. O'Leary."

"You got it, pal." She pivoted to Jesse. "Satisfied?"

"I will be, tonight," he said. "Is seven o'clock all right?"

Robin nodded. "Do you want me to drive?"

Jesse shook his head. His eyes glittered mysteriously as they met hers. In what way would he be satisfied tonight? she wondered. Had he found the activities of the past two days unsatisfying? Would a once-delayed dinner date be enough to satisfy him?

Much as it troubled her to admit it, she hoped that dinner wouldn't be enough to satisfy him. She wanted

more than a meal from Jesse. And the way he was looking at her, the way his eyes seemed to overpower her and
his mouth quirked into that dazzling smile of his, con-
veyed that he wanted more from her, too. "I'll see you at
seven," he promised, giving her shoulder a light squeeze
before he strode from the kitchen.

THIS TIME, HE CAME. Promptly at seven o'clock he arrived at her front door, dressed in a turtleneck, wool
slacks, his tweed blazer and cashmere scarf. He was
treated to the vision Robin had planned for him on Friday night: the gray sweater-dress—which, she decided
after lengthy deliberation, didn't make her appear too
wan or flat-chested—the artfully made-up eyes, the
curled ends of her glistening blond hair. His reaction
convinced Robin that her efforts had been worthwhile.
"You look fantastic," he said as he entered the house.

Philip had already eaten dinner, and he and Kate were
negotiating over dessert while Mrs. Lindblad stood by,
peeking around the bend in the hallway to spy on Jesse
and Robin. Feeling the need to settle the dispute between Kate and Philip before she left, Robin dashed to
the kitchen and pronounced judgment. "One slice of
apple pie, Phil, and you've got to eat it in the kitchen. It's
too messy for the den. Be good, and don't forget to brush
your teeth before bed."

Philip scowled at her maternal admonition. "Of course
I'll brush my teeth. Toothpaste is the only sweet thing I
ever get to eat around here," he grumbled. Perhaps Mrs.
Lindblad was moved by his lament, but Robin and Kate
knew better. Indeed it was hard to feel any pity for the
boy while Kate was slicing him a hefty wedge of pie.

Robin joined Jesse by the front door, pulled her coat
from the closet, and picked up her purse. "Are you sure

you don't want me to drive?" she asked as they strolled down the walk to the driveway.

Jesse's answer was to unlock the passenger door of the small rental car. "I'm not going to drive into any more electrical poles, if that's what you're worried about," he assured her before closing the door and moving around to the driver's side.

That wasn't what Robin was worried about. She was worried about whether he might be nervous about driving, given what he'd recently been through. She knew the old adage about climbing back on the horse after it threw you, but still, she was more than willing to drive if Jesse wanted her to.

Obviously, he didn't. He cruised to the corner, the steering wheel rubbing his knees whenever he turned it, and headed up the hill to the main road. "I want to do it right this time," he answered her unformed question. "That includes my doing the driving. In the words of Phil, I owe you one."

Robin shifted uneasily in her seat. "I wish you hadn't asked me out in front of him," she said. "It kind of put me on the spot."

"Oh?" Jesse halted at a stop sign and turned to her. "If he wasn't there, would you have said no?"

Robin returned his gaze. All afternoon she had been inhaling the tangy perfume of pine tree in the living room, but now that smell was replaced by the scent of Jesse, a warm, musky, undeniably masculine fragrance. His eyes were piercing, his hair thick and velvety, his hands on the wheel strong and certain. No matter what the circumstances, Robin could never have said no to his dinner invitation.

"I just—I'd rather you had asked me in private," she explained. "I mean, so much of what we've done has

been all three of us. If this was just going to be between
the two of us, Jesse, then that's how you should have
gone about it." As soon as she uttered the words, she realized how much she had divulged. Her confusion about
whether Jesse liked her because she was Philip's mother
or because she was herself had to be evident to him.

He contemplated her for a long moment, then nodded. "You're right. I've never been involved with a
mother before, and I guess I've been a little clumsy. I'm
sorry."

"Don't be," Robin said swiftly, elated by his admis-
sion that he was involved with her.

He drove to a Mexican restaurant on the eastern end of
town. After hurrying inside to escape the evening chill,
they were seated at a cozy, candle-lit booth. Robin removed her coat, Jesse his scarf and jacket. A classical
guitarist stationed not far from them serenaded them
with delicate arrangements of Bach fugues.

A waitress approached their table and asked if they
wanted drinks. Robin meditated. What went with Mexican food? A tequila sunrise, maybe, or a margarita, or—

"Have you got any wine?" Jesse asked the waitress.

Robin's jaw dropped. Wine? With tacos and enchilla-
das?

"We've got a house burgundy, chablis and rosé," the
waitress informed him. "You can order it by the glass.
We've also got sangria."

Jesse turned to Robin. "I think beer might go better
with this food," she suggested. "Sangria's too sweet."

"I hate beer," Jesse declared.

Her astonishment increased. The man hated beer.
Well, she wasn't going to drink alone, and she wasn't
going to drink wine with Mexican food. "I think I'll
skip," she said prudently.

Nodding, Jesse accepted two menus from the waitress and dismissed her. He handed one of the menus to Robin, but she didn't bother to open it. She was too busy gaping at him. "Is something wrong?" he asked.

"I don't think I've ever met a man who hated beer before."

"Then I'm your first," Jesse said, unperturbed. Sensing that she was awaiting an explanation, he informed her, "I tried beer in law school. Not only did it taste awful, but it gave me a whopping headache."

"Law school?" she blurted out. "What did you drink in college?"

"Nothing."

"Nothing?" Her gaze narrowed on him. "What were you, a teetotaler?"

"Yes. I'm not anymore, Robin. I do like wine."

She lowered her menu to the table and studied him in fascination. She had never met a teetotaler before. "Why didn't you drink?" she asked.

"I was raised very strictly," he said. "I've already told you my parents are very religious. They raised me to think consuming liquor was a sin."

"In excess, maybe," Robin granted. Then she refuted herself. "No—it's a problem, and sometimes a disease, but it isn't a sin. I've known a lot of heavy drinkers, Jesse. My mother had some rough times with booze—lots of army wives do. It's a lousy life, being uprooted all the time, and they do whatever it takes to help them feel like they fit in. But my mother's problem resolved itself right after my father retired. And it *wasn't* a sin," she stressed.

"I know that now," Jesse granted. "I had my doubts even as a child. But when drinking isn't a regular part of your life, taking that first taste of liquor is a fearsome experience." He shrugged. "I think I can survive the rest of my life without beer being a part of it."

The waitress returned to take their orders. Once they were alone again, Robin regarded the puzzling man seated across the table from her. "I just can't picture you as devoutly religious," she commented.

He chuckled. "I'm not sure I ever was. My parents were. I always had too many questions. There's no room for questions if you're buying into fundamentalism, Robin. You either accept it or reject it. You swallow all of it or none of it."

"And you couldn't swallow it."

"I tried," he admitted, his smile expanding. "But I kept choking on it."

It dawned on Robin that her knowledge of Jesse Lawson was woefully slim. All she knew about fundamentalists was what she saw on television: militant preachers spewing sermons of hellfire and brimstone, orating against sex and the theory of evolution, alerting parents to the perils of exposing their children to certain books and ideas. She could scarcely believe that a man as urbane as Jesse had been raised in such an environment.

You either accept it or reject it. Apparently he refused to recognize any middle ground. Unable to accept any part of it, he'd rejected all of it.

She had to learn more about him. She had to make sense of him. "How did you wind up in Branford?" she inquired.

"I was offered a job with New Haven Legal Assistance," he replied. "It was exactly what I was looking for, so I took it."

"Were you doing legal aid work in Los Angeles?"

He shook his head. "Far from it, Robin. I was raking in the bucks working for a big company."

Robin could imagine Jesse as a high-powered corporate attorney more easily than as a fundamentalist. But the pieces weren't falling together, and she plowed ahead, ignoring the waitress who came to deliver their dinners. "Why did you have to come all the way across the country just to switch jobs? I bet there were plenty of legal aid jobs in L.A."

"I was ready for a change of scenery as well as a change of jobs," Jesse admitted.

"So it seems." She tasted her quesadilla, smiled at its piquancy, and cooled her tongue of the fiery spiciness with a long sip of ice water. "I've lived in so many places," she said, "but never southern California. I know it's wrong to think of Los Angeles as a bunch of movie stars and television production companies and nothing else, but that's what I picture."

"Add a few palm trees and you wouldn't be far from the mark," Jesse joked.

"What big company did you work for?"

"G.C.E."

"Was that a show-biz company?"

Jesse grinned ironically. "In a sense." At her bemused stare, he clarified. "G.C.E. stands for Grace Cathedral Enterprises."

"Grace Cathedral? You mean—that big chapel on television, with the Reverend Robert Shepherd and his famous choir?"

Jesse appeared irritated. "Don't tell me you watch *Blessings at Noon*, Robin."

"I don't," she swore, surprised by the stinging bitterness in his words. "But it's hard not to know about Grace Cathedral. I'm sure everybody's caught a few minutes of Shepherd's shows at least once in their lives. You really worked there?"

"I did."

Perhaps the Grace Cathedral broadcasts were a bit overdone, but Robin found it exciting to think that Jesse actually worked with a certified television star. "What's he like?" she asked. "What's Shepherd really like? Is he just as bombastic when the cameras aren't on him? Or is all that sanctimoniousness just an act?"

Jesse toyed with his fork for a minute, then placed it on the edge of his plate. "He's an actor," he said, laboring over his words. "He plays to his audience."

"But when he's off the air—"

"He's an actor, just like any other TV performer. His concerns are the same—ratings, popularity, audience. He's never 'off'."

The difficulty Jesse seemed to be having in describing his former boss indicated to Robin how uncomfortable he must have felt in his work for the man. "What do all those holy people need a lawyer for?" she asked.

Jesse let out a caustic laugh. "You're an innocent, aren't you. Don't you know what outfits like Grace Cathedral are all about?" He consumed some of his chicken, then elaborated. "Money, Robin. Contributions. Distribution rights, royalties, agency fees, air time and commercials. Money. Whenever you've got that much money pouring in, you'd better have a lawyer handy to protect your interests. And to oversee contracts, to avoid lawsuits. To make sure that the cured cripples Shepherd likes to parade across the screen aren't phonies."

"So you admit that Shepherd does cure cripples," Robin said, pouncing on his words. "You admit that there are miracles, Jesse."

He shook his head. "I admit that people who are injured can sometimes defy their prognoses and get better.

I admit that people facing seemingly insurmountable personal problems can sometimes overcome them. But that doesn't mean that miracles have occurred. It just means that prognoses are sometimes wrong, and that with enough fortitude, most people can overcome their personal problems. It isn't God, Robin. It's people working hard to improve their lives and reach their goals. But…yes, as a lawyer, I had to get affidavits from all of Shepherd's guests, from the doctors and witnesses and all, to avoid legal problems over false claims.''

"Why on earth did you ever take a job like that?"

Jesse ruminated for a while. He was obviously trying to work through his thoughts, to discover a precise response to Robin's reasonable question. "Let's just say it was part of my upbringing," he answered vaguely. "I may have started experimenting with liquor in law school, but there was still too much of the obedient son in me. I questioned a lot, but…there were some things I should have questioned that I didn't."

Robin leaned back and examined the man facing her. Her badgering questions didn't seem to annoy him—if they did, he would have changed the subject. Instead he appeared open to her probing. His gaze was unwavering, his smile hesitant, his bandaged left hand resting palm up on the table, cupped slightly, as if shaped to hold whatever she might give him, to lift whatever might be weighing on her.

"I'm sorry," she mumbled, not sure why she was apologizing. "This is all a bit bewildering."

"It doesn't have to be." Jesse extended his arm across the table and captured her hand in his. "I'm pretty forthright about who I am and what I think," he commented. "I admire you for asking. That's my favorite yardstick for measuring others, Robin. I like people who are willing to ask questions.''

"But still…" She tried to unravel her snarled thoughts. "For someone who choked on religion and rejected it, how come you got into our Christmas tree in such a big way today?"

Maybe Jesse liked people who asked questions, but this question held a genuine challenge. He didn't back away, though. Nor did he release her hand. He simply held it, curling his fingers loosely around her slender wrist. "I'm not quite sure," he said.

"And the shopping trip yesterday, and the visit with Santa Claus…"

"That has nothing to do with religion," he argued. "Visiting Santa made Phil happy, and keeping him entertained while you shopped made you happy. And the tree…" He hesitated, a wistful smile curving his lips. "The tree was beautiful because it means so much to you both. I was honored to be included in something that special to you and Phil. It was fun. And the mall was fun, too. After what happened Friday night, all I wanted was to enjoy life, to have fun."

That hadn't been all Jesse had wanted. Particularly not on Friday night. Jesse had wanted more from Robin, more than he was able to ask for. They both knew that.

Everything about Friday night was etched into her soul. Every excruciating detail, every sensation, every inchoate thought that had flitted through her brain during those few heady moments when she had stood kissing Jesse on his porch—it was all still with her, perplexing her. Her confusion must have shown plainly in her face, because Jesse's hand tightened slightly on hers and his smile disappeared. "Robin, if there's more you need to know, ask."

She raised her eyes to his. "I don't even know what questions I'm supposed to be asking," she confessed with a nervous laugh.

He regarded her for a long, contemplative minute, interpreting her bewilderment, supplying the explanation she seemed to be seeking. "When I was in that accident," he murmured, "it wasn't just the seat belt that saved my life." He paused, his gaze holding hers, uncompromising. "You saved my life, too."

"Me?" she sputtered. "All I did was pick you up at the hospital—"

"You did much more than that, Robin. Or maybe... maybe we did it together." His thumb moved against her wrist, tracing the bones, dancing across her throbbing pulse. "I kept thinking of you throughout the accident, clinging to thoughts of you. And that's what pulled me through. I'm convinced of it."

Stunned, Robin fell back in her seat. She was incredibly flattered by what Jesse had said—flattered and frantic. How had she pulled him through? How had she come to mean that much to him?

The same way he had come to mean something to her, she concluded. Her shopping trip with Philip on Saturday had been one of the most enjoyable she'd ever had, not only because Jesse had kept Philip occupied for her but because Jesse was there. Her outing to purchase a tree that morning had been wonderful because Jesse was there. Decorating the tree had been joyous, because Jesse was there.

She had always believed that what made the holiday special was the tradition of it. Jesse wasn't a part of any tradition for her. Yet his presence had somehow made the traditional activities much more meaningful.

"You look scared," Jesse observed, withdrawing his hand and studying her, concerned.

"I don't think I am." Robin emitted a small, breathless laugh, and then, as she absorbed Jesse's affectionate smile, a more confident chuckle. "What I do think is that you're just too stuck on being an atheist to admit that it wasn't me who pulled you through. It was the Lord, watching over you."

"I think I know the difference between a beautiful blond woman and a bearded old geezer in the clouds."

"Your idea of God is ridiculous," Robin retorted, laughing even harder.

Jesse joined her laughter. "That's probably why I don't believe in Him. Do you want dessert?"

"No." What Robin wanted was time, time to shape all the questions she had for Jesse, time for him to provide all the answers. What she wanted was time alone with him, time to come to terms with the fact that he held her responsible for saving his life.

Time to figure out what it all meant, what Jesse meant, how much he was coming to mean to her.

Chapter Seven

"I'll drive you ladies home," Jesse chivalrously offered as Kate O'Leary and her friend reached for their coats.

"That's very nice of you," Kate disputed him, "but you don't have to. We're only going down the block."

"Then I'll walk you home," Jesse said with a finality that even Kate wouldn't dare to contradict.

The two women exchanged impressed glances behind Jesse's back before allowing him to escort them out of the house. Robin imagined that Kate would be doing penance for weeks to atone for having once implied that Jesse Lawson was no better than vermin. She watched as the trio strolled down the front walk, Jesse turning up the collar of his blazer and tightening his scarf against the frigid December night. Then she closed the door, leaving it unlocked for him, and removed her own coat. She stepped out of her shoes, tiptoed up the stairs to check on her sleeping son, and returned to the living room.

The tree nearly overwhelmed the room, towering regally in its corner. Robin bent down by the wall socket and plugged the lights in. The room filled with a multicolored glow from the tiny sparkling bulbs.

Her gaze wandered to the fireplace. Jesse would be freezing by the time he got back from Kate's house. Her

smile widening, she tugged open the mesh curtain pro-
tecting the hearth, balled up a few sheets of newspaper,
piled on some kindling and applied a lit match to her
construction. It caught instantly, lending the room a cozy
warmth. Robin remained seated by the fireplace, admiring the yellow licks of flame as they flared upward. When
she thought the fire was hot enough she added two sea-
soned logs. They crackled as the flames danced around
them, and then finally caught fire. A feeling of contentment infused her as she inhaled the pungent scent of
burning wood and let the heat wrap around her.

"You read my mind." The mellow sound of Jesse's
voice startled her; she hadn't heard him enter the house.
Flinching, she glanced over her shoulder and found him
standing less than a foot behind her, unwinding his scarf.
"It's cold out there," he announced, sliding off his blazer
and tossing it onto a chair. Then he dropped onto the
carpeted floor beside Robin and extended his hands palm
forward to catch the fire's warmth.

"I'm going to sound like a mother for saying this,"
Robin muttered, "but why do you run around in nothing but a blazer when it's wintertime?"

He grinned. "I'm from southern California, remember? The only coat I own is an unlined raincoat."

"Then it's high time you bought yourself something
warmer," she reproached him. "This is yankee country.
Treat yourself to a coat for Christmas."

"I'll treat myself to a coat out of respect for Mother
Nature," Jesse corrected her with a chuckle. He turned
to face the fire, resting his left forearm across his bent
knee and gazing into the blaze. It cast a golden glow
across his face, delineating the harsh angles of it, em-
phasizing the dynamic lines of his nose and chin, the
planes of his cheeks and brow, and making his hair seem

impossibly blacker in contrast. His lingering smile grati-
fied Robin. She'd been smart to build a fire, to warm this
outlander who didn't know how to dress for a New England winter.

She still harbored many questions about Jesse. She had
assailed him mercilessly with her questions over dinner,
and he'd answered them without hesitation, yet he remained an enigma to her. She wanted to know more; she
needed to. She needed to know, among other things, why
he'd chosen to live in Connecticut, a part of the country
with a climate that required clothing he didn't own and
driving skills he'd had little chance to master. He had said
he was ready for a major change, but a three-thousand-
mile change? "There has to be more to it," she pondered, surprised to hear herself giving voice to her bemusement.

Jesse eyed her, perplexed. "More to what? Mother
Nature?"

She laughed meekly and turned to stare at the fire.
When Jesse had enough of her questions, she supposed,
he'd let her know. But although he wasn't complaining
about her nosiness, she couldn't look directly at him
when she said, "There has to be more to your decision to
move to New Haven. It couldn't have just been the job.
There must be openings in every city in the country for
lawyers willing to do legal aid work. You didn't have to
move so far away from home."

She could feel his eyes upon her, studying her profile
as she continued to face the fireplace. He lapsed into
thought for a moment, then said, "I think I did have to."

"Why?" she posed. "You lived in L.A. for so much of
your life. Your family was there, and your roots... I'd
give my eyeteeth for the chance to have lived in one place
for so long, to really become attached to it. I'm begin-

ning to feel attached to Branford, but it's taken me nine years."

"Maybe I want to become attached to Branford, too," Jesse remarked.

Robin laughed again, and Jesse joined her. Branford was a nice enough town, with some beautiful neighborhoods and a breathtaking coastline bordering the Long Island Sound. But it was too modest to deserve the sort of instant attachment Jesse alluded to. "It isn't Branford," she debated him, finding the courage to turn back to him. "And it isn't New Haven. You weren't coming here—you were only trying to get as far from L.A. as possible."

Jesse conceded with a grin. "Is there anything wrong with that?"

"Of course not," she hastened to assure him. "Only...I can't believe your job was the only reason you left."

His smile faded. This time it was he who turned to the fire, staring at the hypnotic flickering of the flames because it was easier than looking at Robin. "What are you getting at?" he asked, his tone low and even. "Do you want to know if I left a woman behind? I did."

That hadn't been what Robin was getting at, at least not consciously. Without giving it much thought, she had assumed that Jesse would have been seeing women—or, for that matter, a specific woman—wherever he lived. But since he'd introduced the subject, she wasn't about to let it drop. "You came here to recover from a broken heart?" she asked, then felt her cheeks darken with color at her relentless prying. "It's none of my business, Jesse. I don't know why you've put up with so many questions from me—"

He touched her shoulder reassuringly. Ignoring her belated apology, he said, "I didn't have a broken heart, Robin. Just like you and your ex-husband, we grew apart."

"Were you married?" she asked, although she felt safe in presuming that he hadn't been. If he had, he would have said so the evening she'd told him about her divorce.

He shook his head, confirming her guess. "Anne and I were pretty serious, but it didn't get that far."

"Was she in show biz?"

"She was a television producer."

A television producer. Robin imagined someone rich and polished, ambitious and successful. Someone with a magnificent wardrobe, someone who didn't have to worry about clothes making her look flat-chested, someone whose hair didn't require a curling iron to make it appear thick and wavy and lustrous. All in all, Robin concluded, someone who was brainy and gorgeous and everything Robin wasn't.

She was so busy wrestling with her insecurities that she missed part of what Jesse was saying. ". . . for G.C.E., too."

"Hmm?"

"She was one of the producers of *Blessings at Noon*. We met through work. We were together, on and off, for about four years. But she bought into the whole scene and I didn't, and finally we were forced to admit that the differences between us were irreconcilable." He paused, then angled his face to view her. "What's the matter, Robin? You wish I hadn't brought it up, don't you?"

"It isn't that," she said quickly. "It's just . . . I can't help wondering what you're doing here with me when you could be with some glamorous lady who produces television shows.''

He gazed steadily at her, neither smiling nor frowning, simply looking, absorbing her with his eyes. "You know what I'm doing here with you," he said.

He was with her, she reminded herself, because he thought she had saved his life.

If she had, it hadn't been through any intentional action on her part, and she wasn't sure she was ready to accept the responsibility his statement implied. She had heard it said that when you saved another person's life, you owned that person's life, and it was yours to look after forever. The very idea made Robin uncomfortable.

Yet she didn't exactly want to shirk the responsibility Jesse was giving her. She wanted to keep him safe, to protect him, to build fires to warm him. Deep in her heart, she wanted to believe that, however inadvertently, she *had* helped him to survive the crash.

The fact of that crash was brought home to her as Jesse shoved up the sleeves of his turtleneck sweater and revealed the tan Ace bandage around his sprained wrist. "You shouldn't have been lugging around the tree today," she scolded. If she was going to accept responsibility for his life, then she had a right to chide him for taking unnecessary risks with it. "You ought to give your wrist a chance to heal."

His gaze traveled from her to his arm and back again. His smile reached his eyes, imbuing them with a captivating glitter. "If you're really so worried about making it better," he goaded her, "you can kiss it. I saw you heal Phil with a kiss after he took that tumble in the parking lot yesterday."

Seemingly an innocuous request. But Jesse's earlier words echoed inside her: *You know what I'm doing here with you.* Perhaps he was with her because she'd saved his life, and perhaps he was with her only because he wanted to seduce her. Asking her to kiss his sprained wrist sounded more like the latter, and she faltered for a moment, mulling over how best to deal with a seduction attempt. He'd taken her out for dinner and then returned with her to her house. Did he believe sex was next on the agenda?

"I think," she said, fighting against the waver in her voice, "that making an injury better with a kiss works only when you're related by blood."

"Let's try it and find out."

Despite Jesse's light tone, despite the laughter dancing in his eyes, Robin understood his intention. She might be rusty when it came to male-female games, she might be inexperienced, but she wasn't an idiot. She sensed in his attitude not the overpowering need that had compelled him to kiss her the last time they were alone, but rather a strong, healthy attraction, a masculine hunger, controlled but very real, very present.

"If I do try it . . ." She faltered again, unsure of how receptive she should be to his overture. She was just as attracted to him as he was to her, just as anxious to recapture the passion they'd shared on his porch a few nights back. But she was nervous, too, and she bought time by pointing out, "Making an injury better with a kiss is a miracle cure. You've got to admit you believe in miracle cures, Jesse, or it won't work."

His eyes met hers. Perhaps he understood her hesitancy; perhaps he thought she was testing him. His smile vanished but his gaze intensified, searching her face for a clue of how to proceed—if he should proceed. "I'll admit that I do believe in miracles," he said quietly. "Not divinely inspired ones, Robin, but—I believe that people can create their own miracles." He raised his wrist in front of her, daring her to create a miracle for them.

She shyly touched her lips to his exposed thumb. "There. All better?"

"Miraculously." He ran his thumb gently over her lower lip, tracing the full curve of it. "Should I say hallelujah now?" He moved closer, his face a mere breath away from hers. "Should I sing your praises before heaven and earth?"

"No," she answered on a sigh, her entire body attuned to him, yielding, welcoming the kiss she knew was coming. "You only have to believe."

"I believe," he murmured, molding his mouth to hers. His tongue traced the line his thumb had sketched over her lips, but didn't venture farther. Before she could relax fully in the heavenly sensations his kiss elicited, he drew back, patiently waiting for a cue from her to continue.

"I guess some things are allowed," she mumbled with a hazy smile.

"What?"

"Well, you weren't allowed to drink," she said. "But even ultra-religious people must be allowed to kiss. You didn't wait until law school to learn how to kiss did you?"

A soft laugh bubbled up from his chest. "I always assumed this was allowed. Where else would baby fundamentalists come from?" Refusing her a chance to reply, his lips covered hers again. This time his tongue penetrated her mouth, conquering her with an intimacy that was both shocking and tender. Her tongue eagerly met his. Kissing Jesse this way, not in desperation but in sheer pleasure, felt as natural as talking to him, arguing philosophies with him, taunting him about his bizarre beliefs.

He had said he believed. As his kiss deepened, as her flesh melted in the heat of it, she believed, too. She believed that some things defied logic, and that, logical or not, Jesse was the man with whom she wanted to make love, now, tonight, the man with whom she wanted to end her long years of solitude.

Her arms curled around his shoulders as he bowed to her, urging her down onto the carpet beneath him. Her hair splayed out about her head, and his fingers twined through the silky blond tresses, reaching for her earlobes, for the smooth skin of her throat, the nape of her neck. Without breaking the kiss, he shifted above her, his chest moving against hers, his hips settling provocatively between her thighs. She reflexively arched her back, pressing her breasts into the wall of rib and muscle, and he groaned.

Lifting his mouth, he slipped his hand between their bodies and roamed downward to stroke the rounded swell of her breast. Despite the layers of cloth separating his palm from her skin, he easily located her nipple and centered on it, causing it to stiffen against his fingers. The heat roaring through her flesh and gathering below her abdomen had nothing to do with the fire in the hearth. It was a result of Jesse, the weight of him upon her, his sensitive caresses igniting a blazing yearning within her.

Her arms moved down to ring his waist. Through his shirt, she explored the sleek, firm muscles of his lower back, the tension in them as his hips shifted above hers again. She felt his arousal, hard and unyielding as he moved against her, urging her legs to accommodate him.

"Where's your bed?" he whispered, the hoarse rumble of his voice burning against her ear as his lips grazed her hair.

Upstairs, her soul cried out in a silent answer. *Take him upstairs.* Yet the words wouldn't come. Twisting beneath him, she glimpsed the staircase across the room, the polished railing that would soon be draped in garlands, the steps rising up to her bedroom, to the bed in which she'd slept alone for three years. Once more she tried to speak, but her lips refused to shape the words, her lungs refused to support them.

Jesse nudged her face back to his. He peered down at her, his eyes smoky, his lips parted as he struggled with his erratic breath. He couldn't help but discern her irresolution. "Are you worried about Philip?" he asked.

Philip could sleep through a train wreck, Robin knew. Concern about disturbing his rest wasn't what was holding her back. She shook her head, afraid to trust herself to say anything until she knew precisely what it was she had to say.

"Tell me, Robin," Jesse prompted her, sensing her confusion. "Tell me what's bothering you."

"I'm not..." She swallowed, then forced herself to speak. "I'm not sure that I love you, Jesse. Not yet. And if I don't love you...we can't. I know that must sound ridiculously outdated, or infantile, or—"

He cut off the spate of words with a brush of his fingertips over her trembling lips. Then he leaned back, scrutinizing her, his expression revealing nothing. For a long time the only sounds in the room were his labored breathing and the crackle of the fire. "I guess that leaves me with two options," he granted.

"Oh?"

"Either I can say, yes, it's outdated and infantile, and we both want each other, so let's enjoy ourselves." He smiled crookedly. "Or else I can be a gentleman, respect your feelings and go home."

"There's a third option," Robin told him. "You could convince me that I do love you." And it wouldn't take much persuasion on his part to convince her of that, she acknowledged privately. He was such a good man, so thoughtful, so caring, considerate enough to suggest leaving when they were both feeling an imperative desire for each other. He was so generous, accepting her endless questions, providing answers for questions she hadn't even asked. How could she not love him?

It wasn't that she didn't; it was only that she wasn't sure. She'd been single for too long, and her experience so far with Jesse didn't fit any of her expectations about how love was supposed to develop. More than that, she felt ignorant, nervous, frightened by the prospect of making love with someone who wasn't Ray. She didn't love Ray anymore, she hadn't loved him for a long time, but she had never loved anybody else. She was too old to remember how one was supposed to go about falling in love. And she was much too old—or old-fashioned—to think that love didn't matter when it came to sex.

"I can't convince you that you love me, Robin," Jesse said gently. "It's something you'll have to decide for yourself." He rose languorously to a sitting position, his aroused body obviously reluctant to give hers up, and then helped her to sit as well. The flickering light from the fire played across his features, highlighting his eyes for an instant and then casting them in shadow.

"Are you angry?" she asked timidly.

"Angry?" He looped his arm around her shoulders and cuddled her to him, then planted a kiss on the crown of her head. "No, I'm not angry."

"But you think I'm outdated and infantile—"

"I think you're a very wise woman," he said. "If you want to know the truth, Robin... I want your love as much as I want you."

Simply hearing him express such a sentiment was so touching that Robin nearly shouted "Yes! I love you!" How could she not love someone who wanted her love so much?

Love was more than being wanted, she reflected. For her, at least, it took time, commitment, knowledge and understanding. She was willing to invest the time and the commitment. She was willing to do whatever it took to know Jesse fully, to reach an understanding of the man at her side. But right now, as she nestled into his shoulder and shared the fire's beauty and warmth with him, she admitted that she didn't yet know everything she had to know about him—and she definitely didn't understand everything she had to understand. He was so complex, so strange, in many ways as alien to her as a creature from Gleek.

But in time, she vowed, in time she would know him. In time she would understand.

Chapter Eight

"Let me explain this one more time," Jesse said, his patience strained to the breaking point. "Gerald Selby had nothing to do with the outbreak of violence. His commanding officer knows that, you know it, and I know it. Selby has never been friendly with the sailors under investigation. He's a good kid, and it would mean the world to his mother if you could see your way clear to grant him his Christmas leave."

The captain on the other end of the telephone remained unmoved. "And I've outlined our position for you, Mr. Lawson. If we grant a leave for Gerald Selby, we've got to grant leaves for the entire crew."

"I don't care about the entire crew," Jesse snapped. "All I care about is one man."

"We have our rules, Mr. Lawson," Captain Stevenson recited. "This is the way the military operates. Without rules, it can't function. I'm very sorry for your client. But this is the way the investigation is going to proceed. We need the entire crew here for questioning."

"You know what's going to happen," Jesse argued, not bothering to disguise his caustic tone. "The damned investigators are going to go home for Christmas, and Selby and his crewmates are going to sit around twiddling their thumbs on the base in Newport for the day. There's no need for that. The investigators can question Selby some other time.''

''We have our rules, Mr. Lawson.''

Jesse cursed under his breath. ''Newport is three hours from New Haven, where Selby's family resides. All he needs is forty-eight hours. He isn't under suspicion. He understands his obligations. He'll be back on base by December twenty-sixth.''

''That would be contrary to rules, Mr. Lawson. If we allow one man his leave—''

''Yes, I know,'' Jesse interrupted. He didn't think he could stomach another repetition of the Naval Code. Just beyond his open office door, a hysterical client was ranting in Spanish to one of the paralegal volunteers. Outside his window, sleet drizzled against the pavement in a staccato rhythm, glazing everything below—including the cramped white rental car that Jesse had driven to work that morning. He needed a new car. And a coat.

And he needed to talk about Gerald Selby's Christmas leave to someone who didn't respond like an automaton. ''Consider the holiday,'' he implored Captain Stevenson. ''Consider the issue of morale. Depriving Gerald Selby of this one special day with his family—''

''If we grant him his leave, Mr. Lawson, then everybody's going to want their leaves.''

''So what?'' Jesse retorted. ''It's Christmas, for crying out loud. Even the Navy must believe in Santa Claus!''

What was he saying? What kind of fool argument was that? Jesse was a lawyer, and as a lawyer it was his duty to use any and every tactic at his command to turn an opponent around. But Santa Claus?

Captain Stevenson said nothing for a moment. *He's probably running me through his computer,* Jesse thought morosely. *Checking to see if I've ever been committed to a mental hospital. Or else he's sending a telegram to Mrs. Selby, recommending that she seek new counsel . . .*

And then, suddenly, Captain Stevenson started to laugh. Authentic human laughter. The man wasn't an automaton, after all.

Jesse laughed, too. He didn't believe in Santa Claus, but if the Navy did—if this one desk-bound officer did— Gerald Selby might have a chance to spend the holiday with his mother. "I tell you what," Captain Stevenson suggested. "Send me something in writing. And for heaven's sake, ask for twenty-four hours, not forty-eight. I'm not making any promises, Mr. Lawson. I'm operating within a strict hierarchy here. I've got to answer to people."

"Anything you can do for my client will be greatly appreciated," Jesse swore. "I'll get something into the mail right away. With a copy to the North Pole. Thank you for your time, Captain Stevenson."

He hung up and surrendered to another laugh. What some people might call the Christmas spirit, Jesse called goodwill and human kindness. If more people exercised the spirit year-round, it would no longer be associated with one single day, and the world would be a much better place. But such a hope was fruitless; Jesse knew that the goodwill, human-kindness argument he'd just presented to Captain Stevenson would have been utterly ineffective in June or September. But then, if Gerald Selby's leave had been scheduled for June or September, Mrs. Selby wouldn't have been so crushed by its postponement.

She might still wind up crushed, Jesse reminded himself. Captain Stevenson might not be able to arrange

Gerald's release for the holiday. And that was the least of Mrs. Selby's problems.

Jesse had been contacted that morning by the attorney representing Mr. Cabot, the man who owned the New-hallville tenement where Mrs. Selby lived. "We've received a copy of your class-action suit," the lawyer had announced, "and my client has instructed me to inform you that he has no interest in negotiating a settlement. We'll leave it up to the courts to decide whether he's been remiss in fulfilling the obligations of your clients' leases."

It was a ploy, of course. Any court in the country would find against Mr. Cabot, and his attorney had to know that. Their strategy clearly was to bide their time and hope the tenants gave up and moved out. The civil court wouldn't set a date for a hearing for months. By then Mrs. Selby and her neighbors might well be so sick of living in a building without any services that they'd evacuate on their own. Or else the building would be condemned, Cabot would pay a nominal fine, and the tenants would still have to move out.

Perhaps Jesse should have mentioned Santa Claus to Cabot's attorney.

The Spanish-speaking man had stopped hectoring the paralegal in the hallway, and the sleet stopped drumming against the window. Jesse stood and crossed the small room to peer outside. An impotent winter sun was fighting its way out from behind the broken ceiling of leaden clouds. Jesse rooted for the sun to win the tussle. But even if it did, he still needed a coat.

Buying a coat wouldn't be as difficult as buying a car, he assured himself. He'd spent his lunch break at a Nissan dealership, listening to a snappy-looking blow-dried kid tell him that a man like Jesse would truly appreciate the extra power of a 200-SX. The price the salesman had bandied about was less absurd than the stratospheric numbers Jesse had heard the last time he'd bought a new car, six years ago. But at least the Mercedes dealer hadn't treated him like a doddering old fogie.

It had been one of those days, Jesse meditated as he witnessed the ongoing battle between the sun and the clouds. The call from Cabot's lawyer, interviews with two new clients—a handicapped woman being hassled by the Social Security Administration and a distraught teenager who claimed his employer, a gas station owner, owed him back wages—the encounter with the car dealer, and a conversation with a Navy captain. And the sleet, the same treacherous precipitation that had nearly killed Jesse last Friday.

So why was he in such a good mood? "Robin," he said aloud.

He ought to be in a bad mood about her, too, but he wasn't. He ought to be frustrated and resentful of her refusal to make love with him. What they'd begun on her living room floor last night was sensational, and she shouldn't have been so prim and resistant about following through on it. It was obvious that they had both wanted what was happening, that they'd both desired each other.

Yet he wasn't resentful. Frustrated, maybe, but not resentful. He admired the courage it had taken her to put a stop to the situation before she was overwhelmed by it. He admired her willingness to trust her mind and her heart. He admired her decency and her principles. He didn't consider her outdated or infantile.

A woman who wouldn't sleep with a man she didn't love... He didn't know such people still existed. Even the most pious of the folks he'd worked with at Grace Cathedral—sure, they'd claim that a couple ought to be married before they engaged in sex, but love didn't necessarily have anything to do with it. Men lusted, and they had to pay the price by marrying the women they lusted after. Women submitted—that was the price they paid for the security of marriage.

More sophisticated practitioners of the Grace theology, like Anne, didn't feel obliged to sanctify their relationships before allowing them to become intimate. But that made people like Anne even more hypocritical, in Jesse's opinion. "Nobody has to know we're having an affair," she had often said. "We're discreet about it. Nobody's watching."

"What about God?" he'd posed sarcastically. "Isn't He watching?"

"I'm sure God doesn't mind," Anne had maintained. "After all, we're doing His work."

Robin would never make such a ridiculous claim. Jesse didn't doubt that she believed in God, but she didn't cling to the superficial aspects of religion. She hadn't brought things to a halt last night because she was trying to extort a marriage proposal from Jesse. Nor had she brought things to a halt because she was afraid of bringing God's wrath upon her. She had acted in the interest of love. And for that alone, Jesse loved her.

He loved her for more than that, of course. He loved her for having known how cold he would be and building a fire in her fireplace. He loved her for buying her son a Christmas tree. Jesse loved her for listening, for wanting to know, for not condemning him for his beliefs.

He did have beliefs. They differed from most people's, but they were just as valid. He hadn't been exaggerating when he'd told Robin he believed; he believed in the inherent goodness within people, in human strength, in bravery and conviction. He believed in Robin.

And, as the clouds closed in front of the sun again, dark with foreboding, he believed in the practicality of buying a warm coat.

ONE HOUR and two hundred fifty dollars later, he left a men's clothing shop on the Post Road in Branford, wearing a brand-new coat of gray cashmere. The evening air was bitterly cold, and he didn't want to know what the wind chill factor computed to. But with the coat on, he felt snug and toasty. He would have to thank Robin for having talked some sense into him.

In fact, he could thank her now. Woodleigh's was just a few buildings away on the strip, and he was reasonably certain the store would still be open. He climbed into his car, grimaced at the faint rattle of the engine as he revved it, and cruised down the road to Woodleigh's.

Entering the store, he spotted Robin almost at once. She was hard to miss, standing on the top rung of a ladder and reaching for a boxed set of woven place mats on an upper shelf. In her brown pinafore and her buoyant ponytail, her pleated skirt and loafers, she looked surprisingly girlish. But the shapely calves visible between those loafers and the hem of her skirt were exceptionally sexy, and Jesse suffered a fresh twinge of disappointment as he recalled how close he'd come to ravishing her on the carpet of her living room.

He willfully directed his vision to the dwarf Christmas tree on the counter to distract his attention from Robin's sexy legs. By the time he risked glancing back at her, she had descended the ladder and was handing the box of place mats to a grateful customer. Bypassing numerous other shoppers and clerks in a meandering path through the store to the cash register with her customer, Robin noticed Jesse and hesitated. Then she smiled, revealing

her tiny white teeth. Another twinge ripped through him
as he remembered how marvelous it had felt to kiss her.

"I'll be right with you," she said by way of greeting
before she glided around the counter to ring up the purchase. Jesse waited by the counter, gazing at her small
hands as they efficiently punched the buttons on her
computerized register, as they counted the customer's
change and gift-wrapped the box. Those slender fingers
that manipulated the wrapping paper and ribbon with
such finesse had run through his hair and down his back,
had dug into his muscles and compelled his body... No.
He'd come here to show her his new coat, not to pressure her into picking up where they'd left off Sunday
night.

The customer departed, and Robin slipped away from
the register to greet Jesse. "I love it!" she exclaimed,
circling him and examining the coat. "It looks so warm,
Jesse. And the color suits you perfectly."

"It cost a fortune," he complained half-heartedly.

"And worth every penny," she asserted, stroking the
sleeve and sighing at its soft texture. Abruptly she pulled
her hand away, as if embarrassed at having touched him.

He wouldn't increase her embarrassment by com-
menting on it. "Do you have a minute?" was all he
asked.

She surveyed the bustling store and frowned. Apparently she didn't have a minute. "I'm sorry, Jesse, but it's
crazy here tonight. And I've got to work till nine. With
the extended holiday hours—"

"One minute," he persevered.

She raised her eyes to his. He sensed doubt in them,
and wondered whether it was doubt about her feelings for
him or doubt about his claim that he'd take only a minute of her time. Either way, it didn't matter, he decided,

because he also sensed humor in those glittering hazel irises, and joy at seeing him. "One minute," she capitulated, striding briskly to the rear of the store.

He followed her through a door and into a hallway. She stepped through another door, which led into a minuscule lounge, equipped with a coffeemaker, a water-bubbler and a compact refrigerator. A two-seat couch of orange vinyl was jammed against a wall of the window-less room, but she didn't bother to sit. She paced the brief length of the lounge, fidgeting with the tie of her pinafore.

Now that they were alone, Jesse acknowledged privately that he hadn't come here to thank her for pushing him into buying a coat. He came here to see her, to hold her, to reassure her that last night meant everything and nothing, that it meant whatever she wanted it to mean. When she reached the far end of the room and about-faced, he caught up to her and slipped his arms around her narrow waist. "Hello," he murmured, containing the urge to kiss her. Hugging her would have to do for now.

"Jesse." She sighed again, and rested her head against his shoulder. "I'm sorry about last night."

"You have no reason to be."

Evidently she disagreed. "It's just..." Her words were muffled by the thick fabric of the coat and she pulled away. Rotating, she eased out of his arms and began to pace again. "I'm—I'm new at all this, Jesse. I mean, I—I haven't dated much since my divorce. That's a lie. I haven't dated at all since my divorce."

"It's okay, Robin," he tried to console her.

She pivoted, facing him from across the lounge, her arms folded defensively over her chest. "It's more than that, Jesse. Ray—my ex-husband—he was the first...

what I mean is, he was the *only* man I've ever..." Dropping her gaze to the floor, she drifted off.

"Robin." Jesse didn't want to laugh; she might be insulted if he did. But she appeared so ludicrously upset, so worked up over something he considered irrelevant. "I don't care about your past, Robin. All I care about is us."

"I care about us, too," she allowed, toying with the tie of her pinafore again.

Jesse couldn't bear to see her fidget. It indicated that she was nervous, and he couldn't bear the thought that he made her nervous. Closing the space between them, he enveloped her hands in his to immobilize them.

"And it's just—well, we haven't known each other very long, and you aren't like anyone I've ever met before, and—"

"Relax," he whispered, brushing his mouth against hers. He wasn't kissing her to pressure her, he told himself. He was only kissing her as a means of putting an end to her babbling.

She laughed anxiously and turned her head. "What can I say? I'm a dowdy old mother and—"

"And you don't have to say anything," he insisted. "How do I shut you up?"

She laughed again, a genuine, heartfelt laugh this time. "You must think I'm nuts," she mumbled.

"I think you're fantastic," he said. "When can we see each other for longer than a minute? Are you going to have to work late all week?"

She shook her head. "Just tonight and Thursday. But I've got to save some time for Philip. I hate it when I work late and don't get to spend the evening with him. Especially now, at this time of year. I promised him that we'd decorate the rest of the house when I got home tomorrow, and he and I have a hot date at McDonald's lined up for Wednesday. And Joanna's hosting a Christmas party for some of the neighborhood kids after dinner on Friday, and I told her I'd help her out—"

"You're a busy lady," Jesse conceded. "How's Saturday?"

"I don't know yet. Can you call me a little later in the week?"

"I think I can manage that." He kissed her again, a light, lingering kiss on her lips. "My minute must be up," he whispered reluctantly.

"I forgot to time you," she confessed, touching her mouth to his once more and then breaking from him. "I'd better run. Drive carefully tonight, Jesse. It's slippery out there."

"Yes, ma'am." He accompanied her out of the lounge, and the instant she reentered the store she was accosted by frantic clerks. Where were the extra boxes of star-shaped crystal tree ornaments? What should be done about the woman with the overdrawn credit card? Where did Kevin put that morning's shipment of sterling silver napkin rings? Could Robin please deal with the cantankerous old man who wanted to return the beach umbrella he'd bought at the store last July?

Tossing Jesse a beleaguered smile, Robin allowed her employees to sweep her away.

WHAT WAS SHE THINKING? How could she treat the man so shabbily? Sunday night, she'd pushed him away after blatantly encouraging him to seduce her, and today she'd declared that she was all but unavailable to see him for the next century. If he had any brains, he'd wash his hands of her.

By nine-fifteen, she'd waved off the last of her sales-clerks and locked up the store. Trudging through the back door to the employee parking lot, she let out an anguished breath and shook her head. She had essentially told Jesse that she didn't have time for him. He would have to be superhuman to put up with her. And he wasn't superhuman.

The truth was, she didn't have time for him, not now, not during the most important month for business at Woodleigh's. She didn't have time to build a friendship with a man when she scarcely had time for her own son. Whatever free moments she had belonged to Philip.

She hated these late-night schedules. Whenever she had to work past nine, she always gave Philip permission to stay up until she got home. But he would be in his pajamas, and they'd get to spend at best ten minutes catching up on their day's activities before she'd have to send him to bed. If she let him stay up any later, he'd fall asleep in class the following day.

She wanted to make time for Jesse, too. She owed herself the opportunity to develop a relationship with a man. She couldn't let her life revolve entirely around work and Philip. She was a person, too, with her own needs.

Grunting, she unlocked her car and started the engine. "That's a swell thought," she muttered, wondering whether she'd read it in some magazine or book on self-actualization in the eighties. The people who preached that kind of drivel obviously didn't have to contend with the realities of day-to-day living. Robin was a mother first, a breadwinner second. Social butterfly ranked way down there at the bottom of the list, below car-washer and checkbook-balancer.

And yet . . . and yet, for a brief, mystifying moment Sunday night, lost in the awesome power of Jesse's lovemaking, she had forgotten about being a mother, a breadwinner, and all the rest of it. She had been only a woman, a mature, sensual woman reveling in the magic that mature, sensual women were supposed to experience with like-minded men. For those few minutes, nothing had been important but her own physical awakening, her longing... her needs.

All right, so she had needs. Big deal. Ever since she'd made a conscious decision to become a mother, she had voluntarily put her own needs on hold. Philip's needs came first. Right now, he needed his mother, his home, a magnificent Christmas. And that took precedence over anything Robin might want to discover with a man.

Except... except for those few damnably glorious minutes when she'd gazed up into Jesse's face, when she'd felt his body moving passionately against hers... "Don't even think about it," she cautioned herself. "If he's really interested in you, he'll accept your priorities."

Fat chance of that, too, she mourned. Any woman whose priorities had Christmas with her little boy coming before a love affair couldn't hope to hold an atheist's interest for long.

Philip was cavorting around the living room in his pajamas when Robin got home. "Hey, Mom!" he bellowed, racing to her and giving her a boisterous hug. "I got a hundred on my spelling test, and Ms. Becker wrote 'Good job' on it, with a big explanation point."

"Exclamation point," Robin corrected him, returning his hug. "That's wonderful, Phil. I'm very proud of you."

"Yeah, well, she wasn't too boring today. And a bunch of us decided we've got to give Cookie Monster a Christ-

mas present. Like, maybe, a big box of cookies. Will you
bake some for him?''

"Philip!" Chuckling, Robin pulled off her coat and
hung it in the closet. "If I'm going to go to all the trouble of baking cookies, I'm sure not going to let you feed
them to a snake.''

"On Gleek, mommies bake cookies for snakes all the
time," Philip said.

"Then send Cookie Monster to Gleek."

"And—oh, yeah! We got a package in the mail from
Grandma and Grandpa Greer," Philip continued. "Mrs.
O'Leary said it was probably Christmas presents and I
couldn't open it up.''

"She's right," Robin confirmed. "I'll open it, and if
it's presents, they'll go right under the tree and stay there
until the big day."

"Aww!"

"It's way past your bedtime, fella," Robin said, giving Philip an affectionate swat on his backside. "How
about heading up the stairs while I pay Mrs. O'Leary?"

Once Robin had written a check for Kate and sent her
home, she climbed the stairs to Philip's room. He was
seated on his bed, his blond hair tousled and his pajama
bottoms drooping to expose his belly button. That was
the way boys were, Robin reminded herself—they never
grew gradually, but instead stayed the same height for
months and months, and then shot up two inches in a
week. She would have to buy him some new pajamas.

"Where's your spelling test?" she asked, skirting the
bed to reach his desk. She found the paper lying on top
of his arithmetic workbook. A big red 100 appeared at
the top, along with Ms. Becker's glowing message at the
bottom.

Beaming, Robin returned to Philip's bed and gave her son another hug. "I'm so proud of you."

He snorted modestly. "It was easy, Mom. I guess I'm just naturally smart."

"Just last week you were telling me that spelling was dumb," Robin teased, pulling back the blanket for him. As he lay down, she noticed the gap between his pajama top and bottoms again. He was growing up, both physically and intellectually. No matter how much Robin wanted to make room in her life for Jesse, she would never do it at the expense of missing out on Philip's daily growth. Go out on dates, become embroiled in an affair, blink, and your son would change on you overnight. Philip's development was simply too important to miss. "I love you, Phil," she whispered, momentarily overcome by sentiment.

"It was just a spelling test," he said nonchalantly. "Don't get carried away."

Laughing, Robin kissed him and shut off the light.

She stole to her bedroom to change into her jeans and sweat shirt, then headed downstairs. The parcel from her former in-laws was sitting on a counter in the kitchen, and she cut it open with a steak knife. Sure enough, it contained two gift-wrapped boxes, both tagged with Philip's name. Robin was happy that, in spite of the divorce, Philip's paternal grandparents kept in touch with him.

After placing the gifts under the tree, she returned to the kitchen to fix herself a light supper. Given how late it was, she didn't have much of an appetite, and the leftover macaroni and cheese Kate had prepared for Philip and herself hardly looked appealing. Robin wearily opened a can of soup, dumped it into a pot, and set it on the stove. Just as it started to bubble, the telephone rang.

She answered it at once, hoping the bell hadn't roused Philip. "Hello?"

"Hi, Robin." It was Jesse.

Whatever she'd told him, however inanely she'd blabbered in the staff lounge, she obviously hadn't scared him off—yet. A giddy smile shaped her lips as she murmured, "Hello, Jesse."

"There was so much I wanted to tell you today," he said. "A minute wasn't enough."

He *had* told her so much today—he had told her that her inexperience didn't bother him, that she had no reason to apologize for her behavior last night, that all he cared about was "us." Anything else he might say now would seem trivial in comparison.

But she wasn't about to stop him. Instead she shut off the stove, poured the soup into a bowl, and carried it to the table, the phone receiver wedged against her shoulder. "I'm listening," she prompted him.

"I gave the Navy a lecture on Santa Claus," he announced.

"What?" She dropped her spoon, splattering drops of soup across the table.

"I told you about my client whose son is in the Navy, didn't I?"

Robin retrieved her spoon and wiped the surface of the table with her napkin. "Something about how the Navy was denying him his Christmas leave," she recalled.

"That's right. I called up a captain stationed at Newport today and told him that if the Navy believed in Santa Claus, they had to let the boy go home for Christmas."

"You didn't!"

"I did, Robin, and I think it's your fault."

If this was his way of remonstrating with her, he certainly didn't sound terribly angry. Indeed, he sounded quite amused. "In that case, have your client pay me instead of you," she quipped.

"This is legal aid, Robin. The clients don't pay."

"Oh. Right." She sipped her soup, inordinately pleased by this conversation—inordinately pleased that Jesse had felt he had to share his news with her. "What did the Navy say?"

"They asked me to send them a written brief on the matter," he told her. "What do you think, Robin? If I send them an affidavit on the existence of Santa, are they going to blackmail me with it?"

"I wouldn't lose sleep over it," she consoled him.

His laughter faded. "Seriously, Robin. You know more than I do about how the military functions. Do you think the Navy will bend its rules to accommodate Christmas for this one kid and his mother?"

Had he called her up for legal counsel? Astonished, she lowered her spoon and tucked the receiver more firmly against her chin. "I don't know, Jesse. The Navy does things differently from the Army. But there are a few officers here and there who've got hearts. It probably depends on whether the captain you spoke to is one of them."

"Hearts," Jesse echoed, his tone soft and sincere. "That's really what it's all about, isn't it?"

"What Christmas is about? Of course, Jesse," she said firmly. "That's exactly what it's about."

"*I* don't have to be converted," Jesse pointed out good-naturedly. "It's the Navy that has to be convinced."

Robin almost blurted out that, of all people, Jesse *did* have to be converted. But he didn't, really. He'd already gone Christmas shopping with her and Philip, and helped them to buy a tree, and participated in decorating it. If he hadn't gotten sick of the holiday by now, then he probably was half the distance to believing in it.

"Well," she said, "I wish you lots of luck. And your client, too. In her son's place, if the Navy refused me my leave, I'd go AWOL."

"Great," Jesse snorted. "And Mrs. Selby would be begging me to represent him at his court-martial. Something tells me I shouldn't have asked you for advice."

Advice wasn't why Jesse had called her. Nor had he called her to complain about his challenges at work. He had called her for no other reason than to talk, to include her in his day.

She remembered how she and Ray used to talk this way, back when things were good between them. He would arrive home from work, and she would arrive home from one of the various jobs she'd held before Philip was born, and they'd compare notes, describe moments, chatter about anything that crossed their minds, no matter how inconsequential. It had been for Robin one of the nicest aspects of being married.

And now Jesse was offering her that same companionship. He was presenting himself as a kindred soul with whom she could share a few thoughts at the end of her day. An unexpected sense of well-being flooded her, a warmth and contentment she hadn't experienced in years. "I'm close, Jesse," she admitted, startling herself.

"Close to what?" he asked, bewildered.

"Close to loving you."

He said nothing for a moment. And then, "I'm glad, Robin. Very glad."

Chapter Nine

He called again Tuesday evening. Robin and Philip were in the kitchen, Philip pasting together a chain composed of red and green construction paper links, and Robin arranging flexible sprigs of pine around the bases of the red candles she planned to display in the living room and dining room windows. She and Philip had already replaced the willow wreath on the front door with the fresh pine wreath, and spiraled a long rope of holly and red velvet ribbon around the staircase railing. The tree was lit up, and Robin had tuned the television set to a rebroadcast of an old Bing Crosby Christmas special so they could listen to carols while they worked.

"Is it just my imagination," Jesse asked when Robin answered the phone, "or are Japanese cars small?"

When the phone had begun to ring, she'd hoped that the call would be from Jesse, and she was delighted to hear his voice on the other end. "Hello, Jesse," she greeted him.

He regaled her for a few minutes with a tale of his fruitless effort to find a suitable new car for himself. "Either the cars they're making these days are overpriced and underequipped, or I'm too demanding," he concluded.

"A little of both, probably," Robin noted affectionately.

"So," he said. "About Saturday night—are you free?"

"Yes and no," she answered. "The problem is, I've got to work until five on Saturday, and from noon to five Sunday."

"That still leaves Saturday evening," Jesse noted.

Robin knew that she would be exhausted after a full day at the store on a Saturday. She also knew that she would want to spend the evening with Philip. But that didn't mean she had to deprive herself of Jesse's company, too. "Maybe you could come over for dinner," she said. "I won't be able to prepare anything too elegant, but—"

"Better yet, why don't you come here for dinner?" Jesse offered. "After working all day, you shouldn't have to prepare anything at all. Phil can come along, too, if he'd like."

Robin didn't doubt that Philip would like that just fine. "Are you sure that would be all right?" she asked.

"If he likes spaghetti and meatballs, he's my kind of guest," Jesse replied. "I'm not exactly a gourmet cook."

"Spaghetti and meatballs is one of his favorites."

"Great. Come over whenever you're ready after work."

"It'll probably be around five-thirty or six," Robin estimated. "We'll see you then." After hanging up, she went in search of Philip. She found him in the den, switching the TV channel to a police show. "Forget it, fella," she scolded, twisting the dial back to the Bing Crosby special. "I want to hear Bing and the whole Crosby family sing, 'We wish you a Merry Christmas.'"

"He's dead," Philip pointed out. "Why should we watch a dead person?"

"We aren't watching, we're listening," Robin said. "And if you want to decorate this house with me, you'd better steer clear of all those violent shows."

Philip shaped his hand into a make-believe pistol and created an explosive *pow* sound through his lips. "Okay, Mom," he said, his imaginary assassination accomplished. "Let's decorate."

"THERE HE IS AGAIN," Kirsten whispered to Lisa as the two clerks spied on the handsome dark-haired man in the gray cashmere coat who had just entered Woodleigh's and was unknowingly standing beneath the mistletoe by the store's front door.

"Forget it," Lisa whispered back. "He's Robin's."

Robin suspected that she wasn't supposed to have overheard their exchange, but how could she help herself when the three of them were crowded behind the counter, bagging merchandise for customers? Not that Jesse was hers, but she knew instinctively that he'd come to Woodleigh's to see her. She straightened her pinafore, handed her customer a receipt and a bagged package of clove-scented candles, and scooted around the counter to greet Jesse.

"I won't ask for one minute," he said, grinning. "This might take two. Can you come outside?"

"Two minutes, huh," she muttered with pretended dismay, eyeing the frantic shoppers milling about the store. Her gaze alighted on Lisa and Kirsten, who were watching her and Jesse with inordinate curiosity, and she decided to let them think Jesse was hers. Slipping her hand through the bend in his elbow, she said, "Two minutes. I'm timing you."

Laughing, he ushered her out of the store. Parked at the curb, in a no-parking zone, was a sky-blue Volkswagen Rabbit. He gestured at it with his free arm, then grinned proudly at Robin.

For a minute she feared that she was hallucinating. The last time she'd seen this car, it had been smashed fore and aft, with a splintered windshield and a missing bumper. How had Jesse managed to get it repaired? Why had he bothered?

"I just bought it this afternoon," he boasted, guiding her around the car so she could view it from every angle. "It's an '80. What do you think?"

She shivered as a gust of freezing air assaulted her. Jesse opened the flap of his coat and wrapped it around her, snuggling her against himself. It wasn't the coat that warmed her, she acknowledged, but his body, his nearness. The delectable heat that infused her was nearly enough to eradicate her discomfort at the sight of his car.

Nearly enough, but not quite. "Why did you buy a car identical to the one you were driving when you had your accident?" she asked.

"I was looking at new VW's," he explained. "But the dealer had some used ones in the lot. I saw this car, and I thought—why not? I was lucky the last time I was in a car like this. I was so lucky I survived with barely a scratch. It's obviously the right car for me."

She tilted her head back to see his face. The thick collar of his coat rode up beneath her ponytail, soft against the nape of her neck. Jesse smiled down at her, such a sweet, wonderful smile that she couldn't help mirroring it. "So you believe in luck, is that it?" she teased. "What's the difference between luck and God, Jesse?"

"I..." He hesitated, sorting through his thoughts. Then his smile grew even more gentle. "I believe that my life was saved by a blue VW Rabbit and you. Now I've got another blue VW Rabbit.''

And you've got me, Robin almost said. She curled her arms around his lean torso, trying to ward off the encroaching numbness in her hands. "If it's the car you want, then congratulations,'' she mumbled into his shoulder, hating herself for not declaring that she was willing to be part of the lucky package for him as well. If only he would admit that he did believe in luck, if only he would admit that Robin hadn't saved his life, if only he would bend that much...

Did she really need him to bend for her? Did she really need him to say, "Yes, I believe in luck. I believe in Santa Claus. I believe in family and the good Lord and all the things they represent, I believe my life was saved by divine intervention.'' Was that why she was holding back, refusing to give herself over to love?

She wasn't sure. All she knew was that whenever Jesse started talking about her having saved his life, she became edgy. Whenever she analyzed the differences in their outlooks on life, she held back. Whenever she remembered how much she had desired him last Sunday night, she felt scared. She wanted things simple; she wanted the expected routines and rituals. She didn't know how to deal with a man like Jesse.

"You're turning to ice out here,'' he commented quietly, tightening the coat around her and hurrying her back indoors. A blast of hot air from the heating vent by the door slammed into their huddled bodies, and she extricated herself from his coat and rubbed her fingers together to restore sensation to them. "You don't like the car,'' he inferred.

"I do, Jesse,'' she countered, forcing a smile. "I think it's great.''

"But . . . ?"

But I want to love you, and I'm frightened. I want you to make this easy for me. "I think the car's terrific," she said, "and I'm happy you won't have to drive the rental car anymore. Rabbits handle well in bad weather."

"Maybe I should have bought a new car," he mused, glancing through the front window at his illegally parked Rabbit. "But I kept thinking of what it would look like to my clients in Newhallville if I drove up in some flashy sixteen-thousand-dollar car. It would be like shoving their noses in their own poverty."

"And your radio would get ripped off," she observed. "A used car is probably a smart idea for someone in your line of work."

He nodded. "Well. I just wanted to show it to you. I'll let you get back to work." He kissed her cheek, then straightened up and buttoned his coat.

She touched his arm, holding him in place. She had failed to tell him she loved him, but she had to let him know in some way how pleased she was by his impromptu visit. "Jesse . . . I'm really glad you came by to show the car to me."

The corners of his mouth twitched upward. "One of these days, I'll take you for a spin in it."

"Heavens, no!" she cried, groaning at his unintended pun. "The last thing I want to do is sit next to you when you're spinning in a car."

His laughter mingled with hers. "No spins, Robin. Scout's honor. I'll see you Saturday." With that, he left the store.

A heavy sense of loss overtook her as, gazing through the glass, she watched Jesse climb into the blue VW at the curb, fasten his seat belt, gun the engine and drive away. What was wrong with her? Why did she want so desper-

ately to play it safe with him? Why was she so afraid to
let go?

She wanted him, yes. But the thought of any man other
than Ray loving her, knowing her so intimately...

She'd been afraid the first time with Ray, too. Even in
high school she had been aware that some of her classmates slept with their boyfriends. But Robin never had,
not because she was a prude, not because she didn't understand the facts of life or possess a healthy streak of
curiosity, but because she didn't love those boys. She had
dated Ray for a year and a half in college before she finally agreed to spend the night with him. And as excited
as she'd been, she'd also been petrified.

Ray had been gentle with her, and she'd enjoyed the
experience greatly. But her fear had never been based on
the physical aspects of what was occurring. It had been
a matter of emotions: did she love Ray enough to make
the moment meaningful? Was it more than simply sex
they were sharing? She believed that making love had to
be spiritual to be right. It had to entail a joining of souls
as well as bodies.

It had been right with Ray. They'd loved each other
then, and they continued to love each other for nearly
seven more years. After their relationship began to dis-
integrate, they still made love whenever he was home. Yet
it was no longer as satisfying to Robin, no longer as fulfilling. Her love for him was on the wane, and their sexual relationship was no longer spiritual. Their souls were
traveling in different directions.

She didn't doubt that she would enjoy making love
with Jesse, but enjoyment wasn't the issue. The issue was,
how could she make love with a man who claimed to have
no soul at all? How could she ever find something spiritual with him?

ON SATURDAY EVENING, Robin and Philip drove to Jesse's condominium. Philip expressed great relief when Ms. Becker didn't appear on her porch. He galloped down the stairs to Jesse's door and rang the doorbell, causing it to sound incessantly until Robin shoved his hand away.

Jesse opened the door, dressed in jeans and a crisp white shirt. "Come on in," he welcomed them, stepping aside so they could enter the living room.

It was big. Robin could say that much for it. A swanky-looking leather couch stood against one wall, a rocking chair, a table and a lamp against another. An empty modern fireplace consumed a third wall. And that was it. No pictures, no plants, no knickknacks or clutter. Not a single personal touch, nary an idiosyncratic item to personalize the room.

"I like this place," Philip announced, pulling off his jacket and darting to the rocking chair. He sat on it and energetically pumped his legs, giving himself a ride. "I like it a lot better than my dad's apartment in Washington. His living room has books and newspapers lying all over the place, and he gets real mad whenever I touch them. Can I see the rest of it?"

"There's not much to see," Jesse warned, running to catch up with Philip as he raced into the dining room.

Robin followed, and tried to hide her shock. There wasn't a stick of furniture in the room, not a table, not a chair, not a sideboard. A breakfast bar separated it from the kitchen, and four stools were positioned two on each side of the counter to provide an eating area. The kitchen looked like a real room only because it was filled with the cabinets and appliances that had come with the house. "Oh, wow!" Philip hooted, noticing the three neatly arranged place settings on the breakfast bar. "Are we gonna be eating here? It's almost like a restaurant, Mom!''

She laughed sheepishly. "That gives you an idea of the quality of the restaurants I take Philip to."

"Well," Jesse addressed the boy, "we're eating at the counter because we haven't got anyplace else to eat. I haven't bought a dining table yet." He took Robin's parka, scooped Philip's jacket off the floor, and hung them both in the coat closet. Then he returned to the kitchen and filled a pot with water.

"Can I help?" Robin asked.

Jesse shook his head. "The meatballs and sauce are already made, and so's the salad. All that's left is cooking the spaghetti."

"What's for dessert?" Philip asked.

"Ice cream," Jesse told him.

"All right!" Philip flopped onto one of the stools, discovered that the seat revolved, and busied himself with spinning in dizzying circles.

Robin scanned the vacant dining room one last time, then moved around the counter to the kitchen. "Why haven't you bought a dining table yet?" she asked, hoping she didn't sound disapproving. "You've lived here since June, Jesse."

He pulled a fistful of dry pasta from a box, estimated its volume, and dumped it into the boiling water. Then he shrugged. "I guess this place doesn't feel like home to me yet."

"Of course it doesn't," Robin said with a laugh. "How could it feel like a home when you haven't done anything to make it a home?"

Jesse glanced at her, grinning impishly. "You think I should spend a fortune at Woodleigh's?"

"Woodleigh's or K-Mart," Robin answered. "It doesn't have to be a fortune, Jesse. Just a few pictures on the walls, or something..."

He shrugged again, apparently not sharing her concern. "I'll get around to it one of these days," he said, "once I start settling in."

"Are you sure it's not that you're planning to return to California eventually?"

"Are you from California?" Philip interjected. "Wow, that's neat. I've been to California, sort of. Once, when we visited my grandma in Hawaii, we changed planes in Los Angeles. I never got out of the airport, though."

"L.A.X.," Jesse grunted. "What a tourist attraction. I bet Hawaii is much nicer than L.A. Do you visit your grandma often?"

"Uh-uh. It's too expensive. Mostly, she visits us, on account of she's just one person. She comes every summer. She won't come in the winter. She hates cold weather," he added with a disdainful sniff.

"It makes her sick." Robin defended her mother to Philip. "It aggravates her arthritis." She turned back to Jesse, who was vigorously stirring the spaghetti in the pot. "I can't imagine living in a place for six months and not settling in. My family spent only five months on a base in Wyoming, and you wouldn't believe how lived-in my mother made that house."

"It's obviously a knack you've inherited," Jesse praised her. "You know how to make a house a home."

"Because it's important," she asserted, then stifled herself. She wasn't going to torment Jesse with yet another sermon on her feelings about the necessity of having a real home. She had probably already bored him to death on the subject.

Jesse served the meal, including red wine for the adults and soda for Philip. Robin winced inwardly as she recalled her advice to Jesse about purchasing a wine rack. That was the least his condominium needed.

Maybe she could buy him something homey for Christmas. She wanted to get him something he'd like, something he would be able to use. Certainly not a dining table, but maybe a framed print, or some andirons for his fireplace, or a crystal fruit bowl for the table in the living room. A houseplant, perhaps, or...a tree. A full, towering Douglas fir, festooned with lights and tinsel and a huge silver star at its apex, would do wonders for his living room.

Philip's behavior at dinner was exemplary. He even ate half his salad, along with plenty of spaghetti. He sang one of his favorite songs, "On Top of Spaghetti," to the tune of "On Top of Old Smoky," and assessed with Jesse the odds that Ms. Becker could hear their voices through the wall dividing the two condominiums. After dinner, he wolfed down a generous portion of ice cream, and Robin didn't object when Jesse led him downstairs to watch television in the den.

"It was delicious," Robin complimented Jesse once they were alone in the kitchen. Over his protests, she insisted on helping him to rinse the dishes and stack them in the dishwasher. Once the pots were scrubbed and the counter wiped, Jesse refilled their glasses with wine and led her into the living room. No sooner were they seated on the couch when Philip appeared at the top of the stairs to ask, "This guy on the news said something about the deficit, Mom. I forget, which is worse? The deficit or the debt?"

"In twenty-five words or less?" Robin chuckled. "The deficit."

"That's what I thought," Philip muttered, vanishing down the stairs again.

Jesse leaned back into the leather-covered upholstery and arched his arm casually around Robin's shoulders. "You ought to go into politics," he joked. "You sure know how to cut right to the meat of the matter."

"I'll let Philip go into politics for me," Robin rejoined. "I'll explain things for him, and he can carry out the policies. He's got more energy than I do."

"He does have an abundance of energy, doesn't he," Jesse agreed.

Philip might have energy, but he lacked diplomatic skills. Gazing about the austere room, Robin remembered what her son had said as soon as he'd entered Jesse's house; that he liked it a lot better than he liked his father's apartment. "Does it bother you when Philip mentions his father?" she asked Jesse.

"Why should it bother me?"

Robin mulled over her answer. It shouldn't bother Jesse, but she had presumed that most men would feel uncomfortable about the ex-husbands of women in whom they were romantically interested. "You told me all about your ex-girlfriend in Los Angeles," she recollected. "But you never ask me about my ex-husband."

Jesse meditated on her words, then shrugged. "What should I ask? You grew apart, you broke up, he cares about Phil and you aren't bitter. Is there anything else I need to know?"

"You know more than that," Robin recalled, her eyes meeting Jesse's for an instant and then shifting away in embarrassment.

He studied her attentively, reminiscing. Then he nodded. "You mean, that he's the only man you've ever made love with? Robin, that's not important to me. *You're* what's important to me."

"Yes, but—"

"Robin." His fingers floated through her hair, stroking in a consoling rhythm. "The only thing that matters is that you're a woman with strong values. I admire that. I really do."

"Maybe you admire it," she said, smiling timidly, "but you'd rather have gotten me into bed last Sunday, wouldn't you?"

"Not if you were entertaining doubts."

"You weren't frustrated?"

"Of course I was frustrated," he admitted with a short laugh. His thumb reached her earlobe and traced its curve, causing a ripple of longing to twist through her. "I'm still frustrated, Robin, but frustration isn't fatal."

"I'm sorry, Jesse," she confessed. "I'm trying to work it out, I'm trying very hard—"

"Don't try," he urged her. "It's all inside you, and it'll come out when it's ready."

"And in the meantime, you'll get tired of waiting and—"

Jesse leaned toward her, brushing his lips along her temple. "I don't think I'll have to wait that long," he whispered.

The implication in his words was as arousing as the tender caress of his thumb along her ear. She suffered another surge of longing, dark and demanding, and if it weren't for the intrusive patter of sneakered feet on the stairs, she might have been tempted to act on it.

But Philip rescued her from her rashness by barging into the living room. "The guy on the news said something about Koala Lumpy. Where's that, Mom?"

"Koala Lumpy?" she asked. "You mean, Kuala Lumpur. It's a city in Malaysia."

"Malaysia," Philip repeated. "That's in Asia. They rhyme, Jesse. Malaysia, Asia." With that astute observation, he disappeared down the stairs again.

"He's amazing," Jesse commented, staring at the staircase. "You've got yourself an incredible little boy."

"Any little boy could figure out that Malaysia rhymed with Asia," Robin argued, although she was thrilled that Jesse considered her son as amazing as she did. "And never call him a little boy to his face. He thinks he's a big boy."

"Ah, yes. Little boys play with Smurfs, isn't that right?" Jesse deliberated for a minute, his smile deepening. "I don't know much about kids, Robin, but Philip seems so...so free-wheeling, so eager to embrace the world. If I had ever asked my parents about Kuala Lumpur, they would have treated me to a ten-minute dissertation on the good works of the missionaries in Malaysia. And when they were through, they would have told me to spend more time studying the scripture and less time asking so many questions."

"Then you're the amazing one," Robin observed. "You turned out pretty well, under the circumstances."

Jesse chuckled modestly and drew Robin closer to himself, cushioning her head against his shoulder. "Phil's turning out better," he said. "You're lucky to have a son like him. Or maybe he's the lucky one, having a mother like you."

If Robin challenged Jesse, he would swear that he didn't believe in luck. So she simply accepted his observation, letting its truth sink into her and settle comfortably inside her heart. Jesse did believe in luck. And so did

Robin. Like Jesse, she believed, among other things, that she was immeasurably lucky to have a son like Philip.

BUT IF ONE BELIEVED in luck, one had to believe in bad luck as well as good. When Robin's phone rang early Sunday morning, her voice was thick with sleep and contentment when she answered it, expecting to hear Jesse's voice on the other end. Words of gratitude took shape on her tongue, gratitude about the lovely evening she and Philip had had with him, his kindness in making dinner for them, his generosity in choosing to respect rather than despise her. If pressed, she might even confess that he was the finest man she'd ever met, and that she did love him.

The voice she heard in response to her drowsy hello wasn't Jesse's, however. Cutting through the static in the long-distance connection, she heard her ex-husband say, "Robin? It's Ray. I'm going to be stateside for Christmas, and I want Philip with me."

Chapter Ten

She bolted upright in bed, struggling for lucidity. "Ray?" she mumbled. "Where are you?"

"I'm in Buenos Aires right now, but I'm going to be back in the States next week. It cropped up at the spur of the moment. I know you weren't expecting this, Robin, but . . . if I'm going to be in the country, I'd really like to see Philip."

"But—but you just saw him!" That wasn't exactly true. Ray had been stateside in October, and after a couple of days in his Washington, D.C., apartment, he'd flown up to Connecticut and spent a weekend with his son. Whenever Ray was in the country during the school term, he took a room at a motel in Branford so he would be able to see Philip without interrupting his son's class attendance. Usually, however, Ray timed his furloughs for February, when the school system shut down for a week-long vacation to coincide with Washington's birthday, and for August. That way, Philip could travel to the capital to visit his father.

"I know, I know," Ray said. "But, Robin, this is special. An Argentine businessman I've been working with was planning to take his children to Orlando for Christmas, but he suddenly found out that he couldn't take the time off from work. He's passed the reservations along to me, and I was able to wheedle some free time. Robin, it's Orlando."

"Florida?" What on earth did Ray want to do in Florida? She wished she wasn't so muddled, so absurdly drowsy.

"Disney World. I've got the room, I've got the tickets to Disney World, Epcot Center... Mickey Mouse, Robin," he explained. "Phil's going to love it."

Of course Philip would love it. No argument there. But... "Not at Christmas, Ray. You can't take him away at Christmas."

For several seconds all she heard was the scratchy sound of long-distance disturbances on the line. Then Ray spoke again, slowly and precisely. "You have him every holiday, Robin. We've never fought about that. You have him for Thanksgiving, Easter, Halloween, his birthday. You've had him every Christmas since we split."

She couldn't dispute Ray's claim. But the reason Robin had Philip for the holidays was that Ray had left. He had preferred to traipse around the world, living out of suitcases, instead of establishing a home and celebrating the rituals of each season with his family. Ray had never once quarreled with Robin over custody of their child. She willingly accepted the responsibility of raising their son, and one of her rewards was to have him with her for the holidays. Especially Christmas.

"Robin." Ray sounded cajoling. "We're talking about Mickey Mouse. When is Phil going to have another opportunity like this? I'd like to fly him down to Florida and spend a few days with him here. What better Christmas present can we give him?"

"He doesn't want Mickey Mouse for Christmas," Robin retorted. "He wants a rocket ship, and some Masters of the Universe toys—"

"He can have them, too," Ray pointed out. "How can you even consider denying him this? It's a kid's dream come true."

It was Ray's dream come true, too, no doubt. But Christmas without Philip wasn't a dream for Robin. It was the worst nightmare she could imagine.

"Why don't you ask him?" Ray proposed. "Ask him if he'd rather spend Christmas in Connecticut or go to Disney World."

"That's not fair!" Robin raged. "You know damned well he'll choose Disney World."

"Then be Santa for him. Give him his wish."

"Ray." She squeezed her eyes shut, refusing to succumb to tears, trying to force her words past the lump in her throat. "I don't want to deny him Mickey Mouse. But at Christmastime? You know how I feel about Christmas."

"Yes, I know how you feel," Ray said soothingly. "But this was when my colleague had the reservations, and I can't do anything about it." In a firmer tone, he added, "Phil's my son, too."

"Who's on the phone?" Philip shouted through the closed bedroom door.

Robin shuddered. "Your father," she replied.

Philip hurled the door open and scrambled onto the bed beside his mother. He grabbed the phone from her and hollered, "Hi, Dad! Where are you?"

Robin kicked off the blanket, stood and stalked to the window. Pulling back the drapes, she gazed outside. The sky was overcast, gloomy with thick gray clouds hinting at snow. Who cared if it snowed, though? If Philip went

to Florida, he'd have a hot, muggy Christmas. And
without him here, Robin wouldn't want Christmas at all,
let alone a white one.

She let the drapes fall across the window and turned to
study her son. He looked small in the wide double bed,
despite the fact that he was outgrowing his pajamas. His
eyes were bright and round as he clung to the telephone,
his high-pitched voice ebullient. "Yeah, school's okay. I
got a hundred on my last spelling test.... Oh, guess what?
We had dinner at Jesse's house last night. He made spaghetti and meatballs, and ice cream.... He's a friend of
Mom's," Philip reported.

Great, Robin grunted inwardly. Now Ray was going to
find out that Robin had a male friend. The next thing she
knew, he'd be accusing her of moral turpitude, demanding a new custody hearing and taking her child away from
her forever.

"Mickey Mouse!" Philip shrieked, and Robin felt her
stomach twist into a knot. Ray must be telling Philip
about Disney World. Her son's expression was ecstatic.
She'd never be able to keep him home for Christmas now.
"No kidding, Dad? Really? And I could come down to
Florida? Oh, wow!"

The tears rose again, causing Robin's vision to blur.
She hastily looked away. She wasn't going to let Philip see
her cry.

"He wants to talk to you, Mom," Philip announced,
extending the phone in her direction.

Nodding, she swallowed and crossed the room. She sat
gingerly on the edge of the mattress, took the receiver
from Philip and pressed it to her ear. "That was low,
Ray," she muttered. "You shouldn't have mentioned it
to him before we'd worked it all out."

"He wants to come," Ray told her—as if she hadn't already figured that out. "Who's Jesse, by the way?"

"You heard Philip," she said impassively. "Jesse's a friend of ours."

"Don't get me wrong," Ray hastened to placate her. "It's about time you started dating."

"I'm not dating," she said. "He's just a friend." Whether or not that was an honest response, she wasn't about to provide Ray with explanations he didn't deserve. Right now the man deserved nothing, nothing at all. "So, now that you've shot your mouth off to Phil about Disney World—"

"He wants to come," Ray repeated. "He'll hate you if you stand in his way."

And I'll hate you if you take him, she nearly screamed. But she couldn't verbalize such an ugly thought in front of Philip. She couldn't even allow herself to think it. Philip wanted to see Mickey Mouse, and Robin would never stand in his way. Ray was right about that.

A low, tortured breath escaped her as she resigned herself to the miserable promise of a Christmas without her son. "What's the plan?" she asked listlessly, trying unsuccessfully to ignore Philip, who was bouncing on the bed and chanting, "Mickey Mouse! Mickey Mouse!"

"Today's the thirteenth," Ray outlined. "My ticket will get me to Florida on the twenty-second. Phil can fly down the twenty-third, and I'll be here to meet him. I'll arrange for a ticket out of LaGuardia or Kennedy. Which is better for you?"

She sighed. "LaGuardia."

"Fine. I'll call you in a couple of days, after I've finalized things. I don't know whether it'll be warm enough to swim, but the hotel has a pool, so pack his bathing suit."

"Yeah."

"Robin." His tone was ameliorating. "I'm sorry it's happened now. I know you're sad. I know how you feel about the holiday. But think of how much fun Phil's going to have."

"Thanks for the counseling session," she snapped. "I've got to go."

"I'll be in touch," Ray said before hanging up.

Robin dropped the receiver into its cradle and sighed again. She attempted a smile for Philip's sake and twisted to face him. "Quite a surprise, isn't it," she murmured.

He jumped off the bed and performed a giddy dance. "Mickey Mouse! I'm gonna see Mickey Mouse for Christmas!"

"I guess you are," she conceded, wiping her hand across her damp eyelashes and reaching for her bathrobe.

She went downstairs and made Philip breakfast—a heaping bowl of Cheerios, a bagel, two glasses of orange juice and a cup filled half with coffee and half with milk. Exciting events always made him gluttonous. Robin herself barely managed to consume two bites of her own bagel and a cup of black coffee. Some exciting events stirred her appetite, too, but this one left her feeling distinctly nauseated.

After eating, Philip went to his room to get dressed. Robin poured herself a second cup of coffee, stared at it for ten minutes, and then dumped it down the drain. Then she wandered into the living room and glared at the magnificent tree, the ribbon-and-holly-trimmed balustrade, the decorated candles in the windows. She inhaled the tangy scent of pine. Christmas without Philip. She couldn't bear it.

Returning to the kitchen, she reached for the phone. Perhaps ten o'clock on a Sunday morning was too early to call Jesse, but in another half hour, she'd have to shower, get dressed, summon Kate O'Leary and leave for Woodleigh's. She pulled the new telephone book from the shelf, flipped through it until she located Jesse's number, and dialed.

He sounded reasonably awake when he answered; Robin found solace in that. "Hello, Jesse—it's Robin, and I . . ." A fresh lump of tears took up residence in her throat, and she was unable to continue.

"What happened?" he asked, worried.

"Disney World happened," she moaned, then related the details of Ray's call to Jesse. Maybe he thought her divorce hadn't left her bitter, but she didn't bother to disguise her bitterness now. "Of all the times, Jesse—of all the times, it had to be Christmas. Any other time of the year I wouldn't have minded. But to do this—to do this to me at Christmas—"

"It doesn't sound like he's doing anything to *you*," Jesse calmly pointed out. "It's something he's doing for Philip."

"Don't you think I know that? I hate myself for being so angry, Jesse. I want Philip to have this opportunity. But Christmas—" She stopped short. How could she expect Jesse to understand her anguish? He didn't care about Christmas at all.

"Oh, Robin." Maybe he couldn't understand, but he did seem sympathetic. "I wish there was something I could do. I don't suppose it would help to send another Navy captain a legal brief about Santa Claus."

Of course he understood. He had been going through a similiar crisis with the client of his who wanted her son home for the holiday. Just because Christmas signified nothing to Jesse didn't mean he couldn't commiserate with people for whom it signified everything.

"What am I going to do?" she asked, desperate for words of wisdom from him, a straw to grasp at.

He ruminated. "Maybe you could spend Christmas with your mother," he suggested. "Wouldn't she come to Connecticut for the holiday?"

"No, she'll never be able to tolerate the cold weather."

"You could go to Hawaii, then."

"No," Robin said decisively. "Christmas is a time for home, Jesse. I'm not going to leave home."

"Then you'll stay here," he said. "And I'll be here, and we'll make the best of it."

The tension in her gut slowly ebbed, replaced by a shimmering warmth. Christmas with Jesse. Christmas with a man she was only beginning to know, a man who rejected so many of the things she believed in, a man who claimed he had no soul. Christmas with a friend. "You'll celebrate with me?" she asked timidly.

"I'll do my best," he said. "But I'm not going to strap on a false beard and climb down your chimney."

For the first time since Ray's call, a smile teased her lips. It wasn't much of a smile, rather feeble and forlorn, but if Jesse was willing to do his best, she would have to do her best, too. "No false beard," she assured him. "But I make a gingerbread house for Philip every year, and—" she swallowed the catch in her throat "—somebody's got to eat it."

"That I'll do," Jesse volunteered.

"Hey, Mom!" Philip's shrill voice sliced through the air from upstairs. "You'd better shake a leg or you'll be late for work!"

"I've got to go," Robin said.

"I'll talk to you later," Jesse promised before hanging up.

Robin dropped the receiver into placé. Although Jesse was less than a mile away, and Philip was separated from her only by a flight of stairs, she felt lonely. So profoundly, so oppressively lonely that picturing Jesse impersonating Santa Claus made her want to cry.

There would be time enough for weeping once Philip was truly gone. For now, she had little choice but to get herself to Woodleigh's and pretend to be full of holiday cheer.

IF I COULDN'T HAVE PHILIP WITH ME for Christmas, I'd die.

Jesse picked up the piece of toast he'd been in the middle of eating, then dropped it back onto his plate as Robin's words echoed inside his skull. She had ultimately admitted that equating Christmas without her son to death was an overstatement, but her sentiments had been obvious. For a woman like her, Christmas without Philip was life without a purpose.

Why was it that this one day meant so damned much to so many people? That was all it was—a day, a date on the calendar, one three-hundred-sixty-fifth of a year. In honor of that one single day, people became maniacs. They spent money they didn't have, drank more than they could stomach, partied until they were ready to drop. They filled their homes with trees and lights, littered their floors with dead twigs and ran up extraordinary electric bills. They made promises of love and bonhomie that were quickly forgotten.

All right, so there was also some religious import to the day. It commemorated the birth of Jesus Christ—but to accept that, you had to swallow a few myths: the myth that Jesus was the Messiah, the myth that He was actually born on the twenty-fifth day of December, the myth that snow could fall in the Middle East. Jesse was one of those people who believed that Jesus was merely a man, a preacher, possibly mystic and possibly misguided, and that December twenty-fifth was declared his birthday to satisfy a lot of pagans who preferred to celebrate the winter solstice. As for snow falling in Bethlehem—well, Jesse had never seen a shred of proof about that ostensible meteorological phenomenon.

But he *had* read the scriptures as a youth, and the one message that remained with him was that it was essential to give of oneself. Not in the hope of salvation—he hadn't bought that particular aspect of it—but because helping others was a decent, humane thing to do. If Robin was in agony, Jesse would help her any way he could.

He wished he knew what it was he could do for her. Bringing Gerald Selby home for Christmas seemed a cinch in comparison, and Jesse hadn't had much success there yet. He'd received an acknowledgment of his letter to Captain Stevenson, nothing more. And even if he could bring Gerald Selby home, what home could he bring him to? Mrs. Selby's landlord was sending out feelers, but days were slipping away and the elevator still didn't work. The trash was being picked up only sporadically, and the lightbulb in Mrs. Selby's corridor hadn't been replaced.

At least Jesse had the legal training to attempt to straighten out Mrs. Selby's various dilemmas. His legal training wouldn't do him any good with Robin, however. All he could offer her was his companionship, his support, his love.

He rested his head in his palms and gazed at the plate of toast. If he offered her all he could, perhaps it would be enough. Simply thinking of her, thinking of the hope and confidence she exuded, had helped him to survive his accident. Now she was devoid of hope and confidence, and he wasn't sure how to go about giving them back to her.

Maybe Philip could help in some way; he owed Jesse a favor. Jesse had done a favor for him by stopping by the Greer house on Thursday evening, while Robin was still at work, and spiriting Philip's Christmas gift for his mother out of the house so she wouldn't find it. It was a peculiar gift, Jesse had to admit: a statue constructed of modeling clay and painted with a garish orange glaze, supposedly depicting a boy from the planet Gleek. Jesse wondered whether Robin would ever be able to guess what the stout object with the pointy feet, the wings protruding from its shoulders and the seashell-shaped ears was supposed to be. She'd recognize the halo Philip had shaped out of wire and propped up above the creature's head, though. Angels didn't dwell in heaven; evidently, they came from Gleek.

Jesse and Mrs. O'Leary had helped Philip to wrap the awkwardly shaped object in paper, taped a lopsided bow to the package, and fastened the home-made card Philip had written. Then, vowing secrecy, Jesse had brought the gift to his condominium for safekeeping.

How would she feel when she found Philip's gift under her tree Christmas morning? Jesse hoped she wouldn't resent her son for abandoning her. Philip was just a kid. He couldn't know the despair his trip to Florida was going to cause his mother. He shouldn't know.

Jesse would make sure he didn't. He would keep Robin from despairing, somehow.

HE WANTED TO TAKE HER out to dinner, but she kept refusing his invitations. It wasn't only that managing
Woodleigh's through the final Christmas crush consumed a disproportionate amount of her time, but that,
irrational as it was, she felt compelled to spend every
spare second with Philip. She kept thinking that if she
collected as many memories as possible of her son, she
could seal them, store them in her brain, and then cheer
herself up by breaking them open on Christmas morning and using them to get her through the day.

Such a wish was impossible, yet she couldn't seem to
stop herself. She talked to Jesse often on the phone, and
he came to the house for dinner a couple of times, but
even when Philip wandered into the den to watch television after dinner, Robin insisted on being in the room
with him. She and Jesse sat on the couch, and while Jesse
gazed at the screen Robin gazed at her son. She memo-
rized the cowlick at the rear of Philip's head, the sparkle
in his eyes, the scuffs on his sneakers and the faded ovals
on the knees of his jeans. She absorbed his every utter-
ance, his every giggle.

Perhaps Christmas would be tolerable if she tape-
recorded him, she contemplated. She could turn on the
cassette at sunrise on December twenty-fifth, and listen
to Philip's adorable voice plying her with questions:
"What does Dan Rather mean when he says fifteen people are *presumed* dead? Are they dead or aren't they?"
No, that wouldn't work.

"When am I going to see this gingerbread house
you've promised me?" Jesse asked on Saturday evening. It was the third night he'd come for dinner, the
third night he'd had to witness Robin obsessively shad-
owing her son around the house. But eight-thirty had arrived and they had just put Philip to bed. She couldn't

very well hover for the next few hours in Philip's doorway, watching him sleep.

"I haven't made it," she confessed, descending the stairs to the living room with Jesse. She had accumulated all the ingredients required for the house: the molasses, the chocolate wafers she used for the roof, the gumdrops with which she trimmed the windows and door. She should have baked the damned thing by now; ordinarily she baked it a week before Christmas so she and Philip could admire it and pride themselves on their ability to resist temptation until Christmas afternoon, when they traditionally disassembled the house and gobbled it up.

But she hadn't been able to bring herself to make the confection this year. It seemed like so much effort to go through when Philip wasn't going to be around to eat it with her.

"Why don't we make it now?" Jesse proposed.

"It takes hours," Robin warned him, glancing at her watch. She had already put in a full day at Woodleigh's, and Jesse had told her over dinner that he'd spent half the day at his office in New Haven, reviewing a pile of depositions he'd taken from his Newhallville clients. Neither she nor Jesse had the energy to tackle a project like the gingerbread house at this hour.

"We can sleep late tomorrow," Jesse pointed out.

Robin glanced sharply at him. Where, exactly, was he planning to sleep late? Why had he said "we"?

She trudged into the kitchen and slumped on a chair. "Jesse, I'm a horrible person," she muttered, focusing on her clenched fists, which rested on the table before her. "You want to spend the night here, and the last thing I can think about right now is whether I want you to do that."

He glided behind her and began kneading the tense muscles along her shoulders. "I thought we were discussing baking gingerbread," he said quietly.

She closed her eyes to savor fully his comforting massage. "How can you stand being around me? I've been such a pill. All I think about is Philip, Philip, Philip."

"And maybe, every now and then, you think about yourself," Jesse reproached, his tone gentle. "You think about how sorry you are for yourself, and you wallow in self-pity. You go on and on about the importance of the Christmas spirit, but I haven't noticed much of it coming from you."

"I haven't got any," she agreed dolefully. "It's like the bottom's fallen out of my world. I don't expect you to understand it, Jesse. I only wonder why you haven't given up on me and moved on."

"Bottoms fall out of worlds all the time," he noted, ending his massage and circling the table. He took a seat across from her and gathered her hands in his. "If you haven't got the strength to make your world livable again, then I'm here to help you."

"Why?" she asked, genuinely curious. "Why me?"

"Because...because deep down inside you, you do have the strength," he replied, his eyes riveted to hers, a trusting glow emanating from their profound depths. "Because your world—more than any other world I've ever seen—deserves to be repaired."

Her fingers wove through his and curled tight, clinging to him. "I do love you, Jesse," she whispered, returning his unwavering gaze.

He nodded. "I know."

"Then why aren't you pushing things? Why aren't you making demands?"

"Is that what love means?" he shot back. "Pushing and making demands?"

"Is it that you don't want me anymore?"

"Oh, Robin..." He let out an incredulous laugh. "Of course I want you. Every time I talk to you, every time I hear your voice... Every time I leave your house alone, I feel like some sort of oversexed adolescent, half-crazy with fantasies."

"Then why...?"

"Because in my fantasies, you're ready for me. You're thinking only of me—of *us*. Not of Phil and not of some overdressed pine tree. Just us. That's what I want, Robin. That's the way I want it."

His candor touched her, and made her feel even more unworthy of him. "You could have that with someone else," she reminded him in a tremulous voice. The last thing she wanted was to drive Jesse away. She had scarcely survived the past week; without him, she wouldn't have survived at all. But she loved him. She loved him enough to want him happy. And she knew she wasn't doing a good job of making him happy.

He pulled her hands to his mouth and kissed her knuckles. "Don't you think I'm aware of that?" he asked, smiling crookedly. "The problem is, you're the lady in the fantasy."

Robin's eyes glistened with tears. For the first time since she'd come to terms with Philip's leaving, they weren't tears of sorrow and loss. "I don't deserve you," she murmured, sliding her hands from his and pushing away from the table. "But since you're here, I'll make you a gingerbread house."

"Make it right," Jesse urged her. "I don't want the bottom falling out of it, too."

IT WAS RAINING lightly when Robin and Philip left for the airport. The temperature hovered in the mid-thirties, and if anything, it would be warmer at the airport, so Robin wasn't worried about the possibility of ice on the runway.

Nor was she worried about Jesse's having to contend with foul weather during his drive to Newport. He had phoned her last night to inform her that the Navy had finally agreed to release Gerald Selby into Jesse's custody on a two-day pass. Selby would have to be back on base by Christmas night, but Jesse had assured Robin that he didn't mind making the long round-trip drive twice in three days. He was thrilled for his client and her family, delighted that their holiday would be brightened by the presence of their son. Most of all, he admitted, he was jubilant that he'd gotten the United States Navy to come around.

And he didn't believe in miracles?

"Now remember," Robin instructed her son, who was squirming on the seat beside her. "The only people you're going to talk to on the plane are the flight attendants and the officers. No strangers, nobody who isn't wearing a uniform. Right?"

"I've been on airplanes by myself before," Philip scoffed. "I know the rules."

"The only time you're to leave your seat is if you have to go to the bathroom," she continued, undeterred.

He rolled his eyes. Then he twisted to confront her. "You're not going to forget to leave milk and cookies for Santa, are you?" he asked, concerned.

"I won't forget."

"The star-shaped ones. Those are his favorite."

Robin pressed her lips together. She hadn't baked her rolled sugar cookies yet. Baking them was something she and Philip always did together the night before Christmas Eve. She had assumed that she would skip making them this year; the gingerbread house had been a pain in the neck to make, and Jesse had refused to take it home with him. "It belongs here," he had insisted when she'd tried to foist it upon him.

So now it was sitting at the center of the dining room table, growing stale. The cookies would grow stale, too. Why should she bother to make them?

"You listening to me, Mom?" Noticing the glassy look in her eyes, Philip nudged her. "Santa likes—"

"The star-shaped ones. Okay, I'll make them."

Temporarily satisfied, Philip settled into his seat. Then he suddenly looked concerned again. "It's on account of, if you don't leave them for Santa, he might not leave my presents under the tree."

"Of course he will," Robin assured her son.

"Yeah, but I won't be there. Like, what if he leaves them, and then when he finds out I'm not home to open them, he takes them away?"

"He won't do that," Robin insisted, wincing at the slight crack in her voice and hoping that Philip hadn't noticed. "You've been a good boy all year, and your presents will be waiting for you when you get home. I'll make sure of it."

"Because it's not like I don't want them," Philip asserted. "It's just that I won't be there."

Don't, she moaned silently. *Please don't say that again. I already know it.*

The drive to the airport took them less than two hours. Robin parked in one of the short-term lots and, holding Philip's hand in one of hers and his suitcase in the other, she strode stoically to the terminal. It was mobbed with holiday travelers, most of them lugging shopping bags overflowing with gift-wrapped boxes. Obtaining a ticket to Florida for Philip at this time of year, on such short notice, was yet more proof that miracles did happen. But this was one miracle Robin would gladly have done without.

The check-in line zigzagged within a roped-off area, and Robin and Philip took their place at the end. For the forty-five minutes it took until they reached the desk, Philip chattered nonstop about what he would say to Mickey Mouse and Donald Duck, which rides he expected to enjoy, what souvenirs he planned to bring home with him. "Would you like a Minnie Mouse watch, Mom?" he asked. "I could get one for you. I have some money left over from my Christmas shopping, and I could probably borrow the rest from Dad. Would you like that?"

"No, thanks," Robin declined, though moved by Philip's generosity. "I've got a perfectly good watch. I want you to spend your money on yourself, Phil."

"Should I get a Mickey watch? Or maybe a T-shirt. They're probably cheaper. Maybe I'll get an Epcot lunchbox or something. Then I can get rid of that Smurfs one."

And on and on, until they finally checked Philip's bag and he received his boarding pass. Robin accompanied him to a special lounge the airline set aside for children who were traveling without adult escorts, and an offensively cheery woman in an airline uniform promptly showered Philip with a plastic VIP badge, a coloring book and crayons, and a deck of playing cards. "Aren't you a lucky boy, taking a big trip like this at Christmastime," the woman babbled.

"Yeah! I'm going to see Disney World," Philip bellowed.

"And your father," Robin coached him in a brittle voice.

The airline employee offered Robin a rueful smile, then turned her attention back to Philip, filling him in on how long the flight would take and what would be served for lunch. This must be what most divorced parents endured at Christmas, Robin mused disconsolately: losing their children to their former spouses and putting up a brave front about it. For all she knew, Philip's departure today might be the start of a brand-new Greer Christmas tradition... but that thought was too horrible to dwell on.

Eventually, Philip and the other unescorted children were beckoned to board the plane. Doing an estimable job of hiding her depression, Robin kissed him good-bye and wished him a wonderful time in Florida. It pained her to watch him vanish down the connector to the jet, but she waved brightly and shouted another good-bye at his receding form. Then, feeling indescribably mournful, she left the airport.

She drove directly to Woodleigh's. The store was in a state of bedlam. Kevin seemed to have mislaid at least half the items in the stockroom; the customers were short-fused and the clerks were frazzled. None of it bothered Robin, however. She needed the distraction, and she was happy to be surrounded by people with worse tempers than hers.

At five o'clock she was free to leave, but she loitered for a while longer in the store, loath to return home. Meandering among the festive displays of merchandise did little to leaven her mood, not even when she calculated the dwindling supplies of many items and the profits the store was accruing. She was seized with the urge to buy something, but she didn't know what. Capitalizing on her in-house discount, she had already bought one of just about everything she'd ever wanted from Woodleigh's stocks.

Jesse. Robin had to buy something for Jesse. She ambled the length of the store again, considering numerous wares. Linens? No, he didn't even own a dining table—what would he do with a tablecloth and matching napkins? The absence of dining room furniture also precluded candlesticks or a hand-embroidered runner for a sideboard. Given his aversion to hard liquor, she couldn't buy him a bar set. A knickknack of some sort? She hadn't noticed any shelves in his condo. He'd laughed at the stationery. And what could be less appropriate than a Christmas tree ornament?

As it was, most of the ornaments had already been bought. Just a few remained on the green felt-covered table. They looked somehow sad to Robin, lonesome and neglected.

She lifted a tiny crystal angel from the table and studied it. Its face was sweet and cherubic, its wings almost gossamer in their delicacy, its robe smoothly draped and its halo an exquisite circle of clarity, glowing with captured light. So what if Jesse didn't like it? This was one little angel who deserved a home.

Robin carried the figurine to the counter and did a quick job of boxing and wrapping it. Then, having run out of excuses to dawdle at the store, she left for home.

Her house seemed unnaturally dark and still when she entered it. No exuberant welcome from Philip, no long-winded description of schoolwork and snakes' diets, no pleading for sweets. It was like stepping inside a mausoleum, Robin thought with a wretched sigh.

She placed the gift-wrapped angel beneath the tree, took off her coat, and went upstairs to the attic storage area to gather up the gift boxes she'd been hiding there. After changing into her jeans and a loose-fitting sweater, she carried the boxes downstairs and dumped them under the tree as well.

"All right, Santa's been here," she muttered to her absent son. Her voice resounded hollowly in the empty house, and she tried to conjure an image of Philip shrieking with delight at the sight of all the colorful packages.

Instead she was visited with the sound of his voice: "The star-shaped ones. Those are his favorites."

"All right," she said again, marching to the kitchen. She might as well bake the damned Christmas cookies and get it over with. She wasn't hungry—she'd fix herself a snack later, if she felt up to it.

Her fingers were crusted with gooey dough when the telephone rang twenty minutes later. "Have you eaten?" Jesse asked cheerfully.

The sound of his voice invigorated her. She was not going to mope, she was not going to sulk. She was not going to wallow in self-pity, as he had rightly accused her of doing a few days ago. "Not yet," she told him, feeling her gloom dissipate at the realization that she wasn't as alone as she'd feared. She couldn't be alone when she had Jesse. "I haven't gotten around to dinner. I'm too busy making cookies."

"Cookies! If I come over with a pizza, do I get to lick the bowl?"

"Whatever lickings there are, they're yours."

"Give me fifteen minutes," he said before hanging up.

He was coming. He would be here. She wouldn't have to bake the cookies—or face Christmas—all by herself. A wonderful, selfless, arguably too-tolerant man was going to face it with her. And she felt joyous, truly joyous.

Abandoning the kitchen, she hurried to the living room and plugged in the tree lights. Then she lit the red candles in the windows. This was the way Christmas was supposed to be, she reminded herself, striding to the den and turning on the television in search for a Christmas special. She supposed she ought to buy some Christmas records, but until she did, the TV would have to provide the carols.

She flipped through the channels, stopping at the first Christmas music she came to. The screen featured a huge choir robed in blue and standing in a horseshoe formation, singing "Joy to the World" in a cappella magnificence. "Perfect," Robin rejoiced, turning up the volume and detouring to the downstairs bathroom to check her appearance.

Her hair was a mess, but she barely had time to brush it before the doorbell rang. Racing from the bathroom, her face radiant with happiness at Jesse's arrival, she swung the front door open.

His hair and the shoulders of his coat were damp from the drizzle, and his arms cradled a steaming white box from which rose the spicy aroma of the pizza. He was smiling cautiously, peering past her at the tree and then at the flickering candles. She flung her arms around him, nearly knocking the pizza out of his hands, and drew him inside. "I'm so glad you're here," she murmured, planting a friendly kiss on his lips.

"I'm glad I'm here, too," he said, handing her the box and removing his coat. "How are you?"

He must have expected to find her in the doldrums, and she was pleased to have confounded those expectations. "I'm fine, Jesse, really. How was Newport?"

He shook his head and chuckled. "Ridiculous," he told her, hanging his coat in the closet. "It was as complicated as a bail hearing just trying to get the kid released. But I did it." He took the pizza back from her and started toward the kitchen. "Where are those cookies?"

"I haven't baked them yet," she said, following him through the house. "The dough's all ready. We'll get them into the oven after we eat." Jesse seemed to have brought her appetite with him. All of a sudden she wanted to dive headlong into the box and stuff her mouth with melted mozzarella.

He put the box on the table and surveyed the counter where she'd arranged the bowl of dough, her rolling pin, containers of red and green sprinkles and an assortment of cookie cutters. "You've been busy," he observed, impishly plucking a dollop of dough from the bowl and tasting it.

"You're just as bad as Philip," she scolded, slapping his hand away. "Is a fondness for raw dough a sex-linked trait?"

Rather than meet her playful teasing, Jesse abruptly grew tense, a cloud darkening his face. He tilted his head and frowned, listening. "What the hell is that?"

"What? The music?" If Jesse didn't like Christmas carols—especially carols performed so beautifully—then he'd just have to tough it out. Robin wasn't going to shut off the television.

His frown deepening, he spun around and stormed to the den. Robin raced after him, prepared to defend the music to the death. As soon as he saw the television screen he froze, then cursed. "You're not watching this, are you?"

"I'm listening to it," she clarified. "Their singing is absolutely gorgeous."

"That's the Grace Cathedral Choir."

"It is?" She moved to his side and gazed at the robed choristers. They were now singing "Oh, Little Town of Bethlehem," their voices sublimely blended and their harmonies pure. "They're fantastic."

"This is the Grace Cathedral annual Christmas special," Jesse said tautly, not at all moved by the spellbinding music. "Turn it off."

She caught herself before blurting out that she absolutely wouldn't turn it off. Perhaps the show had been produced by Jesse's former girlfriend; perhaps his sudden grimness was a result of some old heartache not yet healed. He had been so sensitive to Robin's sorrow lately; the least she could do was sympathize with his discomfort.

She started toward the television, but before she reached the on-off button, the choir came to the final cadence of the song and was replaced on the screen by the Reverend Robert Shepherd. Robin recognized him only because she'd occasionally caught glimpses of his shows, and because his picture appeared in the newspapers every once in a while, often shaking a politician's hand. He was a fine-looking man, with regally silver hair, dark eyes, a hawklike nose and a sharp, square chin. For this Christmas special he was dressed in a majestic royal-blue velvet robe with gold satin trim, and he stared out from the screen with an almost unnerving expression of omniscience.

"Brothers and sisters," he orated in a rich, melodic baritone. "Thank you for joining us in this, our celebration of the birth of Jesus Christ."

Robin hesitated, unable to turn the television off. Something about the minister's voice, about his towering height, his proud bearing, the piercing darkness of his eyes...

"As you know," Shepherd intoned, "Christmas is a time of giving. At this time of year, we remember what Jesus Christ gave to free us from our mortal ignorance. He gave that most valuable gift—His own life—so that we might know the Lord."

There was something eerily familiar about the man on the television. That smooth, sonorous voice...

"Turn it off," Jesse said softly.

The quiet steel in his tone caused her to flinch. "Not yet," she implored him. She didn't know why she wanted to continue to watch the show. She didn't know what she was looking for, what she was sensing. All she knew was that she had to keep watching.

"I can tell you what he's going to say," Jesse remarked. "It isn't worth your time."

"Not yet," she repeated, turning back to the screen.

"...and so we mark this day by giving. We give to our loved ones, our families and friends, our co-workers and neighbors. The splendor of the Grace Cathedral Choir gives us their inspired music. In the spirit of Jesus Christ, we give."

"What's wrong with that?" Robin defended the sermon to Jesse. Shepherd hadn't said anything she could take issue with.

"He's just warming up," Jesse said, stuffing his hands into the pockets of his jeans and leaning against a bookcase, regarding the television from a distance. "Give him a chance—he'll get to the point soon."

"...and while you're giving, you must ask yourselves, what am I giving to the Lord? What am I giving to those who do His work, who spread His word? You've just spent twenty dollars on a bottle of perfume for your mother, forty dollars on a G.I. Joe toy for your son, fifty dollars on Barbie's dream house and swimming pool for your daughter, a diamond for your wife, golf clubs for your husband . . . and where, in that, is your gift to those who do the work of the Lord? Where is the true gift, the gift that will bring Jesus to those who need Him most?

"Think about it, my friends. Think about what you can give, and then give it. We at the Grace Cathedral have seen with our own eyes the miracles that God can perform, and we ask you to help us. In the spirit of Christmas, in the spirit of Jesus, we ask you to give. Call the toll-free number that appears on your screen, and make a pledge. Or send a check to the address that appears above the phone number. Whatever you can afford—five dollars, ten, twenty, a hundred—every little bit helps us to do our work, to bring God to millions of people around the world, people who need Him as much as you do.

"And now, I'll turn you back to our choir. Let their spirit awaken the spirit within you, the spirit of giving."

The address and telephone number continued to flash on the screen as the camera cut back to the choir. They began a lush arrangement of "The First Noel," but Robin hardly heard them. Closing her eyes, turning out her ears, she pictured the Reverend Shepherd as he'd appeared on the screen, his stunning eyes, his mellifluous voice. His plea for money had been a bit heavy-handed, sure. But it wasn't what he'd said that so unnerved her. It was how he'd said it, how he'd sounded, how his dazzling, thickly lashed eyes had reached out to her . . .

She glanced at Jesse, inexplicably fearful of what she would see. He was staring not at the television but at her. Reaching to her with those same dazzling, thickly lashed eyes. "Well," he said in his distinctive voice, a voice uncannily like Shepherd's. "Now you know."

Chapter Eleven

"What?" Robin asked frantically. "What do I know?"

Jesse's expression was inscrutable. "Don't tell me you didn't notice the resemblance."

She couldn't help but notice it, with the two men so closely juxtaposed, their faces confronting her from opposite ends of the same room, their voices merging in the air around her. That she hadn't noticed the likeness between Jesse and the TV evangelist before was only a result of her never having paid much attention to the Reverend Robert Shepherd. "Are you related to him?" she asked, realizing at once that it was a stupid question.

"He's my father."

"Your father!" For no good reason, Jesse's revelation made her feel even more stupid. "But—but his name is Shepherd."

"His stage name," Jesse clarified. "He legally changed his name to Shepherd when he took the job with Grace Cathedral. In fact, he changed all our names."

"Why did he do that?"

Jesse chuckled dryly. "Shepherd," he emphasized. "What could be a more suitable name for someone leading the flock?"

Robin shook her head, amazed that she'd never made the connection before. "And your name is Lawson, because you're a lawyer," she guessed. "Is that some sort of family gag? You all take last names based on your professions?"

"No," Jesse replied. "The family name was Lawson before my father changed it to Shepherd. I decided to change mine back right after I finished law school. In my case, it was just a coincidence."

"Why did you change it back?" Robin asked, totally at sea. "I don't understand any of this, Jesse."

He stared at her for a minute, his eyes glittering enigmatically, his mouth curved in a humorless smile. "It's a long story," he said. "And the pizza's getting cold."

"Then we'll eat and you'll tell me," Robin resolved, leaving the den for the kitchen. Her appetite had fled her again, but she hoped that if she ate something she would stop feeling so light-headed and addled. She covered the cookie dough with plastic wrap and placed the bowl in the refrigerator—the last thing she could cope with right now was baking—and then gathered plates, glasses, napkins and a bottle of cola and set the kitchen table. Jesse pulled two wedges of pizza from the box, distributed them, and sat across from Robin.

Ignoring the food in front of her, she watched him while he bit into his slice. She was unnerved by the steady force of his dark eyes, so similar to Shepherd's, and equally unnerved to find herself picturing Jesse thirty years from now, when his thick shock of black hair would turn silver, when time would deepen the laugh lines radiating from the corners of his eyes and the creases bracketing his lips. If he took after his father, however, his voice wouldn't change with age. It would remain low and silky and persuasive.

"I'm waiting," she reminded him as he swallowed a mouthful of pizza and reached for his soda.

He drank, then lowered his glass. "He changed his name—he got the job at Grace—when I was nine years old. Before that, he was a minister at a relatively small Baptist church in Oroville, up in the mountains in northern California. He had developed a reputation for being a passionate speaker with a lot of charisma, and he was approached by Grace and asked to audition for the opening they had. They were a local operation then. They broadcasted a half-hour show on an independent station every Sunday morning, but they were thinking of expanding. They had hired another guy for the position, but he wasn't working out well and they intended to fire him. His name was Larsen. When they hired my father, they asked him to change his name from Lawson so viewers wouldn't confuse him with Larsen."

"And he chose Shepherd," said Robin.

Jesse nodded. "Not exactly subtle, but then again, standing before a national audience and haranguing them to send you their hard-earned dollars isn't subtle, either. My father's producers didn't care about subtlety—they cared about effectiveness. And my father's very effective. He raised the money to build that monstrous cathedral. He gave Grace clout. He gave its broadcast the numbers—the ratings to enable it to go national. My father's an emcee, an entertainer and a businessman rolled into one."

"He's also a minister," Robin commented, nibbling on her pizza.

"Right. How could I forget?" Jesse scoffed.

"I'll grant you, a big, gaudy cathedral filled with television cameras isn't the same thing as a cozy white clapboard church on the town green, but still . . . that doesn't mean you have to reject the religious part of it.''

"I was having problems with the religion long before we moved to Los Angeles,'' Jesse confessed. He rolled up the sleeves of his flannel shirt and helped himself to a second slice of pizza. "My best friend in Oroville was a kid named Mickey Santangelo. He lived down the street from me, and we did everything together. My parents told me he wouldn't go to heaven because he was a Roman Catholic.''

"No!'' That parents would say something that cruel to an impressionable young boy shocked Robin, and she laughed. "Roman Catholics believe in heaven.''

"Not the way fundamentalists do. It's such a strict denomination. I began to have my doubts when my father changed our name to Shepherd. I never got used to that. My two younger sisters didn't care—they hadn't spent so many years being Lawsons. But Marybeth and I had real problems with the name change, and the move, and being taken out of public school and sent to a private Christian academy. And then, two years after we arrived in L.A., Marybeth got sick.''

He fell silent, submerged in a memory of his sister's illness and death. Robin's curiosity about his childhood was far from satisfied, but if it hurt Jesse too much to talk about his sister's passing, she wouldn't press him. She brushed her fingers comfortingly over the back of his hand and murmured, "Jesse . . .''

Shaking off his sadness, he pulled his hand from hers and took a bite of his pizza. "Marybeth understood,'' he said. "She had the same doubts I did, the same questions. But once she was diagnosed, she returned to the fold. She kept telling me that she had no choice, that she was too weak to fight it and so she may as well trust in prayer. It was such a betrayal, Robin—it was like losing Marybeth twice, losing her to my parents' church and then losing her to death. If only she had trusted herself, maybe she would have beaten the cancer. Maybe she would have pulled through. Some leukemia patients do. But she gave up. She stopped fighting and prayed for God to put her out of her misery.''

"Jesse," Robin said, "you can't blame her for that. None of us know how we'd react to such a dreadful disease unless we've been through it ourselves."

"I know that," Jesse agreed contritely. "I don't blame her, I don't judge her. All I know is that, once she was gone, what little faith I had was gone as well. My father threw himself even more energetically into denouncing sinners and raising money for the cathedral, and my mother—well, she's just a simple God-fearing woman, a clergyman's wife out of her depth. Whatever my father tells her to do, she does. After Marybeth died, Mom turned our home into a domestic cathedral, with prayer corners and iron-clad rules. She spent most of her time hosting fund raising luncheons and leading parents' groups protesting textbooks that mention evolution or sexual equality.''

"And you became a lawyer for your father's church," Robin remarked.

Jesse nodded. He tossed a crescent of crust onto his plate and shifted in his chair, hooking one arm over the back of it and perusing Robin, trying to gauge her reaction to what he was telling her. She wasn't yet certain of her reaction, other than bewilderment and surprise—and a strange, undefinable relief that, at last, she was learning what she had to know about Jesse.

"You've talked about the importance of traditions," he pondered. "Well, this was ours: you finished your schooling and went to work for G.C.E. Or, at least, that's how it went for me. My sisters didn't take jobs with the company—proper ladies are supposed to marry and stay home and raise families. But they both married G.C.E. people. Lillian's married to the musical director of the choir, and Martha's married to one of the accountants. And I became a lawyer and signed on.''

"But first you became Jesse Lawson again," Robin pointed out. "Didn't that upset your father?"

Jesse glanced skyward and groaned. "My father's spent almost as much of his life being upset with me as he has raising money and praising the Lord. He knew I had a rebellious streak; he was always punishing me for it. When he found out that I was sneaking to the public library after school in order to read all the books that were banned in our house, he locked me in my bedroom for a week. The only time the door was unlocked was to pass in a tray of food. When I met a Jewish girl one summer at the beach and asked her out for a date, I got locked up again. Each time in my room I had only the Bible to keep me company.''

Jesse searched Robin's face. It was turned up to his— open and caring—as she listened intently to him and tried to understand.

"When I was in college," he continued, "we had some ferocious debates about the Vietnam war. I kept asking my father why he wasn't preaching more sermons on peace. He kept telling me that fighting against Communism was the same thing as fighting for Jesus, that our side was God's side and he was doing his part by praying for the lives of our boys overseas. By the time I told him I was going to law school instead of divinity school, he had all but given up on me. Changing my name back to Lawson was anticlimactic.''

"But after all that, you still went to work for him."

Jesse reached for his glass of soda and settled in his chair. He watched the bubbles rising to the surface, drank a bit, and shrugged. "He was my father, and that was the way things were done."

Robin eyed him skeptically. "Not good enough, Jesse," she said. If he could have stood up to his father so many times on so many issues, why couldn't he stand up to the man when it came to his career?

Jesse sighed. His attention remained on the fizzing bubbles in his glass, and his words emerged slowly, falteringly. "I wanted to believe," he explained. "Even after all the rebelling, all the questions...I wanted to. It was so much easier for them, having that structure, having answers to everything, knowing exactly what to do and how to do it, whom to embrace and whom to avoid. They belonged to something, and I—I wanted to belong, too."

He looked so lost, so bereft when he revealed his secret desire. It was almost tragic, this man whose mind wouldn't allow his heart's desperate longing. Robin had wished that Jesse would bend in his views, but now she comprehended how hard bending must be for him. He had spent his entire life trying to bend, aching to bend for his family—and discovering that he couldn't.

"Then why did you change your name?" she asked gently.

He set down his glass and sighed again. "I had to," he insisted. "I had never gotten used to being Jesse Shepherd. It never felt right to me. I was so anxious to figure out who I was—I couldn't believe in anything until I was sure of that. And I was sure that I was Jesse Lawson, not Jesse Shepherd." He smiled pensively, his eyes momentarily losing focus, growing distant. Then they returned to Robin. "Ultimately my father decided that changing my name was a wise idea from a business standpoint. If I was going to be negotiating contracts for him, he thought it would look better if we didn't come across as some hokey family project. He wanted people to think he had lots of outside advisors—it gave him an image of strength and professionalism.''

"So you dealt with his church's legal affairs."

"It was basic contract law. I could handle it." Jesse's smile twisted, becoming cynical. "And then Anne Cotter was hired on as a producer—straight from a stint producing game shows, believe it or not—and we started seeing each other socially. That was all right with my father, too. Anne was a solid employee. The fact that we weren't married bothered Dad, but he rationalized it by saying that, since we were both doing such indispensable work for G.C.E., God would forgive us our sins. Anne viewed things that way, too. I seemed to be the only person who didn't."

"You wanted to marry her?"

"I . . . I wanted to live a consistent life, not a hypocritical one," Jesse explained. "I'm glad I didn't marry her; it would have been a lousy marriage. But I felt strange about our relationship. Obviously, my interpretation of right and wrong differed from Anne's, and from my parents', and from everyone else's at Grace. I finally came to recognize that when I told my father I wanted to take a sabbatical from G.C.E. and work with the poor. He flew into a rage. So did Anne. They told me that I was doing God's work at G.C.E., and that that was where God needed my talents. And . . ." He exhaled and smiled wryly. "At that point, it occurred to me that the indigent might need me even more than God did."

"So you quit God and signed up with New Haven Legal Assistance," Robin summarized. It sounded stark when she put it like that, but she couldn't rationalize his actions any other way. "Jesse, it seems as if you rejected God only because it was a way of rejecting your father."

Jesse grunted a laugh. "I rejected God because I'm me," he argued. "*If* God exists, and *if* He created me, then He created me to have the sort of personality that can't accommodate God."

"Q.E.D.," Robin muttered sardonically. "It's not that simple, Jesse. We all go through torture trying to separate ourselves from our parents. I had a real love-hate relationship with my father for most of his life. I loved him because he was my father, but I hated him because he was always putting his job and his country ahead of the needs of his family. My mother and I had our ups and downs, too. She used to drink too much, I told you that. It wasn't until I grew up and developed some perspective that I could accept that she had a reason for drinking. It's always hard to make the break with your parents, but it's part of becoming an adult." Robin smiled wistfully. "Sometimes, when I look at Philip, I wonder what it's going to be like for him, how he's going to rebel and cut his ties. I don't know what's going to happen, but I know something is. I don't think there's any way around it."

"Maybe," Jesse conceded. "Maybe that's what my rebellion was all about. But when the man you're trying to cut your ties with claims to have a direct line to God, it makes the cut a great deal more complicated."

"I'm sure it does." Robin reached for Jesse's hand again, and this time he rotated it to grasp hers. "Why didn't you ever tell me about this before?" she asked.

"I told you about my work for G.C.E."

"But not about your father." Her gaze met Jesse's and held it. He no longer looked bereft. His eyes were lucid, returning her direct scrutiny, and his smile was receptive and sincere. "Is it...is it that you're ashamed of your father?" she asked.

"No, of course not," he answered swiftly.

"Then what?"

His eyes remained locked onto hers, unflinching. His mouth flexed as he searched for the right words, the right response. "Perhaps...perhaps I'm a little embarrassed that it took me thirty-four years to do what most people do when they turn twenty-one."

"There's no time limit on growing up," Robin assured him. "Besides, growing up isn't the same thing as rejecting your father. It only saddens me to think that after all this, you're left with so little. You haven't got your family and you haven't got any faith, either."

"I have myself," Jesse noted, his tone subdued. "In the end, that's all any of us ever has."

Robin's gaze broke from his. She turned to view the counter, where her rolling pin and cookie cutters still sat, a reminder of the fact that Philip was gone, that every other room in her house was empty, that she was alone. In the end, Philip had departed and all she had was herself.

Jesse's fingers tightened on hers. Her head swung back to him, and she felt a sudden burst of warmth inside her. She wasn't alone. "We have more than ourselves, Jesse," she whispered, her face illuminated with joy at her epiphany. "We have each other."

An unspoken communication passed between them, a tacit understanding of what existed between them—a bond, a friendship, a defense against solitude. Jesse stood, circled the table and pulled Robin to her feet. His lips covered hers and coaxed them apart, permitting the intrusion of his tongue. For an immeasurable instant Robin's identity seemed to blur with Jesse's in the heat of their kiss. When Jesse drew back, his eyes were as bright and clear as hers, his smile hesitant but enraptured.

Without a word, Robin led him to the stairs and up. His fingers remained laced through hers, his hold seemingly unbreakable. Not until they had entered her bedroom did he release her. His hands rounded her shoulders and rotated her to face him. "Are you sure about this, Robin?" he asked.

She peered up at him. "Yes," she swore, convinced that she had never been more sure of anything in her life. She had known for a long time that she loved Jesse, and tonight she knew why. She knew that being with him was the way to stave off her loneliness, that his presence could give her life new meaning just when everything had begun to seem meaningless. She knew that taken separately, she and Jesse were two drifting souls, unsure of what to believe in, but that together, they could believe in each other, in "us." She knew, finally, who Jesse was and why he meant so much to her.

His mouth found hers again, moving possessively, instilling in her the comprehension that he offered an answer to more than just the recent loneliness she had suffered since Philip's decision to go to Orlando. She had been living with a different loneliness, one that she had endured for so long she was hardly conscious of it anymore. From the day Ray had chosen a new job and forfeited their shared dream of creating a home, Robin had been alone.

That loneliness had been evanescing ever since Jesse had entered her life. His visits, his calls, his attentiveness to her... It wasn't merely that she needed a man in her life. It was that she needed Jesse, a true friend, someone who cared, someone who mattered.

And tonight, she would have him. They would have each other.

His arms surrounded her, one ringing her waist and the other her shoulders. Her head fell back, and he raveled his fingers through her hair as his tongue probed deeper. When her fingers groped for the buttons on his shirt, he groaned. "Do you know how much I want you?" he whispered hoarsely, sliding his hand beneath the ribbed edge of her sweater to stroke the skin of her back.

"Not as much as I want you," she replied.

He groaned again, her words obviously arousing him. With a quick movement, he yanked her sweater upward. She lifted her arms, helping him to remove it. He snapped the clasp of her bra, which followed her sweater onto the floor.

His hands floated forward to caress her breasts. During her recent meditations about renewing her sex life, she had wondered, with some worry, about how a man might react to the toll that time and childbirth had taken on her body. Hers were not the firm, perky breasts of a young girl, but were soft and small.

Yet with Jesse, she didn't feel self-conscious about her body. His fingers danced across her flesh with almost reverential sensitivity, exploring the warm valley between her breasts, teasing her nipples. He backed up to the bed, pulling her with him, and lowered himself to sit. Then he brought his mouth to one nipple and sucked.

The friction of his tongue on her caused a sharp spasm of desire to rip through her. She gasped, reeling from the wonderful sensation, then once again reached out to undo the buttons of his shirt. This time, Jesse offered his assistance in opening his shirt. Within an instant, it was gone.

His torso was hard and magnificently proportioned. Robin's hands celebrated the muscular contours of it, twirling through the fine dark hairs that curled enticingly across the upper half of his chest and then rising to the knotted ridges of his shoulders. She bowed to kiss the top of Jesse's head, and he took her kiss as a cue to unfasten her jeans.

As soon as she was naked, he shed the rest of his own clothing. Then he urged her down onto the bed beside him, rolling her onto her back and running his hands the length of her compact body. "This is your last chance," he murmured as he molded his palm to the flaring curve of her hip. His lips grazed her chin, tasting its delicately sculpted angle. "I want you to be sure."

Robin sighed brokenly. It wasn't only the warmth of his mouth on her, the pressure of his fingers against her upper thigh, the erotic tug deep within her, anxious with yearning... It was more than that that made her sure. She was sure of Jesse, sure that she knew him, that they needed each other, that this was right. She wove her fingers into his hair and stroked down to the nape of his neck, to the thick bones of his shoulders. "I am."

"I..." His lips nibbled lower, tasting the underside of her jaw, her throat, the arch of her collarbone. "I didn't come here expecting this," he murmured, his breath caressing her skin. "What I mean is... I didn't come prepared."

She laughed, from both surprise and gratitude. Jesse's thoughtfulness and responsibility only magnified her love for him. "It's all right," she assured him, her hands roaming along his back, following the chain of vertebrae to his waist. "I'm protected. I did assume something like this would happen, sooner or later."

"Did you?" His fingers continued to roam down her leg, describing a circle around her kneecap and then rising along the inside of her thigh again. "I didn't."

Robin's eyes widened. "You didn't?"

Jesse's hand paused, and he raised himself to peer down at her. "I never assumed I'd find someone like you," he explained. "I never assumed I'd find something this special."

The extravagance of his compliment rendered Robin speechless. What Jesse said was true. She hadn't dared to dream she'd find a man as special as Jesse.

She curved her hands around his head and pulled him down to her. Their lips fused in a ravenous kiss. The sheer force of it left Robin shifting impatiently beneath Jesse, her body demanding to share in the intimacy her lips and tongue had experienced. The movement of her leg against his hand prompted him to set his fingers free on her thigh again, sketching a twisting line upward.

His fingers combed through the downy golden hair between her legs. When he found her, every muscle in her body tensed reflexively, then melted into his caress. She moaned, surrendering to the fluid pulsing inside her body, the damp rush of hunger for him.

Her hand slid between their chests and down over the taut stretch of his abdomen. He was already fully erect, and when she tightened her fingers around his swollen flesh he gasped. "Slow," he pleaded on a broken breath, fighting to maintain his self-control. "It's been so long for you. I don't want to hurt you."

Robin began to protest that he couldn't hurt her, that at this point she doubted she could go slow anymore. But as his finger gently entered her, preparing her, the only sound she was able to make was a breathless cry of pleasure. Her body clenched around him, every nerve spark-

ing crazily to vibrant life, every impulse centered on the
need to have Jesse, all of him, to absorb him and sur-
round him with herself, to deliver her soul to him.
"Now," she implored, guiding him fully onto her.
"Please, Jesse..."

He pulled his hand away and covered her body with
his. His hips surged convulsively, pressing, invading,
conquering. For a moment, he became still deep within
her as he struggled to contain himself. Then he withdrew
and thrust again, less wildly this time, allowing himself
to savor the enveloping warmth of her body, the comforting warmth of her love.

Her legs twined around his, and her hands settled at
the base of his spine, resisting him every time he drew
back. Whenever his body left hers, she felt herself
glimpsing her loneliness...and then he would return to
her, plunging deeper, demanding more, and she believed
she would never be alone again.

His pace increased, driving her to a pinnacle, pushing
her to an instant of perfect unity with him. With a sigh,
she surrendered to the deluge of throbbing sensation, the
glorious pulses of completion rippling through her,
transporting her, soothing her. It had been too long,
much too long since she'd felt anything like this—and yet
she willingly would have waited even longer if she'd
known that, ultimately Jesse would be the man to bring
her here.

He peaked as she did, his body wrenched by the explosive force of his climax. Groaning, he sank into her
arms and let her hold him. His heart thudded savagely
against her breast, and his breath was shallow and ragged. She wrapped her arms comfortingly around him,
waiting for him to recover, wondering whether she herself ever would.

Eventually his muscles relaxed. He propped himself up on his arms and gazed down at her. "Are you all right?" he asked in a hoarse whisper.

She answered by raising her head to kiss him. Then she nestled back into the pillow, overcome with resplendent weariness.

He tenderly brushed a few stray golden hairs from her cheeks. His eyes journeyed over her face, examining her, easily comprehending the bliss in her shimmering eyes and her astonished smile. "Angel," he breathed.

"What?" A vision of the lovely crystal angel she'd bought for Jesse flashed across her brain. How did he know what she'd gotten him for Christmas?

Grinning, he shook his head. "Nothing," he murmured, rolling off her and gathering her into a snug embrace. "I was just thinking about how much I love you."

Robin needed no further explanation for his cryptic remark. He loved her. Nothing else mattered.

NOTHING ELSE MATTERED, that is, until she woke up the next morning. Her clock buzzed its alarm through her skull, jolting her awake. She slammed her fist onto the button that silenced the clock, sat up, and looked around.

Jesse was gone. She knew she hadn't dreamed the previous night's rapture, because the pillow next to hers still bore the impression of his head, and the sheets were still warm on his side of the mattress. But whatever had happened last night, this morning she was alone.

Shaking her head, trying to ward off the sudden sense of emptiness that seeped through her, she stood and retrieved her bathrobe from the closet. The house's silence troubled her; she considered turning on the alarm again, just so she would hear something. Stepping into her slip-

pers, she shuffled out of her bedroom, halted at the top
of the stairs, and listened. Not a sound.

She knew she ought to go downstairs, but instead, she
found herself stalking to Philip's bedroom. The door was
open, and she stopped at the threshold to stare in at the
crisply made bed, the closet door, the clear surface of the
desk, the shelves stacked neatly with books and toys that
usually lay scattered across the floor. The irritating hush
filling her house had as much to do with Philip's absence as with Jesse's unexplained disappearance. Right
now Philip ought to be bouncing on the bed, smearing
toothpaste all over the bathroom sink, hollering at Robin
to shake a leg so she wouldn't be late for work, cheering
about the impending arrival of Santa Claus.

Last night hadn't changed a thing. The day before
Christmas had arrived, and Philip was gone.

Robin felt a veil of gloom descend around her, cloak-
ing her in its dreary weight. Sighing, she turned her back
on Philip's uncharacteristically tidy room and plodded
down the stairs. At the foot of the staircase she caught a
whiff of coffee. She followed its tempting scent to the
kitchen.

Jesse was standing by the coffeemaker, filling two cups
with the fresh brew. He was wide awake and fully
clothed. At the sound of her entrance, he spun around.
"Good morning!" he greeted her robustly. "I was going
to surprise you with coffee in bed."

"It's a nice surprise, even if I'm out of bed," she said
with false cheer. Seeing him, remembering the ecstasy
they had shared last night, recalling his confession of
love...why couldn't that dispel the doubt creeping over
her?

Jesse loved her—that wasn't what she doubted. Nor
did she doubt that she felt strongly about him. But was

it love that had drawn her to him yesterday, love that had lured them upstairs and into her bed? Or was it loneliness? Had she come to Jesse in the hope of affirming her love for him, or in the hope of assuaging her misery?

He had pulled out a chair for her at the table, and she slumped into it. "I'm an early riser," he said apologetically, handing her a cup of coffee. "Something tells me you're a bear in the morning."

"Not always," she mumbled, hiding her face behind the cup so Jesse couldn't see the torment and confusion in her eyes. "I'm not used to waking up to the alarm clock, that's all. Usually Philip wakes me up."

"Work today?" Jesse asked, sitting across from her and sipping his coffee.

Robin nodded.

Jesse lowered his cup and appraised her, his smile fading. "That bad, huh," he murmured sympathetically. "If it makes you feel any better, I've got to go to work today, too."

"It isn't work that's bothering me," she corrected him.

Something flickered in his eyes, a flash of fear or annoyance, or something—Robin couldn't tell. "Then what's the problem?"

She offered a bleak smile. "Oh, Jesse... It's just that I'm a novice at this," she explained. "I don't know how to deal with the morning after."

Jesse set down his cup, pulled hers from her fingers, and folded his hands around hers. "There's nothing to deal with," he said gently. "It isn't the morning after. It's the morning *before*."

"The morning before what? Christmas Eve?" Hearing herself enunciate those two emotion-laden words made her shudder.

Jesse continued to study her. After a long minute, he sighed. "Forget about Christmas Eve, Robin," he said dryly. "One day isn't worth torturing yourself over."

His words stung, and she couldn't shake the suspicion that he'd intended them to wound her. Perhaps he was trying to shake her out of her malaise—or perhaps he really meant what he'd said. Christmas was just one day to him, worth nothing more than any other day.

How could she possibly love a man who believed such a thing? How, even after making love with him, even after finding refuge from her loneliness in his arms, could she really love Jesse?

Chapter Twelve

She looked stricken.

Jesse gave himself a mental kick in the rear end. What had possessed him to say such a thing to her?

He'd wanted to drag her out of her torpor, that was all. He'd wanted to rescue her from the depression that was closing in around her. If he'd spoken a bit too sharply, a bit too bluntly, it was only because he couldn't stand to see her sinking into despair about the holiday all over again. Derogating Christmas came as a reflex to him. Robin ought to have grown accustomed to his views by now.

Watching her as she slumped in her chair, her downcast face framed by hair as pale and fine as cornsilk, her slim, lovely body hidden beneath a fleecy bathrobe, Jesse admitted that his harsh words had arisen from an impulse more complex than simply the desire to elevate her mood. As egotistical as it was, he had hoped that last night had been marvelous enough to dispel her misery about her son's absence. He had hoped that one night in his arms had been enough to vanquish her sorrow. Making love with Robin had been so rhapsodic, so indescribably splendid; he had presumed that if it had been half as beautiful for her, she wouldn't need anything more.

What a conceited fool he was. He ought to have enough sense to realize that Robin's passion for him couldn't replace her grief over Philip's absence. At best, Jesse had offered her a delightful distraction for a few hours. He wished he could have offered her more, but apparently he hadn't—and the realization hurt. That was why he'd lashed out.

It was too late for him to retract his bitter words. The moment was gone, beyond salvation. He'd have to make it up to her somehow. "What time does Woodleigh's close tonight?" he asked in a placating voice.

"Six," she said dully. Her eyes were opaque, her lips taut as she shaped the solitary word. A narrow crease lined her brow.

It broke his heart to see her this listless. He would make it up to her. He had promised that he'd do his best to make her Christmas bearable. Now, more than ever, he was determined to live up to that promise.

"I'll see you this evening?" he half asked.

"If you want."

Her unenthusiastic delivery wrenched his heart again. He tried to console himself with the thought that he hadn't personally caused her sadness. No, of course he hadn't. All he'd done was to shoot his damned mouth off and exacerbate her mood.

"I've got to go," he said, gulping down his coffee and rising. "I have to stop off at home and change my clothes for work."

Robin shrugged.

"Robin." He moved to her chair and bent down beside her. He was close enough to notice the teardrops beading along her spidery eyelashes. *Please,* he prayed, not even questioning whom he was praying to, *please, let me make it better for Robin. Please show me the way.* He enclosed her in his arms and kissed her lightly. "I love you," he whispered. "We'll have a good Christmas, Robin."

She nodded, batted her eyes and looked away. Jesse could do nothing more for her now. He straightened up and strode out of the kitchen.

He was scheduled to meet that morning with the gas station owner who had bilked Jesse's client of back wages. It was the kind of appointment that called for a suit and necktie; Jesse wanted to intimidate the proprietor, to compel him to compensate his employee promptly and save them all the hassle of a protracted legal battle. The total amount owed came to less than three hundred fifty dollars—a pittance in the circles in which Jesse used to travel, but a fortune to the young man he was currently representing.

After the session with the gas station owner, Jesse would have to attend to a mess of paperwork at his office. Negotiations with Cabot's attorney seemed to have reached a stalemate, and Jesse feared that not long into the new year his Newhallville clients might find themselves homeless.

In the meantime, however, he could see to it that they had decent Christmas dinners. Jesse wasn't good at celebrating Christmas himself, but he was willing to help others celebrate it. He intended to buy those needy tenants some food.

He wanted to indulge Robin, too. He would do whatever he could to make sure she celebrated her holiday.

His meeting with the gas station owner went better than expected. As he'd hoped, Jesse overwhelmed the tight-fisted man with his impeccably tailored suit and a cascade of awesome legalese gibberish. By the time he was finished reciting his list of contingencies, estoppels and adjurations, the poor man had his personal check-book in hand and was busy punching numbers into his calculator, figuring out the precise amount of wages and interest he owed. Jesse drove directly from the service station to his client's apartment to deliver the check.

The young man's elation at receiving his money bolstered Jesse. But his satisfaction was tempered by the phone message awaiting him at his office, from Cabot's attorney. After investigating the cost of performing the necessary repairs to the tenement, according to the message, the landlord had decided not to improve the building. He'd take his chances in the civil court.

Jesse cursed. Five hundred was a spectacular batting average in baseball, but not in life. Jesse had gotten a gasoline jockey his back wages, but he hadn't gotten Cabot to make his property livable for his renters. Jesse had brought Mrs. Selby's son home for Christmas, but was powerless when it came to Robin's son.

Jesse had won Robin's love last night, but he'd lost it this morning.

On the other hand, he mused, the old guy supposedly pulling the strings from above wasn't doing much better. The sky was a clear, cold blue, the streets clean and dry, the few expanses of grass in downtown New Haven naked, in a frozen grayish-brown state of hibernation. The least God could have done was given Robin some snow for Christmas.

WOODLEIGH'S REMAINED frenzied until five-thirty. Then, as if answering some silent command, the customers vanished, toting their purchases with them. At ten minutes to six, one final, hysterical customer entered, snatched up the last three soldier nutcrackers, paid for them in cash and whisked away. And then it was over.

After bidding her staff a happy holiday, distributing bonus checks and shooing the clerks out the door, Robin locked it and turned to survey the shop. The place was a shambles: merchandise picked over, shelves empty, a pewter pitcher resting upside-down on a table.

There would be time enough for cleaning up and sorting the leftovers, Robin meditated with a sigh as she crossed to the cash register and released the drawer. The store would be closed tomorrow, but she could come in early on Saturday to organize the place before the expected rush of returns. Or she could come in tomorrow, she thought glumly. Other than stopping by at Joanna's house to exchange gifts, Robin had no holiday festivities planned.

Christmas would be easier to live through if she were sure of herself, she thought dismally. But she was sure of nothing at the moment, nothing but the fact that spending the night with Jesse had been sublime. If she didn't love him, she couldn't have responded so gloriously to his lovemaking. Yet if she did love him, she would have to accept some basic concepts about him—most significantly, that he shunned the things she considered most important and valuable.

A tap at the door startled her, and she swore generally at all the idiots who left their Christmas shopping to the last minute. Sliding a stack of ten-dollar bills back into their slot, she shut the register drawer and turned toward the store's entry.

Jesse stood outside the door, cupping his hands around his eyes as he peered through the glass. His coat was unbuttoned, and he had on a suit underneath it, with his tie hanging loose and his shirt collar unbuttoned. His breath emerged as small white puffs of vapor in the evening cold.

The sight of him brought on a sudden rush of happiness within her. She ought to have been just as troubled by him now as she'd been that morning—and she imagined that once the wave of joy receded, she would be. Even so, she darted around the counter and raced to the door to let him in. A transient joy was better than no joy at all.

As soon as she opened the door he pushed inside, eager to escape the frigid evening air. His lips were cool but comforting as he kissed her cheek. Slinging an arm around her, he scanned the store. "If it's closed, how come you're still here?" he asked.

"Maybe I was waiting for you." Robin wasn't certain that was true, but she felt good saying it. Seeing how much her statement pleased Jesse made her feel even better.

"This is a strange place to wait," he argued good-naturedly. "I stopped by your house, assuming that you'd be there. But you weren't, so I cruised over here to see if you'd decided to keep the store open an extra hour."

"You came straight from work," Robin observed, scrutinizing his outfit.

"Yes, well, I've got an errand to run. I thought I ought to take care of it first, and then go home and unwind."

"What errand?" Robin asked. Maybe she could join him. Running around town with Jesse would take her mind off the Christmas decorations and untouched gifts for Philip that were waiting at her house.

"I've got some food to deliver to my clients in New Haven. Would you like to come along for the ride?"

"Food?" she questioned. "Food baskets, you mean?"

Jesse chuckled and glanced through the glass front wall to his Volkswagen, which was parked by the curb. "Food bags, actually. I stopped at the supermarket and picked up a few things I thought they could use. Being their lawyer, I know what their finances are like. I didn't want them to be stuck eating hot dogs and peanut butter for Christmas.''

Robin's eyes narrowed on him. This man, this Grinch who thought Christmas was just one more day, had purchased Christmas feasts for his indigent clients. What a phony he was! Blustering about his lack of faith, his rejection of God and religion—and here he was, the personification of Santa Claus himself!

Jesse met her quizzical gaze and smiled sheepishly, clearly attuned to what she was thinking. "It's just some stuff in cans," he said. "Don't get the wrong idea."

"I'll tell you what the wrong idea is," Robin asserted, feeling her energy and her sense of purpose revive. "The wrong idea is to give people their food in bags instead of baskets. If you're going to do this, Jesse, you'd better do it right."

"Uh-oh," he grunted, his smile widening. "Okay, Robin. How do we do this right?"

"First, we get some baskets," she said, jogging across the store to the display of woven wicker baskets. Most of the fancy baskets, the ones with lids and compartments for chilled wine bottles and glasses, had already been sold, but a few plain, open-top baskets still stood on a low shelf. "How many do we need?"

"Four," Jesse told her, taking the baskets as she handed them up to him.

"They don't match," she said.

"It doesn't matter. We'll use this larger one for the Selbys. They're a big family—I bought them a bigger ham."

"Ham?" Grinning, she stood and marched down the side of the store until she came to the remaining Christmas linens. "You're the one who's a hypocrite, Jesse. Pretending to hate Christmas, and you went and bought these people hams!"

"I'm not a hypocrite," he retorted. "I've never objected to giving, Robin. All I object to is concentrating a year's worth of giving on this one day, and then not giving for the rest of the year."

"Sure," Robin scoffed in disbelief as she plucked four red-and-green tablecloths from a shelf. "And how many other days of the year do you give your clients hams?"

Jesse conceded with a grin. "I think it would mean more to them on Christmas than it would at some other time. They're the ones who are celebrating, not me."

Robin laughed. "Of course, Jesse," she said with fake solemnity. "Your act of giving isn't any sort of celebration, is it?"

"Lighten up," he protested, although he was laughing, too. "You're the one who's fixing up these ridiculous baskets."

"They aren't ridiculous," Robin maintained, folding the linens to a manageable size and then using them to line the baskets. "If you do a thing, you do it right."

"Who's going to pay for all this stuff?" Jesse asked, smoothing out the corner of one of the tablecloths.

"I am," Robin said simply. Before Jesse could object, she went on. "I get an employee discount. Or better yet, I'll convince Jack Woodleigh to give them to us at cost. It's for a good cause."

"Even at cost, this stuff must be expensive," Jesse muttered, running his fingers over the delicate straw weave of the largest basket.

"If your clients deserve a ham dinner, then they deserve to receive it in style," Robin maintained. "Go get the food."

By the time he returned to the store, after two trips' worth of bulging paper bags, Robin had added to each basket a clove-scented candle, a brass candlestick, and a carved wood tree ornament shaped like a snowflake. The truth was, none of the items was terribly expensive at wholesale. If Jesse knew how much Woodleigh's marked up its merchandise he'd be horrified, so she thought it best to leave him in ignorance.

"Here we go," he said, dumping the bags onto the counter and unloading them. Along with the hams, he had bought canned sweet potatoes, canned string beans, and tins of fruitcake and hard candies. Robin and Jesse distributed the food among the four baskets, then folded the flaps of the tablecloths over the tops of the cans.

"Let me get my coat," Robin said, untying her pinafore as she strolled to the staff room at the rear of the store. Humming "We Wish You a Merry Christmas" to herself, she removed her barrette and brushed out her hair, smoothed her cowl-neck sweater into the waistband of her skirt, and pulled her coat from its hanger. After slipping it on, she turned off the light and joined Jesse in the store. "I'll leave my car here," she decided, gathering up two of the smaller baskets while Jesse lifted the third small one and the large one. "We can pick it up later."

It wasn't until they were on the turnpike, traveling to New Haven, that she wondered what had happened to her melancholia. She had been so busy arranging the baskets attractively that she'd forgotten how lonely she was without her son. Delivering food baskets to indigent strangers had never been one of her precious holiday traditions, but she was delighted to be doing it. Indeed, she thought it would be a lovely ritual to add to her annual Christmastime routines.

She wondered, too, what had happened to her doubt about Jesse. That he deliberately twisted the radio dial to a grating rock-and-roll program the minute he heard a fragment of the "Hallelujah Chorus" on another station didn't bother her in the least. She'd gladly provide the carols—over his objections, if necessary. She'd provide the tree and the gingerbread house and the pretty gift-wrapped boxes, as long as Jesse provided the Christmas spirit. And that he was doing, grandly.

Robin didn't often have occasion to visit New Haven, and even less often did she drive through the part of town Jesse was now entering. The multifamily dwellings were by and large seedy, and aged, battered cars were parked along the dimly lit roads. Jesse steered past a public housing project, a block of dilapidated two-family houses and a row of gloomy apartments, finally coasting to a halt in front of a rundown, four-story building with a few cracked and boarded windows gracing its front wall. Robin cringed at the realization that people actually lived inside such a dark, foreboding building.

To her surprise, Jesse seemed inordinately pleased by the sight of the place. "They collected the garbage!" he shouted, swinging open his door. "It's about time!"

"You mean, it could have been worse?" Robin blurted out, trying to picture the building with the added blight of garbage heaped around its front door.

"It *has* been worse," Jesse said, leaving the car and moving around to her side to help her out. They walked together to the back of the car, opened the hatchback and pulled out the baskets. "I wonder what prompted Cabot to pay for the garbage removal. He's the landlord—the guy we're suing.''

The Christmas spirit prompted Cabot, Robin contemplated. But Jesse might think she was needling or nagging him if she mentioned anything that corny, so she only smiled and followed him inside the grim apartment building.

Jesse knocked on a door in the first-floor hallway. A stocky young man holding an open bottle of beer answered. ''Mr. Lawson?'' he asked, speaking loudly to drown out the babble of voices and Salsa music emerging from somewhere inside the apartment. His gaze flew to Robin, and his eyebrows rose. ''Who's this? Another lawyer?''

''Hello, Mr. Martinez. This is a friend of mine,'' Jesse replied. ''We brought you some food for tomorrow, in case you want to make a Christmas dinner.'' He took one of Robin's baskets and handed it to the man, who peeked underneath the linen and whistled in amazement. ''I wish I could have come with good news about Cabot,'' Jesse added, ''but this was the best I could do.''

''If this is the best, it's pretty damned good, Mr. Lawson,'' Mr. Martinez said, his eyes glowing with gratitude. ''*Gracias*, Mr. Lawson. My mother, she's gonna love this, she'll make us a big feast. *Gracias! Felice Navidad!*''

Jesse mumbled something unintelligible, then took Robin's hand and escorted her down the hall to the stairs. He wouldn't dare to say Merry Christmas, she thought, amused. If he did, someone might actually think he believed in what he was doing.

''Can't we take the elevator?'' she asked as Jesse began climbing to the second floor.

''It's broken,'' he told her.

Bracing herself for the steep climb, she inhaled deeply and followed him up the long stairway, glad that she had only one basket to carry.

On the second floor, Jesse knocked on another door. A wizened, elderly woman cracked it open, squinting at him above the chain lock. Satisfied by his familiarity, she closed the door to release the chain, then opened it a few inches more. "What is it, Lawson?" she asked suspiciously. "You got our settlement money?"

"I'm sorry, but that's a long way off, Mrs. Stokes," Jesse said apologetically. "What I've got is some food for tomorrow."

The woman turned her dubious gaze to the basket Jesse extended to her. "Hmm," she grunted. "What's the basket for?"

Jesse turned to Robin for assistance. The baskets had been her idea, after all. "You can use it for whatever you want," Robin noted, figuring that this testy woman was not the sort who would make a habit of going on picnics or picking berries.

"Hmm," the woman said again. She eyed the basket in Jesse's hand. "You brought one for *her*?" she asked, angling her head toward a door across the hall. "She ain't home. She's out doing heaven knows what."

"Well." Jesse took the other small basket from Robin and handed it to Mrs. Stokes. "Perhaps you could give this to her when she comes home."

"Yeah, sure." Mrs. Stokes pulled the basket inside. "Heaven knows when she'll be home, carrying on the way she does," she said with a haughty sniff.

"Mrs. Stokes, it's Christmas," Jesse said awkwardly. "Have a little charity."

"Yeah, sure." Mrs. Stokes grumbled something that resembled a thank-you and slammed her door.

"What a strange woman," Robin whispered as they strolled back down the hall to the staircase.

Jesse chuckled. "She's pretty grumpy, all right. And she never passes up an opportunity to complain about Sheena—she lives across the hall. I think Sheena's a prostitute, but I'm not sure."

Robin didn't know what to say to that. This impoverished inner city environment was a far cry from the safe, wholesome world of army bases where she had grown up.

When they reached the third-floor hallway, Jesse stopped and gaped at the lightbulb glowing in the ceiling. He scowled. "Gerald," he muttered.

"What?"

Not bothering to answer, Jesse knocked on one of the doors. It swung open to reveal a strapping young man in jeans, his hair cropped short. The baby he held on his hip was wearing an oversize sailor cap that drooped adorably across his eyes. "Mr. Lawson!" the man hailed Jesse. "It isn't time to go back to Newport yet, is it? Me and my nephew are having too much fun."

"Tomorrow night," Jesse said, hovering on the threshold. "Gerald, did you replace the lightbulb in the hall? I told your mother—"

"Uh-uh, it wasn't me. Mama said some guy was by this morning, changing the bulbs and checking the lock on the front door. Said Mr. Cabot sent him, and he wanted to take care of a few things. Come on in, ask Mama yourself." The man waved Jesse and Robin inside.

The cramped living room of the apartment echoed with the sound of Bruce Springsteen singing "Santa Claus Is Coming to Town" in his gravelly hard-rock voice. Four teenagers, three girls and a boy, were gathered around a flimsy-looking, propped-up limb of a tree, busily hanging the spindly twigs with tinsel. Next to the tree, a paper cutout of Santa Claus was tacked to the wall. A gray-haired woman was seated in a faded easy chair, but she rose at Jesse's and Robin's entrance. "Mr. Lawson!" she cried frantically, hurrying across the room to him. "You haven't come to take Gerald back, have you?"

"No, he's got until tomorrow, Mrs. Selby," Jesse reassured her, extending the basket to her as the teenagers hung back shyly. "We just dropped by to bring you this."

As soon as Mrs. Selby took the basket, her children swarmed around her. "Ooh, look!" one of the girls shouted, pulling the wooden snowflake from the basket. "Look at this! For our tree!" She swooped down on the bedraggled-looking limb and attached the snowflake.

"Oh, my God," Mrs. Selby gasped, staring at the food in the basket. "Oh, Mr. Lawson, we were gonna have nothing worth eating for supper tomorrow, and now this... I don't know what to say."

"Say thank you, Mama," Gerald coached her. "This is awfully kind of you, Mr. Lawson."

"I praise God you came into our lives, Mr. Lawson," Mrs. Selby babbled, carrying the basket into the kitchen and setting it on the table. "Let me empty out this basket so you can take it home—"

"No, the basket is yours to keep," Jesse corrected her, arching his arm around Robin. "You can thank Ms. Greer for that. And for the candle and the table linen." Two of the girls had already removed the contents of the basket and unfolded the tablecloth. They squealed in delight at the red-and-green pattern of wreaths decorating the cloth.

Mrs. Selby dropped onto a chair, stunned. "You are too good to us," she said, sighing. "I thought all my prayers were answered when you brought Gerald home yesterday. And then that man came and fixed the light in the hall this morning. And now this . . . I just don't know what to say."

"Don't say anything," Jesse suggested, patting her arm. "We're on our way. You'd better get back to trimming your tree."

Robin's gaze passed from the gray-haired woman to Gerald and back again. Mrs. Selby had her son home with her for the holiday, and Robin hadn't. Yet she felt no envy, no resentment of the woman whose many prayers had been answered, thanks at least in part to Jesse. It was Christmas, and Christmas didn't have room in it for jealousy. It had room only for this: giving, making others happy, bringing joy.

Her eyes met Mrs. Selby's. "Merry Christmas," she said softly.

"Bless you," Mrs. Selby murmured. "May God bless you both."

The climb downstairs passed in silence. By the time Jesse and Robin reached the car, she was weeping. When he moved to unlock the passenger door for her, he noticed the tears streaking down her cheeks. "What's this all about?" he asked, drawing her against himself in a consoling embrace.

She rested her head against his shoulder and sniffled away her tears. "It's nothing, really. I'm all right."

He ran his fingers through her hair, thoughtful and concerned. "I'm sorry, Robin—I thought you'd enjoy this. It was something I wanted to do. Now we'll do something you want to do—sing Jingle Bells, roast chestnuts over an open fire . . . go to church, if you insist. Whatever you want—"

"No, Jesse," she said, her voice gaining strength. She tilted her head back so she could see him. "We've just done what I wanted to do."

His frown intensified. "Then why are you crying?"

She brushed her tears away with her fingertips. "It was so beautiful, what you did," she explained, her tone low but fervent. "Even that nasty woman who didn't have the good grace to thank you—I bet you knew she wouldn't, and you gave her the basket anyway. I've never seen anything so beautiful in my life."

Jesse gazed at her, his frown dissolving although his expression remained one of bemusement. "It wasn't so beautiful," he said modestly. "It was just something I wanted to do."

"Because it was Christmas," Robin noted.

"Because it was *their* holiday, and I thought they should have a good one. I don't have to believe in Christmas to do something for someone who does. And now—" he touched his lips to hers "—I'll do something for you. In fact, I'll do anything but put on a false beard. That was the deal we made."

"Listen to me, Jesse," Robin demanded impatiently. "I'm trying to tell you—you've already done something for me."

"What have I done for you? Cleaned out your store's supply of straw baskets?"

"You've made me realize that there's a whole lot more to Christmas than putting the tree in the same corner every year. And I love you for it, Jesse. I love you." Her arms coiled around his waist, beneath his coat, and she rose on tiptoe to kiss him.

He briefly returned her kiss, then pulled back and studied her. "You weren't crying because Mrs. Selby has her son and you don't have yours, were you?"

"No," Robin swore. She was honestly glad that her son was in Florida. As she'd just learned from Jesse, more than anything else Christmas meant doing something for someone who believed. Philip believed, and Robin had let him go. "I was crying, Jesse..." She tightened her arms around him, hugging him close. "I was crying because, for a while there, I was stupid enough to question whether I really loved you."

"Questioning isn't stupid," Jesse argued. "You know I respect people who ask questions."

"Yes, but that was one question that had an easy answer, and I shouldn't have had to keep asking it. I won't have to ask it anymore." She kissed him again. "And the other reason I was crying was because, after all these years, it took an avowed atheist to teach me what Christmas is all about."

"That makes perfect sense," Jesse commented, smiling whimsically. "We atheists have the objectivity you Santa worshippers are lacking."

"I'm not a Santa worshipper," Robin contradicted him. "I happen to like the Santa myth—"

"You admit Santa's a myth, then?" Jesse said victoriously. "That's a start."

"Don't try to convert me," she warned him with a laugh.

"What should I do?" he asked, his voice suddenly husky, his lips nearing hers.

"Take me home," she murmured. "We'll build a big fire in the fireplace, and we'll light up the tree, and—" her smile matched his in mischief "—I'll make a believer out of you."

"I already believe," he murmured before covering her lips in a searing kiss.

"And I believe in you, Jesse." She held him close, strengthened by her faith that they were a part of something bigger than themselves, that they were possessed by it. Maybe it was God, maybe love, maybe the power of two souls coming together, becoming one. Maybe all of those things.

Whatever it was, Robin would believe in it forever.

Epilogue

She was awakened by the ringing of her telephone. Groaning, she rolled out of Jesse's arms and groped for the receiver on the night table beside her bed. "Hello?"

"Hey, Mom! It's me!" Philip said gleefully. "Merry Christmas!"

"Philip!" Robin blinked awake and grinned. "Merry Christmas, Phil. Are you having a good time?"

"Yeah, it's been great. Yesterday we went to see this show at a place called Sea World, I think, and they had a whale that danced in the water, and dolphins that jumped through hoops and everything. It was really neat. We're just gonna hang out today, on account of it's Christmas, and tomorrow Dad's going to take me to Disney World."

"It sounds terrific," Robin said earnestly. "I'm so glad you're enjoying it."

"Our hotel room is neat, too. It's got this big color TV set, and they get the Disney channel here. I've been watching all the shows. Dad says he's going crazy."

"Maybe you'd better let him watch some football," Robin advised, sharing her newfound understanding of the holiday with her son. "Christmas means making other people happy, too, Phil."

"Okay, Mom. Did Santa come?"

"I haven't gone downstairs yet to look under the tree," Robin admitted. "But I'm pretty sure he did."

"Did you leave him some star-shaped cookies?"

Robin winced. The cookie dough was still sitting in a bowl in the refrigerator. It had probably solidified into a granite-hard mass by now. She considered confessing to Philip, then decided that a white lie wouldn't hurt. "I did, Phil, and I'm sure he ate them."

"Yeah, I bet he did," Philip concurred. "Are you going to see Jesse today?"

Robin turned to find Jesse awake, comfortably sprawled out beside her, his head propped up in his hand as he listened to her end of the conversation. His smile cut dimples into his cheeks, which were shadowed by an overnight growth of beard. The broad crest of his shoulder protruded from beneath the cover, reminding Robin of the fine body hidden from her view by the blanket. "I'll definitely be seeing Jesse today," she confirmed, winking at the man under discussion. He clasped her hand and drew her palm to his lips for a kiss.

"Well, listen," Philip said, "when you see him, make sure he does what he promised me he'd do. And tell him that if he sees Ms. Becker, he should tell her Merry Christmas for me, all right? Because she had a nice wreath on her door, and I'm gonna try not to think she's so boring anymore."

Philip's long-winded instructions made Robin dizzy, but she obediently responded, "I'll tell him."

"And tell him Merry Christmas from me, too."

"I will."

"I love you, Mom," Philip said. "I'm gonna go now. Dad said I could have pancakes for breakfast every day. Goodbye!"

"Goodbye, Phil. I love you, too." Robin sensed that her son had hung up before she finished speaking, but that didn't matter. Philip knew she loved him.

"How's he doing?" Jesse asked, pushing himself up to sit.

"Having the time of his life." Robin slid across the mattress to him, wrapped her arms around his waist and planted a kiss on his warm chest. "He said to wish you a merry Christmas, among other things."

"I'll forgive him for that," Jesse said magnanimously.

Robin frowned, trying to decipher the rest of Philip's cryptic message. "He also said that you promised to do something for him."

"Do something for him? I wonder what that's supposed to mean." Jesse frowned as well, but it looked like a fake frown to Robin. "It was sweet of him to take time out from his revels with Mickey Mouse to wish you a happy holiday."

"That's one of our traditions," Robin explained. "You call the members of your family who can't be with you. I'll be calling my mother in a few hours. With the time difference between here and Hawaii, I can't call her this early. And Philip will probably call her from Florida, and he'll call his other grandparents in Arizona. We always run up horrendous phone bills on Christmas."

"Some calls are worth the expense," Jesse allowed. "I can see how much Phil's call meant to you."

Robin leaned back from Jesse and examined his face. She could discern in his features a reflection of his father, the similar eyes, the similar nose and jaw, the thick, softly textured hair. "All parents like to hear from their children at Christmas," Robin remarked quietly. "Why don't you call yours?"

"My parents?" The idea clearly didn't appeal to Jesse. His lips twisted in distaste, and he began to shake his head.

"Jesse, it's Christmas. Your first Christmas away from them. Call them."

"After everything I've told you, Robin . . ." He shook his head again, more vehemently. "It's not that I absolutely refuse to call them ever again. But I can't on Christmas. Any other day, sure, but not today."

"You have to," Robin argued. "Why not today? You keep telling me that Christmas isn't such a special day."

"But they think it is."

"Exactly." Robin bore down on him, her bright, hazel eyes piercing the guarded darkness of his. "Give of yourself, Jesse. Make them happy. Do it because *they* believe."

He met her stubborn gaze, then relented with a nod. "All right, I'll do it. In a few hours—I've got time-zone problems, too. And they may just hang up on me—"

"They won't," Robin predicted. "They'll be as happy to hear from you as I was to hear from Philip. Take it from a mother, Jesse. They'll be delighted."

"They'll chat for a few minutes, say good-bye and pray for my soul," he grumbled. Then he smiled grimly and pushed back the covers, putting an end to the conversation.

Robin didn't press him further. She knew he would phone his parents, and she was proud of him. It would be a difficult call for him to make, but he was strong enough to survive it. More than survive it—he would feel wonderful for having done it.

Standing, she put on her bathrobe. Jesse donned his shirt and the trousers of his suit. Taking his hand, she led him from the bedroom. Perhaps he wanted breakfast, but some traditions wouldn't be broken. The first thing Greers always did on Christmas morning was to hurry downstairs and view the presents under the tree. This year, one of those presents would be for Jesse. Though she wasn's sure how he would react, Robin couldn't wait to give it to him.

What she didn't expect was to find the tree all lit up. She was sure she had unplugged the lights last night. But as she reached the bottom step, she was confronted with the sight of her Christmas tree blazing in all its glory.

And something else—there were two packages under the tree that she didn't recognize. With a bright red envelope lying on the carpet beside them.

"What's going on?" she asked, planting her hands on her hips and turning accusingly to Jesse.

He offered a boyish grin. "This one is my gift to Phil," he said, marching to the tree, dropping down on his knees and lifting the rectangular package. "It's a remote-control four-wheel-drive Jeep. When he threatened to buy one for Mrs. O'Leary, I figured it was something he wanted for himself."

"Oh, Jesse—he'll love it!" Robin was once again overwhelmed by his sensitivity. By now she ought to be used to it; by now she ought to expect such thoughtfulness from him. But every time she caught a glimpse of Jesse's generous soul—the soul he pretended he didn't have—she was amazed, nearly moved to tears.

Not wishing to drown them both in a maudlin display, she effected a matter-of-fact smile and pointed to the other unfamiliar package, which was oddly shaped and crudely wrapped. "What else did you buy him?" she asked.

"That one's for you, from Phil," Jesse explained, setting the rectangular box back on the floor among the other presents for Philip. "Last week, he asked me to hide it at my house so you wouldn't find it. Then he ordered me to smuggle it into your house and under the tree on Christmas morning. I'm a man of my word, Robin, so..." He presented Robin with the oddly shaped package.

"When did you bring it in here?" she asked, sitting beside Jesse and gaping at him.

"While you were still asleep. I had it hidden in my car." At her astonished stare, he elaborated. "As a matter of fact, when I went out to get it, I nearly got run over by some obese old guy in a funny red hat. He kept making this stuttering noise at the back of his throat, kind of a ho-ho—"

"Jesse!" Robin laughed and poked him in the arm.

"Seriously," Jesse maintained, his expression deadpan. "I think the fellow was plastered—his nose was all red. And he drove like a maniac. When he wasn't making that silly ho-ho-ho sound, he was muttering about how Californians didn't know how to stay out of the way of other drivers in winter weather—"

"Snow!" Robin erupted, springing to her feet and hastening to the window. She pulled back the curtain and was greeted by the sight of her front lawn, an expanse of frozen grass, devoid of the picturesque white covering she prayed for every Christmas eve.

She hadn't prayed for it last night. White Christmases made for sentimental songs, but they weren't important when it came to what Christmas was *really* about. "So you ran into Santa, did you?" she said, playing along with Jesse's joke.

"He ran into me. It isn't the California drivers who cause all the problems—it's these hot-shot New Englanders."

"Santa isn't a New Englander—he's from the North Pole," Robin declared, returning to Jesse's side. She tore the wrapping paper off Philip's gift to her and unveiled a bizarre humanoid object made of clay and painted orange. It featured disproportionately large ears, stiletto-shaped toes, wings and a halo fashioned out of wire. "Don't tell me it's an angel!" she blurted out before succumbing to more laughter.

"According to Phil, it's a boy from Gleek," Jesse told her.

"Of course. That was my next guess," Robin said, still chuckling at the grotesque statue. "I love it. I'll use it as a centerpiece in the dining room—once you eat that gingerbread house I knocked myself out making for you." She set the Gleek boy aside and lifted a small, neatly wrapped box. "This is for you, Jesse," she said, abruptly solemn.

One of his eyebrows quirked in surprise as he took the box from her. Robin watched nervously as he unwrapped the box and raised the lid. Cushioned in a nest of tissue paper was the crystal angel she'd chosen for him. Jesse picked it up and raised it to the tree, gazing at the array of multicolored light reflected in its facets. "This," he said soberly, "is definitely not a Gleekian."

"It's an angel," Robin murmured, trying unsuccessfully to read his mind. "That seems to be a running theme this year."

"It certainly does," Jesse agreed, lowering the angel and closing his arms around Robin. He kissed her tenderly. "I don't think you can begin to know how much it means to me."

"You called me an angel once," Robin reminded him, looking down at the figurine cradled in his large hand to avoid having to look directly at him.

"More than once," Jesse acknowledged. "I don't believe in angels—except for you."

"I'm not an angel," Robin protested. "I'm not nearly good enough—"

"You don't have to be good," Jesse asserted. "You just have to be able to work miracles every now and then. And that you do, Robin. That you do." He leaned away and scooped up the red envelope. "This is for you from me. I'm not sure if you'll like it, but . . ." He cut himself off and handed her the envelope.

She scrutinized him. He appeared as nervous as she'd felt when she'd given him her gift. But what could he be nervous about? A gift certificate was a perfectly acceptable present, if that was what the envelope contained. A card would be sweet, too. She doubted that he'd give her money. . .

"Open it," he ordered her.

She drew in a deep breath and pried up the flap. A slip of red paper fell out with the word "ME" written on it.

Puzzled, she raised her eyes to his. "I'm giving you *me*, Robin," he explained haltingly. "Myself. I know it isn't commercial, and I didn't wait in line for hours at a store, but . . . when I thought about giving, when I thought about what I wanted you to have . . . all I could think of was myself. If you'll have me," he added, his voice fading uncertainly.

Jesse. Her and Jesse. *Us.* That was what he was giving her. "I can't think of anything I'd rather have," she whispered. "It's the most extravagant gift in the world. The only problem is . . ." Her eyes sparkled playfully. "You've been giving yourself to me all along. It's not really a Christmas gift."

"That's right," Jesse agreed, his smile gaining confidence. "I'd just as soon give on every day of the year. Today is simply a day like any other."

"It is not," Robin insisted, curling up in his lap and hugging him. "You may have been giving yourself to me every day, but today, I got your gift in writing. And let me warn you, it's one gift I'm never going to return."

"Promise?"

"Promise."

"In that case…" He filled his lungs with air and struck a dramatic pose. "I hope I don't choke to death on the words: Merry Christmas, Robin."

Robin observed him for a moment, her eyes sparkling mirthfully despite her concerned expression. "You didn't choke to death," she noted.

He cuddled her close to himself, folding his arms possessively around her and brushing his lips against the glistening golden tendrils crowning her head. "Thank God for that," he sighed.

"Thank *who*?" Robin pounced on the word.

Jesse's mouth flexed as he considered his reply. "A slip of the tongue," he muttered with a laugh.

Robin smiled and nestled deeper into his embrace. So Jesse Lawson had said "Merry Christmas" without choking, and he'd acknowledged God. And he'd given her the most wonderful gift in the universe.

Just a few more miracles to illuminate this miraculously fine morning.

Make Your Christmas Special

TIPS FROM JUDITH ARNOLD

1. Share your rituals with people of different ethnic and religious backgrounds and let them share their rituals with you.

2. Collect some books you've read this year and deliver them to a local hospital or nursing home for the patients.

3. Exercise patience—with your loved ones and strangers. It's a hectic time; try to keep your blood pressure down.

4. Buy yourself a gift. You'll be guaranteed that at least one package under the tree will contain something you truly want.

5. If you bake up a storm, save one of your specialties to bake after Christmas.

6. (A natural corollary to #5) Don't bother stepping on the scale until January 2.

7. Traditions are wonderful, but add something new to your celebration each year: a recipe, a tree ornament, some small thing to keep the holiday from becoming stale.

8. Relax. Don't aim for perfection in entertaining, gift-giving or any other action. Remember that it's *your* holiday, too, and you should enjoy it as much as anyone else. Crystal and china place settings are lovely, but the table isn't nearly as important as the people sitting around it.

9. Think of winter not as a bitterly cold season of gray skies and denuded trees but rather as Mother Nature's way of regrouping her strength for spring's rebirth. Use this time of year to dig in, burrow down and regenerate yourself.

10. Pray for peace. That's really what Christmas is all about.

Harlequin American Romance

COMING NEXT MONTH

#229 NOTHING IN COMMON by Elda Minger

Burt Thomson shared his home with his two sons, an enormous sheepdog, Wadsworth, and total chaos. When Wadsworth redesigned the neighbor's garden—for the third time—Burt knew he had to get help. Into his home came Sandy Hensley, dog trainer *extraordinaire*. She breezed into his life, too, with the force of a small tornado—and in no time worked her own special magic on the entire Thomson clan.

#230 NOBODY'S BABY by Barbara Bretton

Jill knew she had chosen the wrong man as her driver for the month's trek into the Nevada desert. But was Tony also the wrong man to love? She needed to know, because something wonderful happened, something that gave meaning to all her tomorrows. Despite the medical experts' opinion, Jill had become pregnant.

#231 WHERE THERE'S SMOKE ... by Margaret St. George

Sammy had finally mustered her courage and joined a quit-smoking program, but then she found herself seated next to her old flame. But how could she renege on a promise to her kids? She barely had the willpower to kick the habit; how could she possibly overcome those other cravings, the ones that came straight from the heart?

#232 GOLDEN DREAMS by Leigh Anne Williams

Melissa Lane had never wanted to see her Ohio hometown again after she had left it years ago to make a new life for herself. But a speaking tour had brought her back for a one-day visit and then fate stepped in to lengthen her stay. When Melissa looked into the eyes of the boy—now a man—she had left behind, her homecoming became filled with interesting surprises.